Margery Hargest Jones

The Mabinogion

and

A Tale of Taliesin

Limited Special Edition. No. 10 of 25 Paperbacks

To Imogen.

from
Margery
with love.

Margery Hargest Jones is a retired school and music teacher. She is also a folksong collector and arranger who has had several folksong books published which are on the singing examination syllabus of the Associated Board of the Royal Schools of Music (ABRSM).

In memory of my dear friend the late Janet Yendole (née Richards).

Margery Hargest Jones

THE MABINOGION

AND

A TALE OF TALIESIN

AUSTIN MACAULEY PUBLISHERS™

LONDON · CAMBRIDGE · NEW YORK · SHARJAH

A CIP catalogue record for this title is available from the British Library.

ISBN 9781788480482 (Paperback)
ISBN 9781788480499 (Hardback)
ISBN 9781528954150 (ePub e-book)

www.austinmacauley.com

First Published (2019)
Austin Macauley Publishers Ltd
25 Canada Square
Canary Wharf
London
E14 5LQ

Acknowledgements

My thanks goes to Ann Whomersley for typing the manuscript and to my sister, Pat, for research. I am thankful to Cynthia and Janet for their helpful suggestions. I am also grateful to my son, Jeremy, for all his help and support.

Table of Contents

Introduction

The Mabinogion is a collection of Welsh Medieval folk tales first written down in the Thirteenth or Fourteenth Century in the Red Book of Hergest, now housed in the Library of Jesus College, Oxford. It was first translated into English from the Medieval Welsh by an Englishwoman, Lady Charlotte Guest (1812–1895) in 1838 and first published in 1849.

Her version is in very old fashioned language and, as my name is Hargest, by coincidence, I have endeavoured to transcribe it into more Modern English so that it will be easier for children to follow and understand, but retaining the medieval sense of mystery.

The twelve stories of the Mabinogion deal with the medieval themes of magic, enchantment and the 'Otherworld' (Annwfyn) and take place in Wales when Arthur was King, before the days of Camelot and the Round Table.

The first four are the original Mabinogi, i.e., 'The Four Branches of the Mabinogion' with the next two set in Roman Britain and the last five are Arthurian tales in which Arthur appears.

The first tale, about Pwyll Prince of Dyfed, is in two parts and tells of Pwyll who is persuaded to change places with Arawn King of Annwfyn (Otherworld) but behaves there with loyalty and goodness. The second part deals with his meeting and marrying the beautiful Rhiannon who bears him a son, Pryderi. She is cruelly punished by him after being falsely accused of killing her baby son. All ends happily when, after much adventure and magic, the little boy is returned to his mother.

In the second story, Branwen the daughter of Llyr (Lear) is married to Matholwch, King of Ireland, and suffers greatly at his hands because of a crime committed against him by her wicked stepbrother. She was avenged by her brother Brân the Blest who was injured and instructed his followers, on their return to Britain, to cut off his head and bury it in London facing France. This they do after feasting, as he told them to, in Harlech for seven years. They travelled to Penfro (Pembroke), opened a door which faced Cornwall that showed them all the evil they had encountered. They took the head and buried it in White Mount in London.

In the third story, 'Manawyddan the son of Llyr' or (The Trials of Dyfed), Pryderi, now his father Pwyll is dead, gives his mother Rhiannon in marriage to Manawyddan, who is mourning the death of his brother Brân the Blest. When they find no people or animals left in Dyfed, after a great thunderstorm, they leave for Lloegyr (England) to find work. They try all kinds of crafts in various towns but are so good at them that they have to return to Dyfed because they are threatened. Then both Pryderi and Rhiannon disappear. They are rescued by Manawyddan after many magical happenings and the spells are removed from the Cantrefs of Dyfed.

The fourth branch of the Mabinogi concerns Math the son of Mathonwy who turns his nephews into animals in punishment for hurting his wife. Pryderi is killed but Blodeuwedd (Flower Face) comes into the story – a lady made of flowers, who is unfaithful to her husband Llew. She tricks him into being killed but he takes the form of an eagle and flies off. He is recognised as being Llew by Gwydion – one of the brothers– and turns Blodeuwedd into an owl, which has a face like a flower, as punishment, for other birds shun it. This is why it only comes out at night!

The Dream of Macsen Wledig is the story of a Roman Emperor who dreams of travelling to a beautiful country and sees a lady (Elen) with whom he falls in love. His men set out to find this beautiful country as he describes his journey in his dream. They find the beautiful country of Wales, Elen becomes his wife and they rule Rome together.

Lludd and Llefelys are two brothers who experience the Three Plagues of Britain and overcome them. The elder was Lludd who ruled the Island of Britain after Beli the Great, his father, died. He rebuilt much of London and it was called Caer Llud. Its main gate was called Lud's Gate or Ludgate as it is now called. The youngest brother became King of France after the King of France died and left a daughter who Llefelys married. Between the two, the brothers overcome the three plagues which fell upon Britain.

In the seventh story of 'Cilhwch and Olwen' (or The Quest for Olwen) Cilhwch sets out to marry Olwen, the daughter of a huge, fierce giant. He is set many tasks to do this and with Arthur's help eventually is able to marry Olwen. This is the first story in which Arthur is mentioned.

'The Dream of Rhonabwy' recounts a dream in which Arthur again appears and plays a strange game of chess with Owain who owns ravens which attack Arthur's men. They are stopped when Arthur gets angry because his men are being killed and Britain is now in danger. He crushes the chess pieces and the ravens are called off. No one knows the meaning of Rhonabwy's dream.

In 'Owain, or The Lady of the Fountain', while Arthur sleeps, his knight Cynon tells the other knights a story of an adventure he has which so enthrals them that Owain sets out to find the place and have the adventure that Cynon had. He does and more besides meeting the Lady of the Fountain who returns with him to Arthur's Court. He goes away after a time with his followers (the ravens mentioned in Rhonabwy's dream) and in all he does is victorious.

'Peredur the son of Efrawc' is the tenth story in which Peredur is firstly an innocent boy fiercely protected by his mother because she had lost her husband and six other sons to the perils of war. He becomes a knight, however, who does much killing in all his adventures to prove to Arthur that he is a worthy knight.

'Geraint the son of Erbin' is another of Arthur's knights – in the last story – who treats his lady (Enid) very badly, mistakenly thinking that she loves another man. After many tournaments, which he wins, and adventures, all ends happily for Geraint and Enid who reign together prosperously in his own lands ever after.

'Mabinogion' is not really a word. The word 'mab' in Welsh means 'boy' and Lady Charlotte used it as a plural which could suggest 'a tale of descendants', her translation of which she dedicated to her two eldest sons.

Many of the characters which appear in the Arthurian tales, have their equivalents in the later Round Table of Camelot stories: Arthur's queen is Gwenhwyfar (Guinevere) which means 'white phantom'; Bedwyr is Sir Bedivere; Gwalchmai – Sir Gawain; Cei – Sir Kay and Peredur – Sir Percival (or Parsifal). The English meaning of Olwen is 'The White Track' and Angharad Law Ewrawc is 'Angharad Golden Hand'.

I have changed certain letters from Lady Charlotte's translation since some letters do not occur in the Welsh alphabet: in Evrawc 'v' becomes 'f' but is sounded 'v'; there is no 'x' in the Welsh language so 'Maxen' becomes 'Macsen' and there is no 'k' in the Welsh alphabet so 'Kilhwch' becomes 'Cilhwch', as 'Kai' becomes 'Cei'.

More detailed notes are available to the reader in Lady Charlotte's publications of 1841-50 and a later edition of 1877 has copious notes to each story. I have kept explanatory notes to a minimum hoping that my simplification of the narratives is sufficient without detailed notes, which can be found in the editions of Lady Charlotte Guest.

Margery Hargest Jones
Abergavenny October 2014

1. Pwyll Prince of Dyfed

Pwyll, Prince of Dyfed was lord of the seven Cantrefs of Dyfed. Once upon a time he was at Narberth, his main palace, and he thought he would go hunting in his favourite hunting ground of Glyn Cuch. So he left Narberth that night and went as far as Llwyn Diarwyd. He stayed there overnight and left the next morning and arrived at Glyn Cuch. He let the dogs loose in the wood, sounded the horn and began the chase. As he followed the dogs he lost sight of his companions; while he listened to the hounds, he heard the cry of other hounds, different from his own and coming from the opposite direction.

He saw a level open space in the wood, and as his dogs came to it, he saw a stag in front of the other dogs, which overtook it and brought it down. Then he looked at the colour of the other dogs, and of all the hounds he had seen he had never seen any like this. Their hair was a brilliant shining white and their ears were red. The whiteness of their bodies shone and the ears glistened. He came towards the dogs and drove away the other dogs that had brought down the stag and set his own dogs on it.

As he was doing so he saw a rider coming towards him on a large light-grey horse, with a hunting horn round his neck. He was dressed in hunting clothes of grey wool. The rider came up to Pwyll and spoke to him. "Sir," he said, "I know you but I do not wish to greet you."

"Perhaps," said Pwyll, "you are too dignified to greet me."

"Really," he answered, "it is not my dignity that stops me."

"What is it then, Sir?" asked Pwyll.

"My goodness, it is because of your own ignorance and lack of courtesy."

"What lack of courtesy, Sir, have you seen in me?"

"Greater discourtesy I never saw in a man," he said, "than to drive away the dogs that were killing the stag and set your own dogs on it. This was discourteous and although I don't wish to take revenge on you, I will cause you more shame than the value of a hundred stags."

"O Sir," Pwyll replied, "if I have done you wrong, I would like to gain your friendship."

"How will you gain it?" asked the horseman.

"I don't know who you are," said Pwyll.

"I am a crowned King from the land of Annwfyn*, he answered. *"Arawn, a King of Annwfyn am I."

"Lord," said Pwyll, "how may I gain your friendship?"

"In this way," said the King. "There is a man whose lands are opposite to mine, who is always fighting against me. He is Hafgan, a King of Annwfyn, and by getting rid of this power over me, which you can easily do, you can gain my friendship."

"I will do this gladly," said Pwyll. "Show me the way."

"I will send you to Annwfyn instead of me," said Arawn, "and I will give you the fairest lady you ever saw to be your companion. It will make you as like me so that not a page nor an officer or anyone who follows me shall know it is not me. This will be for a year from tomorrow. Then I will meet you here."

"Yes," said Pwyll, "but when I have been there for a year, how will I know the man you speak of?"

"One year from tonight," said Arawn, "is the time he and I have agreed to meet at the Ford. You will be there looking like me and with one blow that you give him, he will no longer live. If he asks you to give him another, do not, for when I did so, he fought with me the next day as well as ever before."

"So," said Pwyll, "what shall I do about my kingdom?"

Arawn said, "I will go there instead of you and no one shall know the difference."

"I will set out gladly," said Pwyll.

"The way shall be clear and nothing will delay you until you come to my kingdom and I will be your guide," said Arawn. He led him within sight of the palace and its buildings.

---

* Hades, i.e. Lower world, place of departed spirits.

"Look," he said, "the Court and Kingdom in your power. Go in and you will see the customs of the Court."

Pwyll went forward to the Court, where he saw bedrooms, halls and rooms, in the most beautiful buildings ever seen. He went into the hall to take off his outer coat and young men and pages helped and saluted him. Two knights helped him to remove his hunting clothes and put on him a gown of silk and gold. The hall was prepared and the host and the household entered together with the Queen, who was the fairest lady he had ever seen. She wore a yellow robe of shining satin. They washed and went to table where they sat, the Queen on one side of him and an Earl on the other. He began to speak with the Queen, and he thought, from her speech, she was the most interesting and cheerful lady that ever was. They had meat and drink and with songs and feasting, this was the most costly Court supplied with food and drink in dishes of gold and royal jewels.

He spent the year in hunting, music, feasting and conversation with his companions until the night came for the meeting. When the night came the nobles went with him, and as they reached the Ford a knight spoke up and said, "Lords, this meeting is between the two kings so we must leave them to fight for their own land and territory."

Then the two kings met in the middle of the Ford and at the first blow the man who was instead of Arawn struck Hafgan in the centre of his shield so that it was split in two. His armour was broken, and Hafgan was thrown to the ground an arm's and a spear's length over the strap of his horse and he received a deadly blow.

"O Sir," said Hafgan, "what right have you to cause my death? I was not hurting you. I don't know why you should kill me, but since you have begun, finish your work."

"Ah my Lord," Pwyll replied, "I may regret doing this to you, kill you who may, but I will not do so."

"My faithful Lords," said Hafgan, "carry me forward. I am dying. I shall not be able to support you any more."

"My Noblemen," said he who looked like Arawn, "have a discussion and decide who ought to be my subjects."

"Lord," said the Noblemen, "we should all be, since there is no king over the whole of Annwfyn but you."

"Yes," he replied, "it is right that those who come humbly should be welcomed graciously, but those who do not obey shall be forced by the sword." So the men paid their respect to him and he began to conquer the country. By noon the next day the two kingdoms were his. He then kept his promise and went to Glyn Cuch.

When he arrived there, the King of Annwfyn was there to meet him and both men were very pleased to see each other. "May Heaven reward you for your friendship! I have heard what you have done. When you come to your own land," he said, "you will see what I have done for you."

Then Arawn gave Pwyll Prince of Dyfed his proper shape and outward appearance. He likewise took his own and set out for the Court of Annwfyn where he was happy to see his people and household, whom he had not seen for so long. They had not realised his absence and greeted him as usual. The day was spent in joy and merriment and he sat and talked with his wife and his nobles. When it was time to sleep rather than make merry, they went to bed.

When he was in bed with his wife, he talked to her and was very loving to her. She had not been used to that for a whole year and she thought how different he was now. She did not speak to him so he asked her what was the matter. She said, "For a year you have not spoken to me like this or been loving towards me." He thought, 'what a faithful man I found in a friend!'

"Lady," he said, "don't blame me. I have neither slept or lay down with you for a year," and he told her the whole story. She said, "You had a true friend for not being tempted to be with me."

"I thought so too," he said.

"That was not strange either," she said.

Pwyll Prince of Dyfed also went to his own country and asked his noblemen how his rule had been during the past year, compared with how it had been before. "Lord", they said, "your wisdom was never so great, and you were never so kind or generous, or your justice never more worthy than seen before this last year.

"Well," he said, "for all the good you have enjoyed, you should thank him who had been with you, for this is what happened." Then he told them the whole story. "Truly, Lord," they said, "thank goodness that you have had such friendship, and do not change the kind of rule that we have enjoyed in the past year."

"I promise that I will not change it," answered Pwyll.

From then on the two friends made the friendship even stronger and sent each other horses, greyhounds, hawks and all jewels that would please the other. Because he lived all that year in Annwfyn, having ruled there so well and united the two kingdoms in one day by his bravery and skill, he lost the name of Pwyll Prince of Dyfed and was called Pwyll Chief of Annwfyn from then on.

****

Once upon a time, Pwyll was at Narberth, his main palace, where a feast had been prepared for him, and there were many men with him. After the first meal, Pwyll got up to walk to the top of a mound that was above the palace. It was called Gorsedd (throne of) Arberth.

"Lord," said one of the Court, "it is said that whoever sits on it cannot go on without receiving blows or wounds, or else see a wonder."

"I am not afraid of receiving blows or wounds," said Pwyll, "but I would gladly see a wonder. So I will go and sit on it."

So on the mound he sat. While he sat there, they saw a lady on a large pure white horse with a robe of shining gold around her, coming along the road that led from the mound. The horse seemed to move at a slow and even pace, and was coming towards the mound.

"My men," said Pwyll, "do any of you know that young lady?"

"No, none of us Lord," they said.

"One of you go and meet her so that we may know who she is." So one of them got up and as he came on to the road to meet her, she passed by. He followed as fast as he could on foot, but the faster he went, the further away from him she was. When he saw that he could not catch up with her on foot he returned to Pwyll, and said to him, "Lord, it is useless for anyone to follow her on foot."

"So," said Pwyll, "go back to the palace and take the fastest horse you see and go after her."

He took a horse and when he came to an open level plain, he spurred the horse, but the more he did, the further from him was the lady. Yet still she went at the same pace as before. His horse began to weaken and when the horse started to fail him, he returned to Pwyll. "Lord," he said, "it is useless for anyone to follow the lady. No horse is as fast as this one and it can't catch up with her."

"Really," said Pwyll, "this must be an illusion. Let us go back to the palace." So to the palace they went for the rest of the day. The next day they got up and after their first meal, Pwyll said, "We will all go to the mound as we did yesterday." To one of his young men he said, "Take the swiftest horse you know." So he did and they went towards the mound with the horse. As they sat down again they saw the lady on the same horse and in the same clothes coming along the road.

"Look," said Pwyll, "here is the lady we saw yesterday. Get ready, young man, to find out who she is."

"My Lord, I will willingly do that," he said. The lady then came opposite to them, so the young man mounted the horse. Before he had settled himself in his saddle, she passed by and there was a clear space between them. She went no faster that the day before, and although he gave his horse the reins he was still no nearer than if he went at a walking pace. The more he urged his horse, the further she was from him.

When he saw that there was no point in following her he returned to where Pwyll was. "Lord," he said, "you can see what has happened."

"I can see that no one can catch her up," said Pwyll. "She must have an important errand to someone on this plain that she should ride so quickly. Let us go back to the palace." To the palace they returned and spent the night in songs and feasting, as they pleased.

The next day, they amused themselves until it was time to eat. When the meal was finished, Pwyll said, "Where are the men who went to the mound yesterday and the day before?"

"We are here, Lord," they said.

"Let us go," he said, "to the mound again and sit there." He said to the page who tended his horse, "saddle my horse well, bring my spurs and hurry with him to the road." The young page did as he was told and they went and sat on the mound. They had only been there a short time when they saw the lady come along in the same way and at the same speed.

"Young man," said Pwyll, "give me my horse." No sooner had he mounted than she passed by him. He turned and followed her. He let his horse bound along and thought he would reach her, but he came no nearer than before. Then he urged his horse at great speed but it was useless to follow her. Then said Pwyll, "O Lady, for the sake of him that you love best, stop for me."

"I will gladly stop," she said. "It would have been better for your horse had you asked me before."

The lady stopped and threw back the veil that covered her face. She looked at him and began to speak to him. "Lady," he asked, "where have you come from and where do you go?"

"I go on my own errand," she said, "and I am very glad to see you."

"I am pleased to see you also," he said. Then he thought that of all the beautiful girls and ladies he had seen, none compared with her beauty. "Lady," he said, "will you tell me your purpose?"

"I will tell you," she said. "My main quest was to find you."

"O", said Pwyll, "that is the most pleasing quest you could have come on. Will you tell me who you are?"

"Lord, I will tell you," she said. "I am Rhiannon, the daughter of Hefeydd Hên, and they want me to marry a man against my will. I do not wish it and that is because of my love for you. I will not have a husband unless you reject me. I have come to hear your answer."

"O," said Pwyll, "this is my answer. If I had to choose from any of the ladies in the world, I would choose you."

"If that is your intention," she said, "make a promise to meet me before I will be married to someone else."

"The sooner I do, the more pleased I will be," said Pwyll. "I would like you to meet me a year today at the palace of Hefeydd," she said, "I will have a feast prepared for when you arrive."

"I will be happy to keep this appointment," he said.

"Lord," she said, "keep in good health and remember to keep your promise. Now I will go." So they parted. He went back to his men and would not answer their questions about the lady but turned the talk to other matters.

When a year had passed, he gathered together a hundred knights to go with him to the palace of Hefeydd Hên. They came to the palace and there was great joy and preparations for him. The whole Court was at his command.

The hall was decorated and they sat down to eat. Hefeydd Hên was on one side of Pwyll and Rhiannon on the other. All the rest were seated according to their rank. They ate, feasted and talked. Soon there entered a tall auburn-haired young man of royal bearing dressed in satin. When he came into the hall, he saluted Pwyll and his men. "Welcome to you, come and sit down," said Pwyll.

"No," he said. "I am a suitor and I will give my message."

"Do so, willingly," said Pwyll.

"Lord," he said, "my message is for you and it is to ask a favour of you."

"Whatever you ask, you shall have," said Pwyll, "as far as I am able."

"Oh," said Rhiannon, "why did you give that answer?"

"Hasn't he given it in front of these noblemen?" asked the young man.

"My goodness," said Pwyll, "what is the favour you ask?"

"The lady who I love the best is to be your bride tonight; I came to ask that she be mine, together with the feast and the banquet that are here."

Pwyll was silent because of the answer he had given. "Be silent as long as you can," said Rhiannon. "Never did a man make a fool of himself as you have done."

"Lady," he said, "I did not know who he was."

"This is the man they would give me to against my will. He is Gwawl the son of Clud, a man of great power and wealth. You will have to give me to him now because of what you have said, or shame will be on you."

"Lady," he said, "I don't understand your answer. I can never do as you say."

"Give me to him," she said, "and I shall see that I shall never be his."

"How will that be?" asked Pwyll. "I will give you a small bag," she said. "Keep it safely. He will ask you for the banquet and the feast and the preparations which are not yours to give. I will give the feast to the men. That will be your answer. As for me, I will be engaged to him a year from tonight. At the end of the year you must be here. Bring this bag with you and put your hundred knights in the orchard beyond."

"When he is feasting, you must come on your own, dressed in ragged clothes and holding the bag in your hands. Ask for nothing except a bagful of food. I will see that all the meat and drink of the seven Cantrefs are put in it, but it will be no fuller than before. After much food and drink has been put in there, he will ask if the bag will ever be full. You must say that it will never be full until a man of noble birth and great wealth will get up and press the food in the bag with both feet saying, 'Enough has been put in there'. I will then make him tread the food in the bag. When he does so, turn the bag so that it will be up over his head, then slip a knot in the string of the bag. With the bugle round your neck, sound it so that the men hear it and come down to the palace."

"Lord," said Gwawl, "it is right that you answer my request."

"You shall have whatever is in my power to give," replied Pwyll.

"Gwawl," said Rhiannon, "as for the feast and the banquet which are here, I have given them to the men of Dyfed, the household and the warriors that are with us. I cannot permit them to be given to anyone else. In a year from tonight, a banquet will be prepared for you in this palace, so that I may become your bride."

So Gwawl went on to his lands and Pwyll went back to Dyfed. They both spent that year until it was the time for the feast at the palace of Hefeydd Hên. Then Gwawl the son of Clud set out for the feast that was prepared for him. He came to the palace and was received with rejoicing. Pwyll, the Chief of Annwfyn arrived at the orchard with his hundred knights as Rhiannon had told him, having the bag with him.

He was dressed in course and ragged clothes and wore large clumsy old shoes on his feet. When he saw that the celebrations after the meal had begun, he went into the hall and greeted Gwawl the son of Clud and all his company. "Lord," he said, "I have a request to make of you."

"I welcome your request," said Gwawl, "and if you ask of me what is just, I will gladly give it to you."

"That is fair," he answered. "I beg only from want. The favour I ask of you to have this small bag filled with meat."

"That is a reasonable request," he said. "You shall gladly have it. Bring him food."

Many servants got up and began to fill the bag, but for all they put in it, it was no fuller than at first. "Gracious," said Gwawl, "will your bag ever be full?"

"It will not," said Pwyll, "unless one who possesses great lands and wealth and treasure gets up and treads down the food in the bag with his feet, and shall say 'Enough has been put in there'."

Rhiannon then said to Gwawl, "Get up quickly."

"I will, willingly," he said. He got up and put his two feet in the bag. Pwyll then turned up the sides of the bag so that Gwawl's head was in it. He shut it up quickly, tied a knot in the strings and blew his horn. All his men came down to the palace, grabbed the men who had come with Gwawl and put them in his own prison.

Pwyll took off his rags and his old shoes; and as they came in, everyone of Pwyll's knights struck the bag either with his foot or a staff. All of them played with the bag in this way. Everyone asked, "What are you playing?"

"The game of Badger in the Bag," they said. It was then that the game of Badger in the Bag was first played.

"Lord," said the man in the bag, "if you can hear me, I do not deserve to be killed in a bag."

"Hefeydd Hên said, "Lord, he speaks the truth. It is right that you listen to him, for he doesn't deserve this."

"Who will be responsible for him?" asked Pwyll.

"We will vouch for him," said Hefeydd, until his men are free to answer for him."

He was let out of the bag and his men were freed. "Ask Gwawl what he promises," said Hefeydd.

"You draw up the agreement," said Gwawl.

"I am happy that it will be as Rhiannon said," answered Pwyll. So the agreement was made between them.

"Lord," said Gwawl, "I am hurt and have many bruises, I need some ointment; with your permission I will go home. I'll leave my nobles here instead of me to answer to what you need."

"I am quite willing that you should do that," said Pwyll. So Gwawl went home to his land.

The hall was then arranged for Pwyll and his men and they sat down at the tables as they had the year before. They ate, feasted and spent the night in merriment and peace. When it was time to sleep, Pwyll and Rhiannon went to their bedroom.

Next morning at daybreak, Rhiannon said, "My Lord, rise and begin to give gifts to the musicians. Refuse no one your generosity."

"So I will, gladly," said Pwyll, "both today and every day while the feast lasts." So Pwyll got up and called for silence and told the men and minstrels to choose what gifts they would like. This was done, the feast went on and everyone had what they wanted while the feast lasted. When it was finished, Pwyll said to Hefeydd, "My Lord, with your permission, I will set out for Dyfed tomorrow."

"Certainly," said Hefeydd, "may Heaven protect you. Also fix a time when Rhiannon may follow you."

"We will go together," said Pwyll.

"Is this what you wish, Lord?" asked Hefeydd.

"Yes, I do," answered Pwyll.

The next day, they set out for Dyfed and travelled to the palace of Narberth, where a feast was made ready for them. Many chief men and most noble ladies of the land came to them and Rhiannon gave all of them a rich gift, either a bracelet, a ring or a precious stone. They ruled the land prosperously both that year and the next.

In the third year, however, the nobles of the land began to be sad to see the man they loved so much, who was their Lord and brother, without an heir. They came to him at a place called Preseleu, in Dyfed. "Lord," they said, "we know you are not as young as some of the men of this country, and we are afraid you will not have an heir of this wife. Therefore take another wife with whom you may have an heir. You can't be with us always, although you wish it and you need an heir."

"Truly," said Pwyll, "we haven't been together for very long and it may yet happen. Grant me a year, so that we may live together. After that I will do as you say." So they agreed.

2. The Birth of Pryderi

Before the year was out, a baby son was born to Rhiannon and Pwyll at Narberth. On the night he was born, six women were brought to watch the boy as his mother, Rhiannon, slept. The women watched for a good part of the night but before midnight all of them fell asleep. Towards daybreak, when they awoke, they looked at where they had put the baby boy and he was gone. "Oh," said one of the women, "the boy is gone."

"Yes," said another, "and at the very least we shall be burnt or put to death because of it."

One of the women said, "Has anyone a good idea of what we should do?" Another said, "I have a good idea for you."

"What is it?" they asked.

"There is a staghound here and she has a litter of puppies. Let us kill some of the cubs and rub the blood on the face and hands of Rhiannon, lay the bones by her and vow that she has killed and devoured her son. She will not be able to disagree with the six of us." This they agreed to do.

Towards morning Rhiannon woke and said, "Women, where is my son?"

"Lady," they said, "do not ask us about your son, we are covered with bruises from the blows of struggling with you. We never saw anyone as violent as you, but it was useless to compete with you. Have you not destroyed your son? Do not blame us."

"For pity's sake, do not blame me," said Rhiannon. "If you are afraid, I will defend you."

"Truly," they said, "we would not do wrong for anything in the world."

"Tell the truth," said Rhiannon. "If you do, you will come to no harm." But she still had the same answer from the women.

Then Pwyll got up and all his household. What had happened could not be kept quiet as the story went across the land and all the nobles heard it. They came to Pwyll and asked him to send Rhiannon away because of the crime she had committed. He, however, was loath to do this because she had a child, so if she had done wrong she should do a punishment for it.

So Rhiannon sent for the teachers and the wise men and accepted a punishment. It was that she should stay at the palace of Narberth for seven years and should sit by the gate near a horse-block every day. She should tell the story to all who came, who didn't know it and she would offer to carry any guests and strangers on her back to the palace. This rarely happened, but in this way did she spend part of the year.

Now at that time Teirnyon, Lord of Gwent Is Coed, who was the best man in the world, had a beautiful mare. On the night of every first of May, she foaled, but no one ever knew what became of the colt. He said to his wife, "what can be done about the mare that foals and the colt disappears?"

"Yes," she said, "what can be done about it?"

"This is the first night of May," he said, "so I intend to watch and find out what happens to the colt."

He saw that the mare be brought into the house, armed himself and kept watch. Soon the mare foaled a large and beautiful colt. It was standing up when Teirnyon heard a great noise and after it a great claw came through the window and grabbed the cold by the mane. Then Teirnyon drew his sword and cut off the arm below the elbow so that the claw and the colt were in the house with him. Then again he heard a great noise and wailing, both at once. He went outside in the direction of the noise but could not see anything because it was dark. Then he remembered he had left the door open and he returned. In the doorway there was an infant boy in swaddling clothes wrapped in satin. He lifted up the boy who was very strong for his age.

He then shut the door and went to the bedroom where his wife was. "Lady," he said, "are you asleep?"

"No, Lord," she said, "I woke up when you came in. What has happened?" Then Teirnyon told her the whole story. "What clothes are on the boy?" she asked.

"A cloak of satin," he answered.

"He must be of high birth," she replied. "I will tell my women that I have been expecting a baby and this is he," she said.

"I agree," he said. They had the boy christened and called him Gwri Wallt Euryn because his hair was as yellow as gold.

He grew quickly and at a year old he was bigger than a three-year-old. When he was two, he was as big as a six-year-old. Before the end of the fourth year, he was asking the grooms to let him water the horses. "My Lord," said Teirnyon's wife, "where is the colt?"

"I have the grooms taking care of him," he said.

"Wouldn't it be good if he was broken in and given to the boy seeing that we had them the same night?" she said.

"I agree with you," said Teirnyon. So the colt was broken and given to the boy to ride.

While these things were going on, they heard the news of Rhiannon and her punishment. As Teirnyon was thinking about this, he looked at the boy and it seemed to him that there was a great likeness between Pwyll and the boy. He knew Pwyll the chief of Annwfyn because he had been one of his followers in the past. He became very sad that he had kept the boy when he knew him to be the son of another man. When he was alone with his wife, he told her that it was not right that they should keep the boy with them and cause an excellent lady such as Rhiannon to be punished for something she hadn't done. His wife agreed that they should return the boy to Pwyll. "We will gain three things" said his wife, "thanks and gifts from Pwyll for nursing his son and taking him back to him and thirdly, if the boy is of a gentle nature, he will be our foster-son and will do us good." So they agreed to do this.

The next day, no later, Teirnyon was ready together with two other knights and the boy, who rode the horse he had been given. They went to Narberth. As they reached the palace, they saw Rhiannon sitting beside the horse block. When they were near her she said, "Sir, go no further. I will carry you all on my back because that is my punishment for destroying my son."

"Oh, fair Lady," said Teirnyon, "do not think I will be carried on your back."

"Neither will I," said the boy. So they all proceeded to the palace. They had a joyful reception. A feast had been prepared because Pwyll had returned from another part of Dyfed. They went into the hall and washed. Pwyll was very pleased to see Teirnyon. They sat down with Teirnyon between Pwyll and Rhiannon and the knights opposite with the boy in between them.

After the meal they were merry and discussed many things. Teirnyon told them about the adventure with the mare and the boy. How he and his wife had brought up the boy as their own. "Here is your son, Lady," said Teirnyon.

"We are all certain of that," they all said.

"If this is true, said Rhiannon, it is the end of my trouble."

"Lady," said Pendaran Dyfed, "you have named your son Pryderi* well. It suits him."

"Won't his own name suit him better?" asked Rhiannon.

"What is his name?" asked Pendaran Dyfed.

"Gwri Wallt Euryn is the name we gave him," said Teirnyon.

"Pryderi shall be his name," said Pendaran.

"It is more suitable," said Pwyll, "that he should have the name his mother said when she heard good news of him." So it was arranged.

"Teirnyon," said Pwyll, "you should be rewarded for bringing up our boy so well and we should repay you for it."

"My Lord," said Teirnyon, "it is my wife who nursed him and she will be very upset to lose him."

"It is right that he should be aware of what my wife and I have done for him."

"He shall," said Pwyll, "and I will support you and your lands for as long as I can. When Pryderi has the power he will do it also. If you agree I will give him to Pendaran Dyfed to foster as well as you."

"That is good," they all said. Teirnyon then went back to his own country with his knights. He was offered expensive gifts of jewels as well as fine horses and dogs but he would take none of them.

---

* The word 'Pryder' or 'Pryderi' means anxiety

30

From then on they all stayed in their own lands. Pryderi was brought up carefully, as was fitting. He became a fine young man, handsome and the best at games of any in the country. Years passed and Pwyll died. Pryderi then ruled the seven *Cantrefs of Dyfed successfully and was much loved by his people. Eventually he added the lands of the three Cantrefs of Ystrad Tywi and the four Cantrefs of Cardigan. These were called the Seven Cantrefs of Seissyllwch. Soon he wished to be married. The wife he chose was Cigfa, the daughter of Gwynn Gohoyw, the son of Gloyw Wallt Lydan, the son of Prince Casnar, one of the nobles of this Island.

---

* Cantref means district

3. Branwen, the Daughter of Llyr (Lear)

(The Story of Branwen)

Bendigeid Fran (otherwise and from here on known as Brân The Blest), the son of Llyr, was the crowned king of Britain. One afternoon he was sitting on the rock of Harlech, at the Court, looking over the sea. With him was his brother Manawyddan, and his half-brothers from his mother's side, Nissyen and Efnissyen, together with many nobles. Nissyen was a good young man of a gentle nature who kept the peace. The other step-brother Efnissyen was a trouble maker to the brothers.

As they sat, they saw thirteen ships coming from the south of Ireland. The king said to his men, "Arm yourselves and go and see what these ships want." So the men armed themselves and went towards the ships. When they were near, they had never seen such beautifully equipped ships. They had satin flags on them, and one of the ships was more elaborate than the others. A shield was on it facing upwards showing they came in peace. The men went nearer so that they may talk. Boats were put out and came towards the land.

Now the King could hear them from the rock above. "You are welcome," he said. "To whom do these ships belong and who is chief among you?"

"Lord," they said, "Matholwch, king of Ireland is here. These ships belong to him."

"Why does he come" asked the king, "and will he come on land?"

"He has a favour to ask you," they said, "but he will not land until it is granted."

"What is that?" enquired the king.

"He would like to be your friend," they said, "and he asks for the hand in marriage of your sister Branwen, the daughter of Llyr."

"Let him come on land and we will consult about it," said Brân. The answer was taken to Matholwch and he came on land and was received with great joy at the Court. The next day they discussed the request and decided to marry Branwen to Matholwch. She was one of the three chief ladies of this island and was the fairest lady in the world.

They decided upon Aberffraw for the wedding. They all went there, Matholwch by ship and Brân and his men by land. They then sat down to a feast. Brân and his brother Manawyddan on one side and Matholwch and Branwen on the other. They were in tents not a house, for no house could hold the Great Brân the Blest. They had a banquet and made merry and talked. Then they went to bed and that night Branwen was married to Matholwch.

Soon after, Efnissyen, the trouble maker, saw the horses and asked to whom they belonged. "They belong to Matholwch, king of Ireland, who has been married to Branwen, your sister," he was told.

"Have they given my sister in marriage without my consent?" he asked angrily. "There can be no greater insult to me." He then attacked the horses and damaged them so that they were of no further use.

Matholwch heard of this and was told by his men that it was done as an insult to him. "It is strange that they should do this to me when they gave me such a high born lady to be my wife," he said.

"Lord," said one of his men, "there is nothing for you to do but go back to your ship." So return he did.

Brân the Blest heard the news that Matholwch was leaving without telling him and sent messengers to ask him why. The king of Ireland told them what he had said to his men that he was surprised that Brân would insult him and yet had given him his sister as his bride. They replied that it was not the will of the Court that he had had to endure this insult but that it was as much of an insult to Brân as to Matholwch. "Nevertheless," they said, "he cannot take the insult back."

The messengers returned to Brân and told him what had been said. On hearing this he decided to send his own brother Manawyddan and other nobles to Matholwch and say that he shall have a sound horse for every one that was injured. Also a staff of silver, as tall as himself and a plate of gold as wide as his face. "Say also," he said, "that it was my step-brother on my mother's side who did this harm and I could not put him to death. Let Matholwch come to meet me and we will make peace together as he pleases." They went to Matholwch and took the message in a friendly way and he listened to them.

He said, "I will discuss this with my council." He did this and it was decided to accept Brân's offer and so they returned to the Court in peace.

Then the pavilions and tents were put up like a hall and they sat down to eat. Brân thought that Matholwch was not as cheerful as he had been before. Perhaps he wasn't satisfied with what he had been given in compensation for what he had lost. So Brân said to him, "As well as replacing all the horses, I will give you a cauldron, which if one of your men was killed, you put him in it, he was as well as ever but without his speech. The next morning they gave Matholwch all the horses they had as well as colts from other districts to make up the number.

On the second night, when they sat together, Matholwch asked Brân from where he had had the cauldron he gave him. "I had it from a man from your country," said Brân, "and I would not give it except to someone from there. One day I was hunting in Ireland when I came upon a lake called the Lake of the Cauldron. I saw a huge yellow-haired man come out of the lake with a huge cauldron on his back. He was of vast size and had a woman with him who was twice as large. I asked where they were going and he said to me, 'This is the reason for our journey. In a fortnight this woman will have a son who will be a warrior fully armed.' So I took them with me and looked after them for a year."

"They began, however, to behave badly, molesting and harassing the nobles and ladies. My people asked me to be rid of them and have me choose between them and my lands. The people made a room of iron and put coals as high as the room. They gave the man, woman and child plenty to eat and drink and made them drunk. They lit the coals until the house was red hot. The man heaved his shoulder against the white heat of the room and only he and his wife escaped."

"Then," said Matholwch, "I suppose he came to you."

"Yes, he did," said Brân "and he gave me the cauldron."

Matholwch then returned to Ireland with his thirteen ships and Branwen at his side. There was great joy when they arrived and in due time Branwen has a son who they named Gwern son of Matholwch.

In the second year trouble broke out in Ireland and his men remembered the bad treatment they had received in Wales. They were determined to be revenged. They drove Branwen from the Court and put her to cook in the kitchens. She was not allowed to see her son. Every day the butcher would give her a blow on the ear, such was her punishment. Matholwch forbad any ships to go to Wales for three years.

During this time Branwen reared a starling and taught it to speak. She wrote a letter, tied to the bird's feet and sent it towards Britain. The bird came to Wales and found Brân the Blest who saw and read the letter from Branwen. He was very sad at the suffering of his sister and resolved to go to Ireland. He left seven knights behind, the chief one being Caradawc his son. He sailed towards Ireland, but the water was shallow and he had to proceed by foot.

The swineherds of Matholwch were at the sea-shore looking after their pigs when they saw a strange sight coming out of the sea. They went to Matholwch and told him what they had seen. It looked like a forest with a mountain and a lake either side. Matholwch sent for Branwen to tell them what it was. She said, "It is my brother Brân the Blest and his men coming to see what I have suffered. The lakes are his two eyes." The chief men of Ireland went to discuss what to do. They decided to destroy the bridge over the River Shannon so that no one could cross.

Brân and his men reached the river with no bridge to cross. They asked Brân how they should cross. He said, "He who will be chief will be a bridge. I will be that bridge." He lay down and all his men crossed over the river.

As he got up, the messengers of Matholwch greeted him and told him their master had given the kingdom of Ireland to Gwern, his and Branwen's son in compensation for the wrong that was done to her. Brân was not pleased and said, "Why shouldn't I have the kingdom? Take that message to Matholwch." The messengers went back to Matholwch and told him that Brân was not happy with the offer. They suggested building a house, since Brân had never been in a house, with Brân and his men on one side and Matholwch and his men on the other, and offer him the kingdom. "Perhaps he will then make peace with you," they said and returned to Brân with this message.

After discussing this with his men he accepted. The house was built big and strong, but the Irish played a sly trick. At each corner pillar of the house they placed a large leather bag with an armed man inside. Efnissyen, the trouble maker, came in and asked what was in the bag. "Flour, good friend," said the Irishman. Efnissyen felt it until he felt the head of the man inside and squeezed it tightly until he was dead. "What is in this bag?" he asked moving to another bag. "Flour," said the Irishman nervously. Efnissyen felt inside and did the same thing as he did with all the bags until all the men inside were dead. Then he sang a verse:-

There is in this bag a different sort of flour,
The armed man of great might;
With his fellow warriors
Ready for a fight.

When he had finished, the men of both sides came into the house and peace was made. Brân the Blest called the boy Gwern to him and then the boy went to Manawyddan and everybody loved him. He then went to Nissyen lovingly. Then said Efnissyen, "Why don't you come to me?" and the boy went willingly. Then Efnissyen took the boy and threw him into the blazing fire. When Branwen saw this she almost leaped in after him but was prevented by Brân. Fighting broke out between the two sides and many men were killed.

The Irish then made a fire under the cauldron and threw their dead into it and they survived the next day but could not speak. When Efnissyen saw that his own men were not resuscitated he was sorry for what he had done and threw himself into the cauldron which then burst into four pieces and his own heart burst too.

The men of Wales were not completely victorious for only seven men of them escaped including Pryderi, Manawyddan and Taliesin. Brân the Blest himself was wounded in the foot with a poisoned dart. He told them to cut off his head and take it to the White Mount in London and bury it there, with the face towards France. He said, "You will be on the road a long time. In Harlech you will be feasting for seven years with the birds of Rhiannon singing to you all the while. You will find my head as pleasant company as I am. In Gwales in Penfro* you will be four score years and you must stay there until you open the door that looks towards Aber Henfelen and towards Cornwall. Do not stay there any longer but set out for London to bury the head."

They cut off the head and set out, Branwen with them. She looked back to Ireland and said, "Two islands have been destroyed because of me," and her heart broke. They buried her on the banks of the Alaw. The seven men then travelled to Harlech, taking the head with them. There they met many men and women, and asked of news. "The news is that Caswallawn son of Beli has conquered Britain (the Island of the Mighty) and is crowned in London."

"What has happened to Caradawc, the son of Brân and the seven men who were left with him in this island?" they asked.

"Caswallawn killed six of the men and Caradawc's heart was broken with grief." Caswallawn could not be seen wielding the sword because he wore a Veil of Illusion. He didn't kill Caradawc because he was his nephew. Caradawc was the third one whose heart was broken through grief. "Pendaran Dyfed, the young page, escaped into the wood," they said.

The men went on to Harlech and stopped to rest, eat and drink. Three birds came and sang a certain beautiful song and they stayed there for seven years. After the seventh year they went to Gwales in Penfro. There they found a spacious hall overlooking the ocean. Two of its doors were open but the third one was closed. That was the one that looked out to Cornwall. They stayed there for four score years and were not aware of

_____

* Pembroke

the time passing. It was known as 'the Entertaining of the Noble Head'.

One day Heilyn the son of Gwynn said, "It would be wrong if I didn't open that door to see what is the truth behind it." So he opened the door and soon they saw all the evils that had befallen them and all the friends and companions they had lost, as if it had happened on that very spot. Because it made them so troubled they could not rest but travelled on towards London with the head. They buried it in the White Mount and while it was concealed no invasion came to the island.

So ends the story of those who travelled over from Ireland.

In Ireland none were left alive except five pregnant women in a cave to whom there were born five sons who were nurtured until they became young men. Each took a wife of the mothers of their friends and governed the country. So became the five divisions of Ireland and they found gold and silver and became wealthy.

So ends this part of the Mabinogi, all about the blows given to Branwen, the entertainment of Brân the Blest who went over to Ireland to avenge the treatment of Branwen; the seven years banquet at Harlech, the singing of the birds of Rhiannon and the travelling of the head of Brân for four score[*] years.

---

[*] a score is 20, 4x 20 = 80 years

4. Manawyddan, the Son of Llyr (Lear)

(The Trials of Dyfed)

When the seven men escaped from Ireland had buried the head of Brân the Blest in the White Mount in London, with its face towards France, Manawyddan looked at the town and sighed, "Oh dear, everyone except us has a place to sleep tonight."

"Lord," said Pryderi, "don't be so sad. Your cousin Caswallawn is king of the Island of the Mighty (Britain) and although he has done you wrong, you have never claimed land that didn't belong to you. You are the third disinherited prince."

"Yes," he answered, "but although the man is my cousin, I am very sorry to see anyone in the place of my brother Brân the Blest. I will not live in the same house with him."

"Will you take my advice?" asked Pryderi. "I have seven Cantrefs* which I still own where my mother Rhiannon lives. I will give her to you as your wife. She was lovely when she was young and is still as lovely now. I will also give you the seven Cantrefs. There are no better ones than they. Cicfa, the daughter of Gwynn Gloyw is my wife but since I own the Cantrefs you may gladly have them with Rhiannon as your wife."

They set out on a long journey to Dyfed and arrived at Narberth where a feast had been prepared for them by Rhiannon and Cicfa. They sat down to eat and Manawyddan and Rhiannon began to talk to each other. He thought that he had never seen a lady more graceful and beautiful than she. "Pryderi," he said, "I will do as you say."

"What is that?" asked Rhiannon.

---

* Cantref means district or a division of land.

"Lady," said Pryderi, "I have offered you as wife to Manawyddan the son of Llyr."

"I shall gladly agree to that," said Rhiannon.

"May Heaven reward you for your perfect friendship," said Manawyddan.

Before the feast was over she became his bride. Pryderi said, "You stay here. I think I will go into Lloegyr (England) to pay my respects to Caswallawn the son of Beli."

"He is in Kent," said Rhiannon. "Better to wait here until he comes nearer." So he waited. They finished the feast and soon were hunting and fishing and enjoying the countryside of Dyfed with its plentiful honey and fish. Their friendship was so great that they didn't like to be parted from one another day or night. Pryderi then went to Oxford to pay his respects to Caswallawn.

After his return, Pryderi and Manawyddan feasted and hunted and soon all four of them went to the Gorsedd (throne) of Narberth – which was a mound – and sat there. Then there began a great thunderstorm and a fall of mist so that they couldn't see one another. When the mist lifted, there was a great light all around but as they looked back they saw nothing. All was gone. The people, animals and houses – all were gone except them.

"Good gracious," cried Manawyddan, "where is everyone?" They went to the castle but it was all empty. Even in the kitchens there were just wild beasts. They managed to survive by killing the wild beasts for one and two years but in the third year they grew tired.

"We can't go on like this," said Manawyddan. "Let us go into Lloegyr (England) and look for work to support us. So they went to Hereford and started making saddles for horses. They made them so well trimming them with blue enamel that the other saddlers of Hereford were losing business. Everyone bought their saddles from Manawyddan. So they decided to kill him and his companions.

Pryderi heard of this and they discussed whether they should leave the city. He suggested that they should kill the saddlers but Manawyddan said not because they would be put in prison. "It would be better to go to another town to make a living," he said. So they went to another town. (Ludlow?)

"What shall we make?" asked Pryderi. "We will make shields," said Manawyddan. So they began to make shields and became so good at it that the other shield makers in the town were going out of business and resolved to kill them. They heard of this and Manawyddan said to Pryderi, "Let us kill them."

"O no," said Pryderi, "for Caswallawn would hear of it and we would be finished. Let us go to another town." So to another city they went. (Gloucester?)

"What craft shall we do?" asked Manawyddan.

"Whatever you like," answered Pryderi.

"Let us make shoes. The shoemakers will not trouble us," said Manawyddan. So they made shoes with dressed leather and gold clasps. They did it so well that the other shoemakers were being put out of business and resolved to kill them.

"These men mean to kill us," said Manawyddan.

"We will not put up with that," said Pryderi, "let us kill them."

"No," said Manawyddan, "let us stay here in Lloegyr (England) no longer but go back to Dyfed." They went to Narberth and built a fire and hunted and stayed there for a year.

One morning they both got up to hunt and the dogs went ahead of them and came to a small bush, but the dogs drew back, with their hair bristling. "Let us go near the bush," said Pryderi, "and see what is in it." As they neared the bush a pure white boar came out. The dogs were set on the boar by the men. He ran away and the dogs followed it until they came upon a huge castle which they had never seen before. The boar quickly ran into the castle with the dogs after it. From the top of the Gorsedd they could not hear the dogs at all.

"Lord," said Pryderi, "I will go into the castle to see where my dogs are."

"I don't think that it is wise to go into a castle you have not seen till now," said Manawyddan. "Someone has put a spell on this land to put a castle here."

"I must see about my dogs," said Pryderi. So into the castle he went.

Inside the castle there were no animals or men, no boar or dogs, but in the middle of the floor he saw a fountain with marble around it. On the edge of the fountain was a golden bowl with chains hanging from the air. He was so pleased with the beauty of the bowl that he put his hands on it. They stuck to the bowl and his feet to the marble floor. His pleasure left him and he just stood there speechless.

Manawyddan waited till the end of the day and realising that he would not hear any news of Pryderi or the dogs he returned to the Palace. Rhiannon looked at him and asked, "Where is Pryderi and the dogs?" Then he told her what had happened. "You have been a bad friend and lost a good friend," she said and went towards the castle. As she went in she saw Pryderi holding the bowl and took hold of the bowl as well. As she did so her hands became stuck to the bowl and her feet to the floor and was not able to speak. Night came with thunder and in a fall of mist the castle vanished and mother and son with it.

When Cicfa – the wife of Pryderi – saw that no one was in the palace except herself and Manawyddan she was very sad. He comforted her and vowed great friendship to her, but suggested since they had no food or dogs they should go into Lloegyr (England) to take up a craft. He said he would be a shoemaker again. He did so well making shoes from fine leather and decorated with gold clasps that the other shoemakers in the town were put out of work and decided to kill him. "We will go back to Dyfed," said Manawyddan and to Dyfed they went.

Manawyddan took with him a bundle of wheat. He went to live at Narberth where he had happy memories of hunting and fishing with Pryderi. There he prepared some ground and sowed three fields of wheat which grew extremely well. When harvest time came he went to look at one of his fields of wheat and it was ripe. "I will reap this tomorrow," he said. The next morning at dawn he went to reap the field of wheat but found nothing but bare straw. He was amazed to see all the ears had gone and the bare straw left.

He then went to look at another field of wheat and that was also ripe. "I will reap this tomorrow," he said. The next morning he came intending to reap the wheat but again found nothing but straw. "Oh," he said, "someone is ruining my livelihood." Then he went to look at the third crop and it was as fine as he had ever seen and was ready to reap. "I will stay here tonight," he said, "and watch the field so I will know who is doing this." He told Cicfa about it and said he would watch all night.

He took his weapons and watched and at midnight there was such a loud commotion. He looked and saw the largest army of mice in the world. The mice climbed the stalks of the wheat and bent them over. Each stalk had a mouse on it and each carried away the ears. In great anger he rushed towards the mice, but he could not catch them except one which was slower and fatter than the rest. He caught it, put it in his glove and tied it up with string. He then returned to the palace.

He went into the hall where Cicfa was and lit a fire. He hung the glove by the string on a peg. "What have you there, Lord?" asked Cicfa.

"A thief," he said, "who I found robbing me."

"What kind of thief is that, that you can put it in your glove?" she asked.

"I will tell you," he said, and told her about the fields of wheat and the mice eating them. "I caught this one which was less nimble than the rest," he said, "and now I will hang it."

"Surely it is not seemly for a man of your dignity to hang a creature such as this!" said Cicfa.

"It is what I intend to do. I would hang them all if had caught them," said Manawyddan.

The next morning he went to the Gorsedd (mount) of Narberth taking the mouse with him. He set up two forks on the highest point of the mound. While he was doing this, he saw a scholar coming towards him in old and poor tattered clothes. It was now seven years since he had seen man or beast. "My Lord," said the scholar, "good day to you."

"And to you," he answered. "From where do you come?"

"I come from singing in Lloegyr (England)," said the scholar. "I go through this land to my own, but what are you doing?"

"I am hanging a thief that I caught robbing me," said Manawyddan.

"It does not become a man of your rank to hang a creature such as that. Let it go free," said the scholar seeing the mouse.

"I will not," said Manawyddan. "I caught it robbing me and I will hang it."

"Lord," said the scholar, "I will give you a pound if you set the creature free."

"I will not let it go free, neither will I sell it," he said.

"As you will," said the scholar and went on his way.

As he was placing a stick across the two forks, a priest came along on a richly dressed horse. "Good day to you," said the priest.

"And to you," said Manawyddan. "May I have your blessing?"

"You may," said the priest, but what are you doing?"

"I am hanging a thief that I caught robbing me," he said.

"What sort of thief?" he asked.

"A creature in the form of a mouse," he answered.

"Lord," said the priest, "rather than you should kill this creature, I will buy it from you."

"Neither will I sell it or set it free," said Manawyddan.

"I will give you three pounds to let it go," said the priest.

"I will not take any money for it, it should be hanged," he said.

"As you will," said the priest and went on his way.

Then he tied the string around the mouse's neck, and as he was about to tighten it, he saw a bishop's retinue with his pack-horses and attendants coming towards him. He stopped what he was doing. "Lord Bishop," he said, "may I have your blessing?"

"You may, but what are you doing?" asked the bishop.

"Hanging a thief that has been robbing me."

"Is that a mouse I see in your hand?"

"Yes and she has robbed me," he answered.

"I don't like to see a man of your status destroying so worthless a creature as this. Let it loose and I will give you seven pounds for it."

"I will not set it free," said Manawyddan.

"I will give you twenty pounds to set it free," said the bishop.

"I will not, for double that," he said.

"I will give you all the horses you can see and the seven loads of baggage and the seven horses it is upon."

"I will not," said Manawyddan.

44

"What price will you take to set the creature free?" asked the Bishop.

"I would like Rhiannon and Pryderi to be free," said Manawyddan.

"That you shall have," he answered.

"I will not set it free yet," he said.

"What else do you want?" asked the Bishop.

"I ask that the spell and magic be removed from the seven Cantrefs of Dyfed."

"That you shall have, now set the mouse free."

"I will not until I know who the mouse may be."

"She is my wife," answered the Bishop.

"Why did she come to me?" asked Manawyddan.

"To ruin you," he answered. "I am Llwyd the son of Cil Coed and I cast a spell over the seven Cantrefs of Dyfed. It was to avenge the treatment of Gwawl the son of Clud because he is my friend. I also had revenge upon Pryderi for the game of Badger in the Bag that Pwyll played upon Gwawl. My servants transformed themselves into mice and ruined your corn on two nights, then my wife and her ladies did the same on the third night. Now she is pregnant, or you wouldn't have been able to catch her. I will give you back Rhiannon and Pryderi if you will now set her free."

"Promise that no more magic shall be on the seven Cantrefs of Dyfed, then I will set her free," said Manawyddan.

"Then set my wife free," said the bishop.

"Not until I see Rhiannon and Pryderi," said Manawyddan.

"Look, here they come," he answered. They came and were greeted by Manawyddan. "Now set my wife free," said the bishop. So he did. Then Llwydd struck the mouse with a magic wand and she was changed back into a beautiful young woman.

"Look at your land," he said, "and you will see it as it was full of crops, herds, people and houses." It was as he described.

Manawyddan asked what Pryderi and Rhiannon had to suffer in their slavery. "Pryderi had a part of the gate of my palace hung around his neck and Rhiannon had the collars of the horses after they had been carrying hay about hers." This was their punishment.

5. Math, the Son of Mathonwy

Math, the son of Mathonwy was lord over Gwynedd, and Pryderi the son of Pwyll was lord of the twenty-one Cantrefs of the South; these were the seven Cantrefs of Dyfed, the seven Cantrefs of Morganwc, the four Cantrefs of Ceridigiawn and the three of Ystrad Tywi.

Now Math loved to rest his feet in the lap of a lady, except when he was at war. The lady was Goewin, the daughter of Pebin of Dôl Pebin in Arfon and she was very beautiful.

At that time Math always lived at Caer Dathyl, in Arfon and was not able to go all around his land. His nephews, however, Gilfaethwy the son of Don and Gwydion the son of Don went instead of him.

Although the lady was always with Math, it was Gilfaethwy who was also in love with her, so much so, that his appearance and spirit changed for love of her.

One day his brother Gwydion looked hard at him and asked, "What is the matter with you?"

"Why, what do you see?" he replied.

"I see that your expression has changed," said Gwydion.

"It is because if Math knew the truth it would be dangerous for me," he said.

"I know," said Gwydion, "don't say anymore, you love Goewin don't you?" His brother sighed deeply, but Gwydion said, "Don't be unhappy, I will help you."

So they went to Math the son of Mathonwy and Gwydion said, "Lord, I have heard of some animals that have never been known in this island before."

"What are they called?" asked Math.

"Pigs, Lord. They are small and their meat is better than that of oxen."

"Who owns them?" he asked.

46

"Pryderi, the son of Pwyll; they were sent to him from Annwfyn by Arawn the King of Annwfyn."

"How can we get them from him?" asked Math.

"We will go, disguised as bards*," they said. "Never fear, we shall not come back without them."

With ten other men they set out for Ceredigiawn to a place called Rhuddlan Teifi where Pryderi's palace was and was welcomed there. That night they told tales and sang songs and pleased everyone in the court. After that they asked Pryderi a favour and he asked what it was. "Lord," said Gwydion, "would you let us have the animals you have had from Annwfyn."

"Oh," said Pryderi, "that would be the easiest thing in the world to do but for the contract between me and my land concerning them. They shall not go from here until I have doubled their number."

"I can free you from the contract," said Gwydion. "Give me until tomorrow."

That night he and his men went to their lodgings and he said, "We shall not have the pigs just by asking."

"How can we get them?" they asked.

"I will make it easy for us to have them," he answered. He then cast a spell and made twelve horses appear and twelve black greyhounds, each of them with a collar and leash which looked like gold. On the horses were twelve saddles and all that should have been iron was made of gold and so were the bridles well made.

He took them to Pryderi and offered them in exchange for the pigs. He also offered twelve gilded shields. Pryderi accepted and exchanged the pigs for the horses, dogs and shields. Then Gwydion left and travelled on with the pigs. He said, "We must go very quickly because the spell will not last until the same time tomorrow."

That night they travelled through many towns for many men were following them. "We must push forward to the safety of Gwynedd," said Gwydion. They reached a town called Arllechwedd where they made a sty for the pigs. Then they

---

* Welsh minstrels or poets

went to see Math the son of Mathonwy at Caer Dathyl. "What is the news?" asked Gwydion.

"Pryderi is gathering twenty-one Cantrefs to pursue you," they said. Just then they heard the trumpets and the army of many men. They armed themselves and went to Penardd in Arfon.

The two brothers, Gwydion and Gilfaethwy returned to Caer Dathyl and Gilfaethwy went to Math's apartment and turned out many ladies rudely but forced Goewin to stay against her will.

The next day they went back to where Math was with his men and waited for Pryderi and his men to arrive. Between Maenor Penardd and Maenor Coed Alun they took their stand. There Pryderi attacked them and a battle took place. Many men were killed. Pryderi's men fled to a place called Nant Call and many more men were killed. The rest fled to Dol Pen Maen where they stopped and tried to make peace.

So that there would be peace Pryderi gave up hostages including Cwrgi Gwastra and many sons of nobles. He then sent a messenger to Math to stop his people fighting and to leave it to between him and Gwydion, who started all the trouble. So it was agreed and they armed themselves and fought. By force of strength, fierceness and by the magic and spells of Gwydion, Pryderi was killed. He was buried at Maen Tyriawc above Melenwyd. His men sadly returned to their land having lost their lord, his best warriors, as well as most of their horses and armour.

The men of Gwynedd were joyful at their triumph and now released the hostages who were set free to follow the men of the south.

Math went back to his home at Caer Dathyl and went into his apartment so that he could lie down and put his feet on his lady's lap. "Lord," said Goewin, "put your feet on someone else's lap for now I am a wife."

"What do you mean?" he asked. "I was attacked unawares and everyone knew about it. It was your nephews Gwydion and Gilfaethwy who hurt me and shamed you."

"Really," he exclaimed, "I will do my utmost to put this matter right. I will compensate you and make you my wife.

You shall have possession of all my lands. Then I will have my own revenge."

The two brothers kept away from the Court and stayed on the land until it was forbidden to give them food or drink. At first they didn't come to Math, but at last they came. "Good day to you Lord," they said.

"Well," he said, "have you come to pay me compensation?"

"We are at your mercy," they said. "You cannot make up for my shame – apart from the death of Pryderi, but since you are at my mercy, I will begin your punishment." He then took his magic wand and struck Gilfaethwy so that he became a deer. He did the same with Gwydion before he got away. "You are now in the form of animals and will stay as such until you must come to me a year from now," he said.

At the end of a year there was a loud noise and a barking of dogs outside the apartment wall. "Lord," said one of his men, "there are two deer and a fawn outside." Math got up and went out. When he saw the animals he said, "As you were deer last year, now will you be wild pigs for the next year." He struck them with the magic wand. "The young one I will take to be baptised," he said. The name he gave him was Hydwn. "Go and be wild pigs," he said, "but come back under the wall a year from now."

When the year had passed, the barking of dogs was heard under the wall of the apartment. Math and his Court went out and saw two wild pigs as well as a well-grown one with them. "This I will take to be baptised," said Math. "As for you, you were wild pigs last year, now you will be wolves for the year to come." He struck them with his magic wand and they became wolves. "Be just like wolves," he said, "but return here a year from today."

On the same day at the end of the year, he heard a great noise and the barking of dogs under the wall of the apartment. He went outside and saw two wolves and a strong cub between them. "This I will take," said Math, "to be baptised and his name shall be Bleiddwn. Now these three are they:

The three sons of Gilfaethwy the false,
The three faithful warriors,
Bleiddwn, Hydwn and Hychdwn the Tall."

Then he struck the two brothers with his magic wand and they became themselves again. He said, "For the wrong you have done me this has been your punishment and your shame. Prepare precious ointment for these men and dress them," and it was done.

After they were dressed and armed, they came to him. "So," said Math, "we will now have peace and friendship between us. Give me your advice. What lady shall I look for?"

"Lord," they said, "that is easy. Look for Arianrod, the daughter of Don, your niece, your sister's daughter."

They brought her to him and he said, "Are you the lady?"

"I don't know, Lord, other than I am me." He took his magic wand and bent it. "Step over this wand," he said, "and I shall know if you are the lady I look for." She stepped over the wand and straight away there appeared a fine chubby fair-haired boy. When he cried out, she went to the door, and they saw a small form there, but before anyone could get a second glimpse of it, Gwydion had taken it, wrapped a velvet scarf around it and hidden it in the chest at the foot of his bed.

"Well," said Math, about the fine fair-haired boy, "I will have this baptised and will call him Dylan." So the boy was baptised and immediately plunged into the sea and was a natural swimmer. He was then called Dylan, the son of the wave.

As Gwydion woke in his bed one morning, he heard a cry from the chest at his feet. He quickly opened the chest and there was the baby boy stretching out his arms from the scarf. He lifted up the boy, carried him to a woman who could nurse him and he was nursed by her for a year. At the end of the year he seemed like a two-year-old. In the second year he came to the Court and Gwydion noticed him and became friendly with him and loved him better than anyone else. When he was four he seemed as big as if he were eight.

One day, Gwydion went out with the boy to the Castle belonging to Arianrod. She welcomed him to the Court and asked, "Who is the boy with you?"

"He is your son," he answered.

"Why do you shame me in this way?" she asked.

"Unless you suffer greater shame than that of my bringing up such a fine boy as this, you will have very little shame," he replied.

"What is the boy's name?" she asked.

"He has no name yet," he replied.

"Well," she said, "I will make it his destiny that he will have no name unless given it by me."

"You are a wicked woman," he said, "but the boy shall have a name however displeasing it is to you. As for you, you can no longer be called a lady." With that he returned in fury to Caer Dathyl with the boy and stayed there the night.

The next day he got up and took the boy to the seashore between there and Aber Menei. He saw some sedges* and seaweed and he turned them into a boat. Out of dry sticks and sedges he made some Spanish leather. Then he made a sail for the boat and he and the boy sailed to the port of Castle Arianrod and they started making shoes. He was seen from the castle so he put a spell on himself and the boy so that they could not be recognised. "What are those men in that boat doing?" asked Arianrod.

"They are shoemakers," answered her men.

"Go and see what kind of leather they have and what kind of work they can do," she said.

They went to the shore and saw that the man and boy were colouring and gilding the leather. They went back and told Arianrod. "Well," she said, "measure my foot and ask the shoemakers to make shoes for me." He made shoes for her but larger than the measure. They were taken to her and she said, "These are too large. I shall pay for them but ask him to make a pair smaller than these." Then he made a pair smaller than her foot and sent them to her. "Tell him that these are too small," which they did, but he said, "I will not make any more shoes until I see her foot." This she was told and she answered, "I will go to him."

She went down to the boat and he was shaping the shoes and the boy stitching them. They greeted each other, but Arianrod said, "I am surprised that you cannot make shoes to measure."

_____

* A grasslike plant growing by waterside

51

"I could not," he replied, "but now I shall be able to."

Just then a wren landed on the deck of the boat and the boy shot at it and hit it in the leg between the sinew and the bone. "Really," she said, "with what skill has the boy hit it!"

"Yes," said Gwydion, "for now he has a name and a very good name. He shall be called Llew Llaw Gyffes." (Llew – fair; Llaw – hand; Gyffes – skilful.)

The leather and shoes disappeared and he and the boy were changed back to their normal appearance. "Well," she said, "I will make it his destiny that he will not bear arms until I give them to him."

"He will bear arms," said Gwydion, "despite your meanness."

Then they went to Dinas Dinllef where Llew was brought up to ride any horse and he was a perfect, strong young man in every way. Gwydion said to him, seeing him pining for his own horse and weapons. "Tomorrow we shall go on a journey, so cheer up."

"I will," said Llew.

At dawn the next morning, they got up and travelled to the castle of Arianrod. They changed their appearance and became two young men, but Gwydion was the stouter of the two. When they got to the gate he said, "Porter, go in and tell your lady that there are two bards (poets) from Glamorgan to entertain her."

"Let them in," said Arianrod, when she was told, and she greeted them joyfully. They feasted and told tales, for Gwydion was an excellent story-teller, until it was time to go to bed.

In the early hours of the morning, Gwydion called up his magic powers and by the time day broke, there was such a commotion outside with shouting, trumpets and a great uproar. Arianrod knocked at their door and told them of a great sight of ships coming towards the land. "What can we do?" she said.

"Lady, we must defend the castle as well as we can," he said.

"Will you help the young man to put on his armour and I will arm myself with the help of the ladies?" he said.

"I will gladly do so," she said and Gwydion said,

"Have you finished?"

"I have," she said.

"So have I," he said. Let us now take off our armour since we have no need of it."

"Why," she asked, "there is an army at the door."

"Oh Lady," he said, "there is no army!"

"What was this commotion then?" she asked.

"The commotion was to break your prophecy. Now he has armour thanks to you," and he changed their appearance back to normal.

"Oh, you are a wicked man," said Arianrod. Many young men could have lost their lives today. Now I will make a third destiny upon the young man, that he will never have a wife of all the women on this earth."

"You were always an evil woman," said Gwydion, "to treat your son so. He shall have a wife despite you."

They then went to see Math the son of Mathonwy, complained bitterly about Arianrod and Gwydion told him how he managed to get arms for the young man. "Well," said Math, "we will try to make a wife for him with spells and charms out of flowers." So they took the flower of the oak, the broom and meadowsweet and made from them the most beautiful girl that man had ever seen. They called her Blodeuwedd (flowers).

After they were married, Math said, "It is not easy for a man to manage without property. I shall give him the best Cantref I have," and Llew lived from then on at a place called Mur y Castell (the wall of the castle) and he ruled the land and was beloved by all.

On day he went to visit Math at Caer Dathyl. Blodeuwedd was left in the Court and heard the sound of a horn. She then saw a tired stag go by and dogs and huntsmen following it. Then came a group of men on foot and she sent a lad to ask who these people were. He came back and told her it was Gronw Pebyr, the lord of Penllyn and his men.

He killed the stag, fed his dogs and it was nearly nightfall when she decided to ask him to stay the night as it would be discourteous not to. He accepted her invitation and thanked her for her kindness. When he had changed his clothes, they sat down and as she looked at him she became full of love for him. As he gazed on her, he felt the same and they talked that evening of their love for each other.

The next day he was going to leave, but she begged him to stay with her. So he stayed another night. The next day they wondered how they might be together always. Gronw said they would have to kill Llew, but she said only Llew would know how he might meet his death. So before he left her the next day, he asked her to find out from Llew how his death may come about while all the time pretending to care for him.

That night Llew Llaw Gyffes returned home. The next day they spent talking, feasting and making music. He noticed that Blodeuwedd was very quiet and asked her what was the matter. "I am not ill," she said, "but I do worry about you getting killed."

"I will not be easily killed," he said.

"Tell me how you might be killed," she said, "for my memory is better than yours."

"I can only be killed by a spear that took a year to make," he said, "and no work should be done on it except on Sundays when people go to church. I cannot be killed in a house or outside it, on horseback or on foot."

"Tell me how you could be killed," she said.

"I will," he said. "By making a bath for me beside a river and putting a roof over it, covering it tightly and bringing a he-goat to the side of the cauldron. Then if I place one foot on the he-goat's back and one on the cauldron, whoever strikes me with the spear will cause my death."

"Well," she said, "thank goodness, it will be easy to avoid that."

She immediately sent a message about this to Gronw at Penllyn. He worked at making a spear for a year and let her know when it was ready.

"Lord," said Blodeuwedd to Llew, "I am still worried about the manner of your death. Will you show me how it could be done if I prepare a bath for you?"

"I will," he said.

She then sent a message to Gronw and told him to be on the hill above the river. She also collected all the goats that were in the Cantref and brought them to the riverside. She said to Llew, "I have prepared the bath, will you go and look at it?"

"I will," he said.

"Will you go into the bath, Lord?" she asked, and he did. She brought the he-goat to the bath. Then Llew got out, put on his trousers and put one foot on the edge of the bath and the other on the goat's back.

Immediately Gronw rose on one knee on the hill, took aim and fixed the poisoned dart which hit Llew in the side, who then flew up in the form of an eagle, gave a fearful scream and wasn't seen again.

As soon as he left, Gronw and Blodeuwedd went back to the palace. The next day Gronw took possession of Ardudwy and ruled over it and Penllyn together.

When this news reached Math and Gwydion, they were both terribly sad and Gwydion said, "Lord, I must go and find my son." He set out through Gwynedd and Powys but found no sign of him. He went into Arfon, came to a peasant's house and stayed there the night. The swineherd was the last to come in and the man of the house asked him if his sow had come home. "She has and has returned to the pigs," he said.

"Where does the sow go to?" asked Gwydion. The swineherd answered that no one knows where the sow goes when she leaves the sty in the morning.

"Will you not open the sty until I am with you?" asked Gwydion. The swineherd agreed.

At dawn's early light, the swineherd woke Gwydion and they went outside to the sty. The swineherd opened it, the sow leaped forward and was off at speed. Gwydion followed her. She followed the course of the river and made for a brook – now called Nant* y Llew. There she stopped and started feeding under an oak tree. Gwydion looked at what the sow was feeding on and saw that it was rotten flesh and maggots. He looked up into the tree where he saw an eagle which when it shook itself, rotten flesh and maggots fell to the ground and the sow was eating it. He thought that the eagle must be Llew so he sang a verse:-

---

* Nant – brook of Llew or Llew's brook

Oak that grows beside the brook,
With the darkened sky in view,
Can I not tell with upward look
Could it be that it is Llew?

When he heard this, the eagle came down until he reached the middle of the tree. Then Gwydion sang another verse:-

Oak that grows on river plain,
Storm and tempest of nine score,
Is not wetted by the rain?
In its branches Llew Llaw.

Then the eagle came down until he was on the lowest branch of the tree and Gwydion then sang a third verse:-

Oak that grows beneath the hill,
Shall I not say it might be he?
Tall, majestic is it still
That Llew will then come down to me.

The eagle then came down on to Gwydion's knee. He struck him with his magic wand and he returned to his old self. No one saw such a pitiful sight. He was all skin and bone.

Llew was taken to Caer Dathyl, to Math's Court and good doctors were called from Gwynedd to treat him, but it was a good year before he was healed. He then said to Math, "It is time I had revenge on him that gave me this injury. The sooner I do it the better I shall be pleased."

They called all the men of Gwynedd together and set out for Ardudwy. Gwydion was ahead of them and reached Mur y Castell. When Blodeuwedd heard they were coming, she and her ladies fled to the mountains and came to a river in which they all drowned except Blodeuwedd. Gwydion caught up with her.

"I will not kill you," he said to her, "but I will do worse than that. I shall turn you into a bird and because of the shame you have brought on Llew you will never show your face in daylight for fear of other birds attacking you. You will not change your name. You will always be Blodeuwedd (Flower

Face) for that is the name for the owl you will become." That is the reason why all other birds hate the owl and why the owl is called Blodeuwedd even now.

Then Gronw Pebyr went back to Penllyn and sent a messenger to Llew to ask him if he would take land, or gold, or silver for the hurt he had received. "I will not." he said. "The very least I will accept is that he comes to the place where he wounded me with the dart and that I stand where he did so that I can take aim at him."

This was told to Gronw. "So," he said, "it seems that I must do this. Will any of you go in my place?"

"No," they said. Because of this refusal, they are known as the third disloyal tribe to this day.

"Well" he said, "I must go."

They both went to the bank of the river Cynfael and Gronw stood where Llew had stood when he struck him and Llew stood where Gronw had stood. Then Gronw said to Llew, "Since it was through the cunning of a woman that I did what I did to you, I beg you to let me put that great stone between me and the blow."

"I will not refuse you that," said Llew. So Gronw placed the stone between him and Llew.

Llew then took aim with the spear which pierced the stone and went through Gronw's back and killed him. There is still the stone on the bank of the river Cynfael with a hole through it known as Llechgronw (Gronw's Stone).

After this Llew ruled the land prosperously and was eventually Lord of all Gwynedd.

6. The Dream of Macsen Wledig

Macsen Wledig was Emperor of Rome. He was the most handsome man and wiser than any emperor before him. One day he met with a council of kings and said, "Tomorrow I wish to go hunting." The next day they all set out and came to a valley of the river that flowed towards Rome. There were thirty-two kings, all his servants, with him, not just for hunting but so that he could be friends with them.

The sun was so hot that Macsen felt sleepy and his men put up their shields to protect him from the sun. They put a golden shield under his head and he slept. While he slept he had a wonderful dream. He was travelling along the valley of the river when he came to the highest mountain in the world. He saw great rivers flowing into the sea and came to the mouth of the largest river ever seen. There he saw a great city with a huge castle in the city with towers of various colours. He also saw a fleet of ships, one larger than the others in gold and silver with a whale bone for a bridge. He went across the bridge onto the ship. The sail was hoisted and he set sail.

As he slept it seemed that he came to the fairest island in the world which he crossed until he came to another smaller island across a strait of water. There he saw a beautiful castle. The gate was open. He went into the castle which had a hall with a roof of gold, doors of gold and he saw two auburn-haired young men playing chess. The chess board was silver and the pieces were golden. The young men wore clothes of jet black satin and had bands of red gold with precious stones around their heads. They wore shoes of the finest Spanish leather on their feet.

Beside a pillar in the hall sat a grey-haired man in a chair of ivory with two eagles of red gold carved on it. He wore rings and bracelets of gold and a gold collar around his neck. His hair was bound with a gold band. He was a powerful looking man. A chessboard was in front of him and he was carving chessmen out of gold.

Before him, sitting in a chair of red gold he saw a lady. She was so beautiful that it was easier to look at the bright sun than to look on her beauty. She wore garments of white silk with clasps of red gold and a mantle of gold silk. She wore a band of red gold on her head but this one was studded with rubies, pearls and precious stones.

She got up from her chair, he put his arms around her and they sat together on the chair cheek to cheek. With the noise of the dogs, the clanking of the shields and the neighing and stamping of the horses, the emperor awoke. He felt so sad and miserable that he had lost the lady of his dream. He was asked, "Isn't it time for your meal?" So he mounted his horse and rode towards Rome.

He was in this way for a whole week. He did not take part in the feasting with his men or the music and entertainment. All he wanted to do was sleep. One day, a page of his – who was king of the Romans– came to him and said, "Lord, the people dislike you."

"Why is that?" he asked.

"Because we can get no response or reaction from you."

"Page," he said, "call all the wise men of Rome together and I will tell you why I am so sorrowful."

The wise men of Rome came to the emperor and he told them, "I have had a dream of the most beautiful lady and because of her I have no interest in anything in life any more."

"Lord," they said, "let us advise you to send messengers for three years to the three parts of the world to look for your dream."

So the messengers travelled for a year and found nothing, so when they returned the emperor was extremely sad. Then the page, who was king of the Romans spoke to him again.

"Why not go hunting in the same place as before?" he said, which the emperor did. He came to a bank of a river and said,

"This is where I was when I had the dream." Thirteen messengers were then sent out and they saw a very high mountain and eventually came to a large river flowing into the sea and the vast city with many-coloured towers. Then they saw a fleet of ships, with one ship larger than the others.

"Look," they said, "this was the dream our master had."

The great ship crossed the sea and came to the Island of Britain. They crossed the country until they reached Eryri (Snowdonia).

"Look," they said again, "the mountain that our Lord saw."* Soon they saw Môn (Anglesey) facing them across the strait.

"This is what our master saw in his sleep," they said. They saw a huge castle. Its gates were open so they went inside. They saw a hall in the castle and said, "This is the hall he saw in his dream." They went into the hall and saw two young men playing chess and a grey-haired man beside a pillar in the ivory chair carving chessmen. Then they saw the lady sitting on a chair of red gold.

The messengers went down on their knees. "All hail, Empress of Rome," they said.

"Good sirs," said the lady, "I see you are highborn messengers but why do you mock me?"

"We do not mock you, lady, but the emperor has seen you in his dream and is miserable and lifeless without you. Will you go with us and be made Empress of Rome or shall the emperor come to you and make you his wife?"

"I think you speak the truth, kind sirs, but if the emperor loves me, let him come here to find me."

The messengers returned to Rome and had to change their tired horses on the way. When then reached Rome they told the emperor that they had found the lady he loved. "We will guide you, over sea and land to the place where she is. We know her name (Elen-Helen), her family and her race, they said.

Immediately the emperor set out with his army. The men who had found her were his guides. They went towards the Island of Britain over the sea and he conquered the land from Beli, the son of Manogan, drove him into the sea and went to Arfon. The emperor recognised the land when he saw it and he saw the castle of Aber Sain. There, in the hall, he saw Cynan

---

* See the Welsh folksong 'O Mountain White' in my songbook Songs of Wales – Boosey & Hawkes

the son of Eudaf and Adeon the son of Eudaf playing chess. He saw Eudaf the son of Caradoc sitting on a chair of ivory carving chessmen. Sitting on a chair of gold he saw the lady.

"Empress of Rome," he said, "all hail!" He threw his arms around her neck and that night she became his bride.

The next morning the lady asked for her dowry. He told her to name what she wanted. She asked for the Island of Britain for her father from the English Channel to the Irish Sea together with three islands for the Empress of Rome. She also asked for castles to be built at Caernarvon, Caerleon and Carmarthen. They had soil brought from Rome so the emperor would feel at home. She had three roads built between each castle called the Roads of Elen Llyddawc (of the hosts) because the Empress came from the Island of Britain.

The emperor stayed on the Island for seven years. At that time, there was a custom in Rome that if an emperor stayed on in a foreign country for over seven years, he should not return and another emperor would rule in his place. The new emperor sent this letter to him at Caerleon, 'If you come and if ever you come to Rome'. He replied in these words, 'If I come to Rome, and if I come'.

Then he and his army set out for Rome. He conquered France and Burgundy on his way and came to the city of Rome. He was outside the city for a year and was no nearer taking it than the first day. They heard this in Britain and Elen's brothers went to help him. The emperor welcomed them. They were a handsome army but not large.

They measured the height of the wall of the city and had carpenters make a ladder for every four men. At midday both the emperors took their midday meal so in the morning the Britons ate and drank and while the emperors were eating they scaled the walls. The emperor of Rome had no time to repel the attack and was killed and many others with him.

Then Macsen came to Elen and said, "I am surprised that your brothers didn't take the city for me."

She replied, "Lord, my brothers are the wisest men in the world. Go to them and they will give you the city willingly." The gates of the city were then opened and the Emperor sat on the throne and all Rome was under his rule.

The emperor told the brothers that they may go and conquer any lands, castles and cities, which they did until Adeon decided to go back to Britain, but Cynan remained in a country which is now called Brittany. The emperor and empress ruled over Rome for many years, and there was peace between Rome and Britain from then on. This was the outcome of Macsen Wledig's dream.

7. The Story of Lludd and Llefelys

(or The Three Plagues of Britain)

Beli the Great, the son of Manogan had four sons. The eldest was Lludd and the youngest was Llefelys. After his death the Island of Britain was ruled by Lludd, and he ruled well. He rebuilt the walls of London and put up many great towers. He also had the people build houses inside the walls. He lived there for the best part of each year and that was why it was called Caer Lludd. Its main gate was called Lludd's Gate or Ludgate as it is now known.

Lludd loved his brother Llefelys best of all his brothers and when the king of France died leaving no heir but a daughter, it was decided that Llefelys married her and ruled France which he did.

After a time, three plagues fell on the Island of Britain. The first was a race of people called the Coranians who caused much trouble, for however low the people of Britain spoke, they heard it – the wind carried it to them – so they couldn't be got rid of.

The second plague was a shriek which came on every May-eve over all the houses of the Island of Britain. It so frightened the people that the men lost their strength and the women their beauty. The trees, animals, earth and waters were left barren and desolate.

The third plague was that however much food and provisions were prepared in the king's court, after the first night's feast, none was left. King Lludd thought that it was easier to be free of the first plague than the other two. He discussed the problem with his nobles and it was decided to go to France to seek the help of Llefelys king of France. When he heard of this he went to meet his brother in a large fleet of ships, but only one ship went forward to meet Lludd and they welcomed each other with brotherly love.

Lludd told his brother the purpose of his journey and Llefelys said that they must discuss the problem, but that the wind might take their words and the Coranians hear them. So he built a large brass horn, but they could not hear each other for there was a moaning sound and Llefelys said that it was a demon in the horn. He sent for some wine to pour through it. The demon was then driven out of the horn and they were able to speak to each other clearly.

To get rid of the first plague Llefelys gave Lludd some insects which he should crush in water. He said that it would have power to destroy the Coranians if poured over all the people, but not hurt his own.

"The second plague," he said, "is a dragon which is fighting with a foreign dragon. That is why it is screaming. You must measure the length and breadth of the Island to get its central point. There dig a pit and pour the best mead* you can find and cover it with satin. You must watch it yourself – for no other person will do – and the dragons will fight furiously, then change their form into pigs and fall into the pit. They will drink up all the mead and fall asleep. You must then cover them and bury them in a stone coffer and they will never bother you again."

"The cause of the third plague," he said, "is a mighty magician who takes your food and drink for his own use. He sends everyone to sleep with a spell so you yourself must stand watch again and if you start to get sleepy have a tub of water standing by and plunge into that to keep yourself awake."

Lludd then returned to his own land. He immediately summoned all his people together, including the Coranians. As Llefelys had taught him, he crushed the insects in water and threw it all over them. It destroyed the whole of the Coranians but did not hurt any of the Britons.

Sometime after this, Lludd had the Island of Britain measured in length and breadth. In Oxford he found the central

---

* An alcoholic drink made from honey and water

point, had a pit dug and filled it with the best mead that could be made. He covered it with satin and sat down to watch the night. Soon he saw the two dragons fighting. When they were tired they turned into little pigs and fell into the pit. When they had drunk all the mead and fallen asleep, Lludd covered them, put them into a stone coffer and buried it in the safest place he could find – Snowdon. That was the end of the screaming that had terrified his people and made his land barren and desolate.

When this was done he had a great feast prepared. When it was ready he placed a tub of cold water by him and kept watch over it himself. There was much music which made Lludd feel very drowsy and he was tempted to sleep, but each time he dozed he put himself in the water to keep awake.

Soon a huge man appeared in strong, heavy armour carrying a hamper. He began to put all the food of meat and drink into the hamper. Lludd was amazed that the hamper could hold so much. "Stop," he cried, "stop!" The man put down the hamper and they began to fight first with swords and when they were broken, by hand to hand fighting which Lludd won.

After he had overcome the huge man, the man asked for mercy. "How can I be merciful to you after all the injuries and wrongs you have done me?" asked Lludd. He answered, "I will make good all the injuries and wrongs I have done you and will promise never to do it again. I will be your slave forever."

Lludd accepted this. So was the Island of Britain freed from the three plagues and Lludd ruled in peace and prosperity for the rest of his life.

8. Cilhwch and Olwen
(or The Quest for Olwen)

I. The Curse

King Cilydd wished to have a wife and he chose the Princess Goleuddydd, the daughter of Prince Anlawdd. It was hoped, in the land, that they would have a son and heir. When she became pregnant, however, she became ill in her mind and went away to the countryside where a swineherd* was keeping a herd of swine*. Before she gave birth to a boy her reason returned and the swineherd took her back to the king's palace.

They named the boy Cilhwch because he had been found in a swine's burrow. He was first cousin to Arthur and was put out to be nursed.

Soon his mother Goleuddydd became ill and was afraid she would die. She made her husband promise that after her death he would not take a wife until he saw a wild rose with two blooms growing on her grave. She asked him to see that the grave was cleaned every year so that nothing grew on it. He promised this and then she died.

He kept his promise and also sent an attendant to the grave every morning to see if anything was growing there. At the end of the seventh year he failed to do this, and as he was out hunting one day he passed her burial ground when he saw the wild rose. He immediately took advice as to who he should marry. One of his advisors said, "I know of a wife that would suit you well. She is the wife of King Doged." So they went to find her. They killed her husband the king, brought back his

---

* pig keeper
* pigs

wife and only daughter and she became his wife. No one thought to tell her about his son Culhwch.

One day the Queen was out walking when she came to the house of an old crone[*] with not a tooth in her head. "Old woman," she said, "tell me, where are the children of the man who so violently carried me away?"

"He has no children," said the old crone.

"Oh dear, how unhappy that makes me," said the Queen, "to be with a man with no children."

The old crone took pity on her and whispered in her ear, "Don't be sorrowful, he has one son."

The Queen returned happily to the palace and asked the King why he had kept his son from her. He duly sent messengers for the boy who was brought to the court. "What a handsome young man I have for a stepson!" said the Queen. "It is time for you to marry. I have a daughter who will be just the wife for you."

"I do not want to marry," said Culhwch. "I am too young to take a wife."

"I declare I shall put a curse upon you that you will not marry anyone until you marry Olwen, the daughter of Ysbaddeden Pencawr – the Chief Giant," said the Queen.

At the mention of the name Olwen, Culhwch blushed and was suddenly filled full of love for her. He went to his father and asked him where he could find her. "My stepmother has put a curse on me," he said, "that I may not marry until I marry Olwen. Where can I find her?"

"I am sorry, I do not know where you can find her. Have courage my son," he said. "Arthur is your first cousin[*]. Go to his court and get him to cut your hair, then he must grant any favour you ask of him. You can ask him where to find Olwen."

II. At Arthur's Court

Culhwch set out on a horse with a head of dappled grey which was four years old, with a bridle of linked gold on his head and a saddle of precious gold. In his hand he held two

[*] a withered old woman

[*] Arthur was a legendary King in Wales before the later tales of Camelot

spears of silver well-tempered with steel, three ells[*] in length with an edge to cut the wind and swifter than the dewdrop in the month of June. A gold hilted sword was on his thigh with a gold blade, and he held a buckler[*] with an ivory boss[*]. With him were two brownish greyhounds with white fronts and having strong collars of rubies around their necks. The left one bounded to the right and the right one to the left, jumping around him. The clods of earth from the horses' hooves flew around him like swallows.

He wore a four-cornered cloak of purple with an apple of gold in each corner. Every one of the apples weighed the value of a hundred kine (cows). There was precious gold to the value of three hundred kine on his shoes. He travelled so lightly that not a blade of grass was disturbed beneath him as he approached the gates of Arthur's palace.

The young man said, "Is there a porter?"

"There is," came the reply," but if you don't be quiet, you will not be welcome. I am Arthur's porter on every first day of January, but during the rest of the year, the duty is taken by Huandaw, Gogigwe, Llaesgymin and best of all, Penpingion who goes on his head to spare his feet; neither upwards or downwards but like a rolling stone upon the floor of the court."

"Open the gate," demanded Cilhwch.

"I will not," said the porter.

"Why not?" he asked.

"Because Arthur is having his meal and there is merriment in the court. Only the son of a king of a privileged country or a craftsman bringing his craft may enter," answered the porter. "There is refreshment for your dogs and horses and hot peppered chops for you with delicious wine and happy songs. Tomorrow the gate will be opened for you."

"This will not do," said Cilhwch. "If you open the gate, all will be well. If not, I shall make such a noise that all your pregnant women will miscarry at the sound."

"Make all the noise you will," said Glewlwyd, the porter, "you shall not enter until I have spoken to Arthur."

---

[*] 45" an old British measure
[*] a small round shield held by the handle
[*] a raised centre

Glewlwyd then went into the Hall. Arthur asked him if he had news from the gate. He answered, "We have been all our lives together and travelled the world, fought together in battles, which you have won, but I have never seen such a handsome man who is at the gate."

"Then bring him in," said Arthur, "and let him be served with wine from gold drinking horns and hot peppered chops until food and drink can be prepared for him."

"If you would take my advice," said Cei*, "you would not change the customs of the court for him."

"But we should," said Arthur, "the greater our country, the greater our renown, fame and glory."

Glewlwyd went back to the gate and opened it. Cilhwch then rode into the Hall on his horse and greeted Arthur. Arthur greeted him also and offered him food and drink. "I have not come here for food and drink," said Cilhwch, "I come here to ask a favour of you."

"Name it," said Arthur.

"I would ask you to trim my hair," said Cilhwch.

"I shall willingly," said Arthur.

He took a gold comb and scissors of silver and cut his hair. "Tell me who you are," he said. "I feel you are related to me."

"I am Cilhwch, the son of Cilydd and Goleuddydd, my mother, the daughter of Prince Anlawdd."

"Then truly you are my cousin. What ever you ask, I will grant," said Arthur.

"I ask that you obtain for me the hand in marriage of Olwen, the daughter of Ysbaddaden Pencawr. I ask you in the name of all the great warriors of this Island of Britain and of the golden chained women too."*

Then Arthur said, "Oh, I have never heard of this lady you speak of, but I will gladly send messengers to find her."

The young man said, "I will give you a year to find her." So the messengers set out, but at the end of a year they had no more news of her than when they set out. Cilhwch was so disappointed that he said that Arthur had failed to honour his promise to find Olwen.

---

* Cei – Sir Kay
* Please see Lady Charlotte Guest's translation for the full list.

"Do not blame Arthur," said Cei. "Come with me and we will not rest until we either prove that the lady does not exist or that we find her." Cei was peculiar in that his breath lasted nine nights and nine days under water and he could exist for nine days and nights without sleep. A wound from his sword no doctor could heal. When he pleased, he could become as tall as the tallest tree in the forest. Also, when it rained, whatever he had in his hand remained dry from the heat of his body so it could be used to make a fire.

Then Arthur called Bedwyr* who was always willing to follow Cei. No one was swifter than he. Although he only had one hand he was brave in battle.

Arthur also called Cynddylig the Guide who was as good a guide in a foreign land as he was in his own country.

Fourthly Arthur called Gwrhyr, who knew all the languages of men, beasts, birds and fishes too.

He called Gwalchmai – (Sir Gawain), his nephew– because he never returned home without finding what he had been looking for.

Lastly he called on Menw, so that if they came upon savage monsters, he would cast a spell over them, so that they could not see Arthur's men but they could be seen themselves.

III. In Search of Olwen

They travelled until they reached a vast open plain, where there was a great castle which seemed the biggest in the world. As they moved towards it, it seemed it was no nearer than when they started. On the second day it was the same, but on the third day they came upon a large flock of sheep which was being kept by a shepherd standing on a green mound. The mastiff* that was beside him took their attention. It was as big as a nine year old stallion and its breath had killed all the trees and bushes around.

Then Cei said, "Gwhyr, you are our interpreter, go and have a word with the shepherd."

"My job is to only go where you go," said Gwhyr.

---

* Bedwyr – Bedivere
* a large strong dog with droopy ears and sagging lips.

"All right, we will go together," said Cei.

"Do not be afraid," said Menw, "for I will cast a spell over the dog so that it will not harm you."

They reached the mound and asked the shepherd how things were with him. "As well as they are with you," he answered.

They then asked, "Whose sheep are these and to whom does that castle belong?"

"You must be stupid," was the reply, "not to know that that is the castle of Ysbaddaden Pencawr Chief Giant and these are his sheep."

"And who are you?" they asked.

"My name is Custennin and the Chief Giant has taken all my possessions and so you see me as a shepherd," he replied. "Who are you?" he asked.

"We are messengers from Arthur come to find Olwen, the daughter of Ysbaddaden Pencawr," they said.

"Do not attempt it," he said, "for no one has returned from such a quest alive, but surely you are Cilhwch, the son of Prince Celyddon and Goleuddydd, your mother. You are my wife's sister's son. Come to the house to see her and she will help you. Be careful, though, because she is the strongest woman in the world."

They approached the shepherd's cottage and his wife ran out to meet them. She went to put her arms around the neck of Cei, but he, just in time, pulled a log from a pile of wood and put it between her hands. The log was splintered into small pieces. Cei joked that if that had been him he would not have survived to be loved by anyone.

They entered the house and were supplied with food. Then the woman opened a big stone coffer and out came a young lad with golden hair. "This is my son," she said. "The Chief Giant has killed all twenty-three of my other sons."

"Let him come with us," said Cei, "he will be safe, for if he dies, I shall have been killed first."

The woman asked what they were seeking. "We come to find Olwen, the daughter of the Chief Giant for Cilhwch," said Cei. The woman was astonished and advised them to return to Arthur's court.

"We will not return until we have found Olwen," said Cei.

"Does she come here?" asked Cilhwch.

"She does come every Saturday to wash her hair and she leaves her gold rings in the bowl and never comes back for them," said the woman.

"Will she come if sent for?" they asked.

"If you promise not to harm her, I will send for her," said the woman. So she was sent for and she came.

She wore a flame-coloured silk robe and a collar of red gold studded with precious emeralds and rubies. Her hair was more yellow than the flower of the broom*. Her skin was whiter than the foam of the wave and her fingers fairer than the blossoms of the wood anemone. The eye of the trained hawk was not brighter than hers. The breast of the white swan was not whiter than hers and her cheeks were more red than the reddest foxglove. Four white trefoils* sprang up wherever she walked and was so called Olwen (white-track).

She entered the house and sat near Culhwch. Immediately he knew that he loved her. He said, "Lady, it is you that I love. Come away with me."

She shook her head and said, "I cannot do this for I have promised not to marry without my father's permission, for when I do, he will die. What you must do now is this. You must see my father and perform all the tasks he sets you. If you accomplish that, then I can marry you. If not, your very lives will be in danger."

"I will do this," said Cilhwch.

She left then and they followed her to the castle. They killed the nine porters that were at the nine gates of the castle and also the nine dogs which did not bark.

They greeted Ysbaddaden Pencawr the Chief Giant. "Who are you?" he shouted, "and why do you come here?"

"We come for the hand of your daughter Olwen for Cilhwch the son of Cilydd," they answered.

"Where are my servants?" he shouted again. "Put up the forks under my eyelids so that I may see my future son-in-law." Forks like trees were put under his eyelids so that he could see.

---

* a yellow shrub growing on sandy banks
* three-leafed plants

He said, "Come back tomorrow and you shall have your answer."

As they rose to leave, the Giant picked up one of three poisoned darts that were beside him and threw it after them. Bedwyr caught it and flung it back. It pierced the Giant's knee. "Oh, oh," cried the Giant, "cursed be you, son-in-law. I shall not walk very well because of this. The dart has hurt me like the sting of a gadfly*. Cursed be the smith who forged it and the anvil on which it was made!"

That night they stayed in the shepherd's cottage. The next day they again went to the castle. They entered the hall and said to the Giant, "Give us your daughter for her dowry which we will pay you and for her two female relatives. You will die otherwise."

The Giant said, "Her four grandmothers and four grandfathers are still alive. I must consult with them. Come back tomorrow for your answer." As they turned to leave he took up a second dart that was beside him and threw it at them. It was caught by Menw who flung it back at him. It went through his chest and out of his back. "Oh cursed son-in-law," the Giant cried, "I was never in such pain. It is like the bite of a blood sucking leech. Cursed be the hearth on which it was heated. I shall have no breath when I walk up a hill and pain in my chest." Then they left.

They returned on the third day to the castle. "Shoot at us no more," they warned the Giant but he said,

"Don't you shoot at me any more unless you want to die. Where are my servants? Lift up my eyelids which have fallen over my eyes so that I may see my future son-in-law," which they did. "Come back tomorrow for your answer," he said again. As they left Yspaddaden Pencaw, the Chief Giant took the third poisoned dart and threw it at them. This time Cilhwch caught it and flung it back at the Giant. It pierced his eyeball so that the dart came out of the back of his head.

"Cursed son-in-law," shouted the Giant. "My eyesight is affected and I shall have headaches and giddiness every month. Cursed be the fire on which it was forged. The pain is like of the bite of a mad dog." They all left the castle for their meal.

---

* a cattle-biting fly

73

On the fourth day they reached the castle and said to the Giant, "Shoot at us no more, unless you wish to be damaged more. Give me your daughter or you will die because of her."

"Where is he who wants my daughter? Come nearer so that I may see you. Oh, it is you!"

"Yes, it is me, Cilhwch, son of Cilydd."

"Then you must accomplish all I demand," said the Giant.

"I will do all, I promise," said Cilhwch.

"You see that hill over there?"

"I see it."

"I want it uprooted and burnt, then sown and ploughed in one day for bread for your and my daughter's wedding," said the Giant.

"It will be easy for me to do, although you may think it is not easy," said Cilhwch.

"You see that red-tilled ground over there?"

"I see it" said Cilhwch. "When I first met Olwen's mother, nine bushels of flax were sown there but nothing came up. I need it to be grown to make a veil for my daughter's head on her wedding day," said the Giant.

"It will be easy for me to accomplish this, although you may not think it easy," said Cilhwch.

"There is something you will not get," said the Giant. "Honey that is nine times sweeter than the ordinary honey from the swarm. I require it for mead to drink at the wedding feast."

"It will be easy for me to get this," said Cilhwch, "although you may not think it is easy."

"The horn of Gwlgawd Gododin to serve us that night is very valuable. There is no other vessel that can hold this drink. He will not allow you to have it of his own free will."

"I will get it easily," said Cilhwch, "although you may not think it easy."

"Though you get this, yet there is something you will not get. The harp of Teirtu to play for us that night. It plays itself when a man wants it to. When he wants it to stop, it stops. He will not give it of his free will and you will not be able to force him."

"It will be easy for me to obtain that, although you may think it not easy," said Cilhwch.

"Then I must wash my head and shave my beard. I must have the tusk of Ysgithyrwyn Penbaedd (Chief boar) to shave myself. It must be plucked alive out of his head."

"I can do this easily, although you may not think it easy."

"I will not trust anyone with the tusk except Cadw of North Britain and he will not leave his kingdom for any man, nor can you force him."

"I can accomplish that easily, although you may not think it easy."

"I need to spread my beard in order to shave it, but that cannot happen unless I have the blood of the Black Witch, the daughter of the White Witch from Pen Nant Gofid (Valley of Grief) on the borders of Hell."

"It will be easy for me to get that, although you may think it is not easy."

"Also there is no comb or scissors to arrange my hair except those between the two ears of Twrch Trwyth – the boar which cannot be hunted until you get the whelp[*] Drudwyn. No leash can hold him except the leash of Cwrs Cant Ewin; there is no collar that will hold the leash except the collar of Canhastyr Canllaw (Hundred-hands) and you will not get the chain of Cilydd Canhastyr to fasten the collar to the leash."

"I shall get all these easily, although you may think it not easy," said Cilhwch.

"There is no huntsman in the world who can manage this dog except Mabon the son of Modron. He was taken from his mother when three nights old from between his mother and the wall. No one knows where he is now or whether he is living or dead. Nor will it ever be known unless his relative Eidoel is found and he is in Glini's secret prison, no one knows where. Even Mabon cannot hunt the boar Twrch except on the horse which is swift as the wave – Gwyn Dun-mane. He belongs to Gweddw who will not give him up of his own free will."

"It will be easy for me to do these things although you may not think it easy."

"Also, the boar Twrch cannot be hunted except by two dogs Aned and Aethlem and there is no huntsman in the world who can hold those two dogs except Cyledyr who is nine times

---

[*] young dog

75

wilder than the wildest beast on the mountain. You will not obtain him unless you first get Gwyn son of Nudd whom God has placed over the demons of the Otherworld (Annwfyn)."

"It will be easy for me to obtain these although you may not think it easy."

"Besides," said the Giant, "no leash in the world will hold these two dogs unless it is made from the beard of Dillus, the bearded. It will be useless unless it is plucked from him while he is still alive but he will not allow it and when he is dead it will be too brittle.

"It will be easy for me to do this although you may think it not easy," said Cilhwch.

"Although you would do all this," said the Giant, "Twrch Trwyth – the boar – cannot be hunted without the sword of Gwrnach the Giant and he will never be killed without it. He will not give it up for anything nor can you force him."

"Lastly, the boar cannot be hunted without Arthur and his huntsmen. He is a mighty warrior and lord of all his kingdom. He will not help you nor can you force him."

"Arthur is my cousin and he will get me all the things you name. I shall have your daughter for my wife and you will die," said Cilhwch.

"If Arthur is your cousin, a curse be on him and you! If you do all those things, you will win my daughter for your wife," said the Giant, who then knocked the forks from under his eyelids to show the talk was over. Cilhwch left with his friends, looking carefully behind them.

IV. Fulfilling the Tasks

(a) The Sword of Gwrnach the Giant

They travelled all that day until the evening and came upon a huge castle which was the largest in the world. Coming out of it they saw a black man bigger than three ordinary men. They asked him whose castle it was. "You are stupid men if you don't know that this is the fort of Gwrnach the Giant and no one ever came from here alive," he said. "No one enters unless he has a craft."

They went towards the gate. "Is there a porter?" Cei asked.

"There is," came the answer, "and you are cursed for asking."

"Open the gate."

"I will not."

"Why won't you?"

"Because they are all eating and drinking and making merry. Only someone who has a craft may enter."

"Go tell your master," said Cei, "that I am the best polisher of swords there is in the world."

"I will go and tell the Giant and will bring you your answer," said the porter. He went into the hall and Gwrnach asked if there was any news from the gate. "There is, my Lord," said the porter. "I have a man there who says he can polish swords."

"Bring him in," said the Giant, "I need to have my sword polished." The porter returned to the gate and opened it.

Cei went in by himself. "Is it true that you can polish swords?" asked the Giant. "It is," answered Cei. His sword was brought to Cei who took a whetstone[*] from under his arm and polished one half of the sword. "Does that please you?" he asked passing the sword to the Giant. "I would give all that is in my lands for it all to look like this," said the Giant.

The sword was now polished. Cei gave it to the Giant to see if he were pleased with his work. The Giant was pleased but Cei said, "I think it is the scabbard which has damaged your sword. Let me see it. I will take out the wooden side pieces and replace them with new ones." He stood by the Giant with the sword in one hand and the scabbard in the other, looking as if he were putting the sword into the scabbard, but with the sword he struck the Giant and cut off his head. They ransacked the castle and took the sword of Gwrnach the Giant back to Arthur's Court.

(b) The Oldest Animals

They told Arthur how their adventure had gone. He asked them which task they should attempt next. "We should try to find Mabon, the son of Modron," they said, "but first we have to locate Glini's prison where his cousin Eidoel is."

_____

[*] a stone for sharpening

They travelled together to the outer wall of Glini's prison where Glini said to Arthur, "What do you want of me? I have no food or riches in this place."

"We wish you no harm," said Arthur, "we just want to free the prisoner Eidoel. Give him to us and we will all leave." Eidoel was freed and went with them.

Arthur asked Eidoel, "How can we find your cousin Mabon?"

"You must ask the birds and the beasts and maybe the fishes too," answered Eidoel. The men laughed and were rebuked by Arthur who decided to return to his court, but not before he chose the four men to take on the next task. He chose Gwyhyr Interpreter of Tongues – he could understand and speak the languages of all men and animals on the earth. He chose Cei and Bedwyr as well as Eidoel who was Mabon's cousin.

They went first to find the Ouzel* of Cilgwri. Gwyhyr asked her if she knew the whereabouts of Mabon, who when he was a baby, was taken from between his mother and the wall. "When I first came to this place," answered the Ouzel, "there was a smith's anvil here. No work has been done on it except the sharpening of my beak and now it is worn away to the size of a nut. I have never heard of the man you are looking for, but since you are Arthur's messengers, I will guide you to the creature who is older than me."

They came to the place where the Stag of Rhedynfre was. "Stag of Rhedynfre," Gwrhyr asked, "we have come as messengers from Arthur to look for Mabon, son of Modron, who was taken from between his mother and the wall when he was three nights old."

The Stag said, "When I first came to this place, there was only one tine* each side of my head. There were no trees here except a single sapling of an oak which grew to have a hundred branches. In time it fell and all that is left is a withered stump. From that day to this I have never heard of the man you are seeking. Nevertheless, since you are messengers from Arthur, I will guide you to an animal which was formed before I was."

---

* Ring Ouzel, a small bird, a close relative of the blackbird
* point of antler

They were taken to the place where there was the Owl of Cwm Cawlwyd. "Owl of Cwm Cawlwyd", said the Stag, "here are messengers from Arthur that wish to find Mabon, son of Modron, who was taken from his mother after three nights."

"When I first came here," said the Owl, "this wide valley was a wooded glen. Some men came and laid it waste. There grew a second wood. This wood is the third. Even my wings are withered stumps. Yet in all this time I have never heard of the men you are looking for. However, I will take you to the oldest creature I know, the one who has travelled most, the Eagle of Gwernabwy."

They came to the place where the Eagle was. "Eagle of Gwernabwy," said Gwythyr, "we are messengers from Arthur looking for Mabon, the son of Modron who was taken from his mother when he was three nights old."

The Eagle said, "I have been here a very long time for when I came here first, I used to perch on a rock and pecked at the stars. Now it is hardly a hands breadth high, but I have never heard of the man of which you enquire, except once when I went in search of food to Llyn Llyw. There I struck my claws into a salmon thinking he would be food for me for a long while. He dragged me down into the depths of the lake. It was difficult to get away from him. Later he sent messengers to make peace with me and asked me to take fifty fish spears out of his back. Unless he knows something of which you speak, no one else will. I will guide you to where he is."

Then they came to the place where the Salmon of Llyn Llyw was. The Eagle said, "Salmon of Llyn Llyw, I have with me Arthur's messengers to ask if you know anything of Mabon, the son of Modron, who was taken from his mother when three nights old."

"As much as I know, I will tell you," said the Salmon. "With every tide I go up the River Severn till I come to the bend of the wall of Caer Loyw (Gloucester), where I have heard such distressing noises. Come with me and you will hear it for yourselves."

So Cei and Gwrhyr went on the shoulders of the Salmon. They reached the wall of a prison and heard such a wailing coming from there. "Who is that lamenting in this house of stone?" asked Gwrhyr.

"It is Mabon, the son of Modron," came the answer. "I am imprisoned here in most cruel circumstances."

"Will you be released for gold or silver?" they asked.

"I will only be freed by fighting," answered Mabon.

They returned to Arthur and told him of this. He summoned his warriors and they set out for Caer Loyw (Gloucester). Cei and Bedwyr went on the Salmon's back. Arthur's men attacked the castle and Cei broke the wall into the dungeon where Mabon was. He travelled home with Arthur, a free man.

(c) The Lame Ant

Despite all these adventures, no one knows where to find the nine bushels* of flax seed that the Giant had asked of Cilhwch for the veil for Olwen's wedding. Before the year was out, Gwythyr was walking across a mountain when he heard a dreadful cry. He saw before him an anthill red with fire. He took his sword and cut it off level with the ground and so saved the ants from a terrible death. There was one ant which was lame but Gwythyr carried it to safety. The ants repaid him with nine bushels of flax seed, which he needed to give to the Giant, which they had carried off years before. One flax seed was missing but the lame ant brought it in before night-fall.

V. The Beard of Dillus the Bearded

Not long after this, Cei and Bedwyr were sitting on the summit of Plinlimmon*, in the highest wind in the world, when they saw, in the distance, a great plume of smoke which was peculiar in that it was not blown about by the wind but stood up like a pillar in the air. They hurried towards the smoke and as they neared it, they saw it was Dillus the Bearded singeing a wild boar.

"Do you know him?" said Bedwyr to Cei.

"I do," said Cei, "and no leash in the world will hold the dogs Aned and Aethlem but a leash from his beard. It must be taken from him while he is still alive with wooden tweezers, or

---

* a measure of capacity, i.e. liquid – 8 gallons
* a high mountain in Cardiganshire

it will be useless. We must wait until he is full of meat and he will fall asleep. We shall make wooden tweezers until then."

When Dillus fell asleep, they dug a deep pit under him. Cei struck him a heavy blow and he fell into the pit. Then they pulled out his beard with the wooden tweezers and killed him.

They took the leash they had made back to Arthur who then sang this song:-

This leash was made by Cei
From Dillus' beard we see;
Who, if he were alive
Would cause Cei's death to be.

This taunt made Cei so angry that the other men could hardly make peace between Cei and Arthur; but thereafter Cei and Bedwyr would have no more to do with these quests.

(d) The Tusk of Ysgithyrwyn Chief Boar

After this Arthur went across the sea to Brittany to obtain the two dogs needed for the hunting of the boar – Twrch Trwyth. Then he went back to the North of Britain to find Cyledyr the Wild – the huntsman. When he got these and the rest of the men and tasks and marvels the Chief Giant had demanded, he pursued the Chief Boar. He and his men found him in the open and Cadw of Pictland (North Britain) mounted Arthur's horse and with his axe, split the boar's head in two and took the tusk to shave the Giant's beard.

(e) The Hunting of the Otherworld Boar (Twrch Trwyth)

Arthur sent Menw to Ireland to find the Twrch Trwyth (boar) and see if the comb and shears were still between his ears. Menw found the boar and transformed himself into a bird. He alighted on the head of the boar and tried to snatch the things from off his head. Twrch twitched his ears and all Menw got was a single bristle. He tried a second time but the boar was angry now and shook himself and his foam touched the bird's feathers. From that day onward Menw was always ill.

Then Arthur gathered all his warriors together and sailed to Ireland where Twrch the boar was, with seven piglets round him. They fought for nine days and nights to no avail. Not a piglet was killed but the boar laid waste much of the province of Ireland. His tired men asked Arthur what was the history of the boar.

"He was a king," said Arthur, "but he was transformed into a swine because of his wickedness."

While the men rested and saw to the wounds, Arthur sent Gwrhyr Interpreter of Tongues to speak with the boar. Like Menw he went in the form of a bird and alighted about Twrch's lair. "Will not one of you speak with Arthur?" he asked. Twrch only grunted. It was his son who answered. He had silver bristles. You could see them glittering in the wood.

"Because we have been made like this, we will do nothing for Arthur. We have enough trouble of our own without you attacking us," he said.

"You must know," said Gwrhyr, "that Arthur is determined to have the comb and scissors between the ears of Twrch."

"Until he is dead, those treasures will not be taken," was the answer. "Go back to Arthur and tell him that, in the morning, we will go to his land of Wales and do all the mischief that we can."

The next day they swam over the sea to Wales. Arthur pursued them aboard his ship. Twrch landed at Porth Cleis in Dyfed and killed all the cattle there, also all the men and beasts of the countryside except a few who escaped.

As soon as he heard of Arthur's landing in Wales, Twrch made for the mountains of Preseleu (Mynydd Preseli) (or Prescelly). Arthur followed him with all his men to hunt on both sides of the River Nyfer. Twrch the boar escaped and killed many of Arthur's men including his young son Gwydre. The boar was wounded for the first time with a spear. He went on and killed many more of Arthur's men including many champions and even a King of France. He escaped again and the dogs and men lost him.

Then Arthur summoned Gwyn, son of Nudd to him and asked him if he knew anything of Twrch and where he was hiding. He did not. The huntsmen went on but were attacked by Grugyn Silver Bristle and Llwydawg the Hewer. There was such a noise of barking and squealing that it roused Twrch who was resting under an oak tree. He came to their defence. He was attacked by men and dogs and eventually all the piglets were killed. Both Grugyn Silver Bristle and Llwydawg the Hewer were killed but not before they had killed four champions and Arthur's uncle.

Only Twrch Trwyth was left now and Arthur said, "Twrch has wasted much of my land and killed many of my men. While I am alive he shall not escape into Cornwall. I mean to fight him to the death." The horsemen and dogs pursued the boar back to the River Severn. Mabon son of Modron went with him into the Severn on his dun*-maned stallion, as well as Custennin's son Goren and the hurt Menw yelling for revenge.

Arthur attacked the boar with the champions that were left. They drowned him in the Severn and Mabon and Cyledyr the Wild plunged at him and between them snatched the shears from between his ears. Before they could get the comb, he had got onto the land and raced into Cornwall.

For the rest of the day they had to rescue Arthur's men from drowning. His manservant carried two millstones to grind meal for Arthur's food around his neck and this weighed him down. While Osla Big-Knife, who carried a knife in a sheath nearly drowned when he lost the knife and the sheath filled with water.

Soon, however, they were all dry and rested and sat on the bank of the River Severn. Then Arthur went, with his men, into Cornwall and caught up with Twrch. What trouble they had had was child's play compared with the task of getting the comb, but get it they did and they drove him out of Cornwall into the sea. No one knows what became of him or the two dogs Aned and Aethlem who went into the water after him. Arthur then went to rest himself in Cornwall.

(f) The Blood of the Black Witch

For a while, Arthur rested at Celli Wig in Cornwall. Then one day he said to his men, "Is there any task we have not fulfilled?"

---

* dull greyish-brown colour

"There is," they said, "the blood of the Black Witch, the daughter of the White Witch of Pen Nant Gofid (The Valley of Grief) in the depths of Hell.

Once more Arthur and his men set out; this time to the witch's cave in the North Country. He sent two of his servants in to fight against the witch, but she grabbed them and caught one by the hair and flung him to the ground. The other attacked her, but she turned again upon them both and drove them off with many blows and knocks. They crawled away painfully.

Arthur was angry to see his own men treated like that and made to go into the cave himself. He was persuaded that it would not be seemly for him to be squabbling with a hag so he sent two other of his servants into the cave. They were treated far worse than the first two and all four were rescued by putting them on the back of Arthur's horse.

Arthur, himself, went into the cave and with his sword struck at the witch and severed her in two parts. Cadw of Pictland took the witch's blood and kept it for the shaving of the Giant Yspaddaden.

VI. Cilhwch Marries Olwen

Cilhwch then set out for the Chief Giant's palace with Goren, the son of Custennin and many men who wished harm to the Giant. Cadw of North Britain dressed his beard and shaved his beard, skin and flesh from the very bone, ear to ear. "Are you shaved now?" asked Cilhwch, "I am shaved," he answered, "and my daughter is yours. Don't thank me though, thank Arthur who has helped you accomplish this. If it were up to me you should never have had her for now it is time for me to lose my life."

Then Goren, the son of Custennin grabbed him by the hair and took him to the mount, cut off his head and set it on a stake to avenge his twenty-three brothers. He took possession of the castle and land with his father's permission.

That same night Olwen became Cilhwch's bride. She was his only wife as long as he lived. In this way did Cilhwch fulfil the destiny which was laid upon him by his stepmother.

9. The Dream of Rhonabwy

When Madawg, son of Maredudd ruled over Powys, his brother
Iorwerth had journeyed into Lloegyr (England), killing the
people, burning houses and carrying away prisoners. Madawg
wished to put a stop to this and sent three men, one of whom
was named Rhonabwy, on a mission to do just that.

Late one evening they came to a house of Heilyn Goch
(Heilyn the Red) where they were to lodge for the night. It was
a terrible place; filthy dirty with holes and puddles of water on
the floor and holly instead of rushes underfoot, which the cattle
had eaten. On the first dais there was an old hag in the hall of
the house, who, when she felt cold, put a lapful of husks onto
the fire which had such a putrid smoke that they could hardly
breathe.

On a second dais, they saw a yellow calf-skin. Although
they didn't know it, it had magic properties for anyone who sat
on it. They asked where were the people of the house but the
hag only muttered. Just then the people of the house came in. A
man with a ruddy complexion and a bundle of faggots* on his
back. The woman was pale and thin with also a bundle under
her arm. They did not speak but made a fire and gave them
stale bread, sour cheese and watered down milk.

A great storm came up so they decided to stay there for the
night. They were shown to a flea-ridden couch made of straw
which the cattle had mostly eaten. A threadbare rug was spread
out with a sheet full of holes and a badly-stuffed pillow. They
were so tired, however, that Rhonabwy's companions were
soon asleep and snoring whereas he could not get to sleep at all.
He saw the yellow calf-skin laid out and thought that it would

---

* Sticks or twigs for fuel

be more comfortable. As soon as he lay down to sleep, he began to dream.

He saw that he and his companions were crossing the plain of Argyngroeg and travelling towards Rhyd y Groes on the River Severn. As they journeyed they heard a great commotion behind them and saw a young man with fair curly hair and a newly-trimmed beard. He was mounted on a chestnut horse and wore a coat of yellow satin sewn with green silk. The yellow of his clothing was as yellow as the blossom of the broom* and the green as green as the needles of the fir tree. On his thigh was a gold hilted sword in a scabbard of Spanish leather, clasped with gold. He wore a scarf of yellow satin trimmed with green silk. So strong was the breath of the horse that when it breathed out, it threw the men away from him, but when it breathed in, it brought them back. They asked the fair-haired youth for his mercy and he gladly gave it in Arthur's name.

"What is your name?" asked Rhonabwy. "I am Iddawc, the son of Mynyo but am best known by my nickname," he answered, "which is Iddawc Cordd Prydain."

"Why are you called that?" asked Rhonabwy.

"I was one of the messengers between Arthur and his nephew Medrawd at the battle of Camlan," he said. "Arthur sent me with a message to ask for peace so that the men of the Island of Britain should not be killed. I changed his friendly words into unfriendly ones, so I am called Iddawc Cordd Prydain (Iddawc the Embroiler* of Britain). So the battle ensued, I left three nights before the battle and went North."

As he finished speaking, they heard a greater commotion than before and when they looked round, they could see a young man with auburn hair but without beard or moustache riding on a stately horse. He wore clothes of red satin trimmed with yellow silk. The trappings of his horse were of the same colours – the yellow as yellow as the blossom of the broom and the red as red as the reddest blood.

---

* The yellow broom was very popular in the Middle Ages, as was the colour yellow – the colour of gold. Geoffrey of Anjou, born in 1113, the father of the first Plantagenet king, Henry II, wore a sprig of yellow broom in his hat. The Latin for 'broom' is planta-genista – thus Plantagenet.
* Involves in hostility i.e. making trouble

As he approached them, he asked Iddawc if he could have a share of the little men with him. "You shall," called Iddawc, "but it is to protect them." The rider promised and rode away.

"Iddawc," said Rhonabwy, "who was that horseman?"

"Rhwawn Bebyr," he was told, "a mighty warrior of the Island of Britain."

They went on their journey over the plain of Argyngroeg as far as the ford of Rhyd y Groes on the River Severn. There, for about a mile they saw an encampment of tents and the noise of a great number of men. Then they saw Arthur on the bank with a bishop on one side and a warrior on the other. A tall auburn haired youth stood before him, with a sheathed sword in his gloved hand. He wore a coat and hat of jet black satin. His face was a white as ivory, his eyebrows black as jet. The part of his wrist that could be seen between his glove and his sleeve was whiter than the lily and thicker than a warrior's ankle.

Iddawc and the men with him came before Arthur and saluted him. Arthur also greeted them and asked Iddawc where he had found these little men. "I found them along the road," answered Iddawc and Arthur smiled.

"Lord," asked Iddawc, "why do you laugh?"

"I am not laughing," said Arthur, "rather I am sad to see such small man guarding this island compared with the men of the past."

He dismissed them and then Iddawc said to Rhonabwy, "Did you see the ring on the Emperor's hand?"

"I saw it," answered Rhonabwy.

"It is one of the properties of the precious stone in it that you will be able to remember what you have seen here tonight. If you had not seen it, you would not remember anything," said Iddawc.

Then they saw a troop of men coming towards the ford. "Iddawc," asked Rhonabwy, "whose troop is that?"

"They are the comrades of Rhwawn Bebyr, your protector. They have mead and honey ale and are loved by the daughters of the Kings of the Island of Britain. They deserve this because they are always in the front and rear of all battles." All the men were coloured red. If one of the knights separated from the troop, he looked like a pillar of fire reaching to the sky. Their tents were also coloured red.

Then they saw another troop coming towards the ford. These, from their horse's chests upwards were as white as the lily flower and below blacker than jet. One of the riders came forward in such a way that the water of the ford splashed over Arthur and the Bishop. The young man who stood before Arthur struck the rider's horse on the nostrils with his sheathed sword.

"Why did you strike my horse?" the rider asked. "Was it an insult or a warning?"

"It was a warning," answered the young man, "and no warning is severe enough for a rider so reckless as to splash water all over Arthur and the holy bishop till they are as wet as if they had just been dragged out of a river."

The rider thought for a moment, then said, "Then I will not take it as an insult," and rode off towards his army.

"Iddawc," said Rhonabwy, "who was that knight?"

"The most eloquent and wise youth that is in the island; Adaon the son of Taliesin."

"Who was the man who struck his horse?"

"A young man who is very pushy; Elphin, the son of Gwyddno."

Then a tall handsome man said in flowing speech that it was marvellous that so large a gathering should be held in so small a space and even more so that they were there at all, since they were to be, by midday, in the battle of Baddon, fighting against Osla Gyllellfawr (Osla Big Knife). "You are right," said Arthur, "let us be on our way."

Iddawc took Rhonabwy up behind him on his horse and they all set out for Cefn Digoll. When they were in the middle of the ford Iddawc turned his horse's head so that Rhonabwy could see the whole valley. He could see troops of riders coming towards the ford. One troop was all in white brocaded silk with fringes of pure black. The other was all in jet black except the fringes of their cloaks which were pure white.

"Iddawc," asked Rhonabwy, "who are the pure white troop over there?"

"They are the men of Norway with March the son of Meirchion, their prince. He is Arthur's cousin."

"Iddawc," asked Rhonabwy, "who are the jet black troop over there?"

"They are the men of Denmark. Edeyrn the son of Nudd is their prince."

By the time they had overtaken Arthur's men, they were below Caer Faddon when they heard a terrible noise and commotion among the men. They could see that at one moment the men at the side were in the centre and the men at the centre were on the side. Then they saw a knight coming. Together with his horse he was dressed in mail with the rings whiter than the whitest lily and the rivets redder than the reddest blood.

"Iddawc," asked Rhonabwy, "will the men run away?"

"King Arthur never ran away and if you are heard saying that you will not be safe," answered Iddawc. "The knight you see is Cei, the most handsome man in Arthur's court and the best rider. The men at the side are closing in to see Cei's horse and the men in the centre go outward to avoid being trampled by Cei's horse. That is the cause of the noise and commotion."

With that, they heard Cadw, Earl of Cornwall being called for and they saw him come with Arthur's sword in his hand. On the sword was the image of two serpents in gold. When the sword was drawn from its scabbard, it seemed as if two flames of fire burst out from the jaws of the serpents. The sight was so amazing that it was hard for anyone to look at it. The commotion stopped as the Earl returned to his tent.

"Iddawc," said Rhonabwy, "who is the man who held Arthur's sword?"

"He is Cadw, Earl of Cornwall, whose duty it is to arm the King in days of battle and warfare."

Then they heard a call for Eiryn, a big, rough, ugly fellow with red hair and whiskers. He came upon a red horse, its mane straggling down its neck and with a pack on its back. He dismounted as he reached Arthur and pulled a golden chair out of the pack together with a carpet of brocaded silk. He spread this before Arthur and all could see an apple of red gold at each corner. He placed the chair on the carpet. It was so big that three men could sit on it.

When Arthur had sat down, with Owain son of Urien standing before him, he said, "Owain, will you play chess with me?"

"I will, my Lord," said Owain. The red young man brought a chessboard of silver and golden chess pieces and they began to play.

They had been playing chess for only a short time, when a young man with fair hair and blue eyes came out of a white tent with the image of a jet-black serpent on top with red eyes and a red flaming tongue. He wore a coat of yellow satin and stockings of a greenish-yellow with shoes of many-coloured leather on his feet. He had a sword with a golden hilt in a scabbard of black leather tipped with fine gold. He greeted Owain who was amazed that he had not greeted Arthur first, but Arthur said, "Do not worry about that, he has already greeted me. His message is for you."

The young man said to Owain, "Have you given permission for the young pages and attendants of the emperor to molest and torment your ravens?"

"Lord," said Owain, "you hear what the youth says. Would you please tell them to stop harassing my little ravens?"

"Play on," said Arthur and the young man returned to the tent.

They finished the game and had started another, when another young man, with auburn hair of ruddy complexion, well built with a beard newly shaved, came from another tent which was yellow with an image of a bright red lion on its roof. Like the previous one he greeted Owain but Arthur was not offended. "Lord," said the youth to Owain, "the attendants of the Emperor are worrying and in some cases killing your ravens. Would you ask him to prevent this?"

"Lord," said Owain, "please call off your men."

"Play on," said Arthur.

They finished that game and were starting the first moves of another when yet another young man with crisp fair hair came from a yellow speckled tent with the figure of an eagle of gold on it with a precious stone in the eagle's head. He was a handsome noble youth with a scarf of blue satin on him with a brooch of gold on his shoulder. He carried a lance with a banner. He was fiercely angry, came quickly up to Owain and told him that most of the ravens had been killed and the rest were so hurt that they were not able to fly or lift their wings from the ground.

"Lord Arthur," said Owain, "call off your men."

"Make your move, if it pleases you," said Arthur. Then Owain said to the young man, "Go back and wherever the trouble is at its worst, raise the banner and we will see what will happen."

So the young man returned to the place where the trouble was at its worst and lifted the banner. As he did so, the ravens all rose up into the sky and if by magic, which it was, were strong and powerful again, attacked the men and damaged their heads, eyes and ears and carried them into the air with a huge flapping of wings. There was a great noise and commotion with the fluttering and croaking of the ravens. There were also the groans of the men, some of which were badly injured and some killed.

Arthur and Owain heard this and were amazed at all the noise. As they looked up another rider came towards them. He was on a brightly coloured horse and had a gold-hilted sword on his thigh. He wore a helmet of gold on his head set with precious stones for the eyes of the flame-coloured leopard that was on it. He was obviously tired and in a bad temper. He told Arthur that Owain's ravens were destroying his men.

The Emperor said to Owain, "Call off your ravens."

"Lord," said Owain, "it is your move." The rider returned to the battle. The ravens were not called off.

As they went on playing, they heard a greater noise than ever, of men shrieking and ravens croaking as they carried the men into the air and tore them apart sending them lifeless to the ground. Out of this commotion came another rider towards them on a light-grey horse in heavy blue armour. He had a gold helmet on his head set with sapphires of great value. On top of the helmet was the figure of a flame-coloured lion with a fiery-red tongue coming out of its mouth and evil eyes in its head. He greeted the Emperor.

"Lord," he said to him, "your men are now all dead. It will be difficult to defend this Island of Britain without them."

"Owain," said Arthur, "call off your ravens."

"Lord Emperor," said Owain, "it is your move."

So they finished that game and started another. Then they heard more shrieks of men and croaking of ravens and the sound of armour crashing to the ground as the men fell. They saw another rider coming towards them on a piebald* horse with a brass helmet on his head. On top of it was the image of a blood-red griffin* with valuable stones in his head for eyes. He was in a rage and told Arthur that all his men had been killed by the ravens and had left Britain at the mercy of its enemies.

Arthur glared at Owain. "Call off your ravens," he commanded angrily. In his rage he crushed the golden chess pieces on the board until they were dust. Then Owain ordered that his banner be lowered. This was done and all was peaceful.

As peace was declared, twenty-four horsemen came from Osla Big Knife to ask Arthur for a truce. A meeting was held with Cei, Bedwyr, Gwyhyr, Interpreter of Tongues and March son of Meirchion. It was decided to grant Osla a truce for a fortnight and a month.

Cei then got up and said, "Let all who wish to follow Arthur to Cornwall come now, and whoever will not, let him join Arthur after the truce."

"Iddawc," said Rhonabwy, "what was the meaning of the game of chess and the battle between Arthur's men and Owain's ravens?" Before Iddawc could answer, a great commotion woke Rhonabwy up. He had been asleep three nights and three days on the yellow ox-skin. No one will ever know the answer to his question because that was the dream of Rhonabwy.

---

* two coloured – usually black and white
* a fabulous creature with an eagle's head and wings and a lion's body

10. Owain, or the Lady of the Fountain

King Arthur was sitting in his royal apartment at Caerleon-upon-Usk, with Owain the son of Urien, Cynon the son of Clydo, Cei the son of Cyner and Gwenhwyfar* (Guinevere) – his wife, with her ladies doing needlework by the window. Glewlwyd Gafawlfawr was acting as a porter at Arthur's palace to welcome guests and strangers and to inform them of the manners and customs of the court.

In the centre of the room, King Arthur sat upon a seat of green rushes, spread over with a covering of flame-coloured satin. He was leaning his elbow on a cushion of red satin.

Arthur said to all that were there, "If I thought you would not think badly of me, I would like to sleep before I have my meal; you can entertain one another telling stories and you can have a flagon* of mead and some meat from Cei." The king then went to sleep. Then Cynon the son of Clydno asked Cei to tell a story. "I will have a good story to tell you," said Cei.

"No," said Cynon, "it would be better if you went to get the food which Arthur promised us and then we can tell you the best tale we know."

So Cei went to the kitchen and to the mead-cellar and returned with a flagon of mead and a handful of skewers with slices of meat on them. They ate the meat and began to drink the mead. "Now," said Cei, "it is time to tell me your story."

"Cynon," said Owain, "tell your story to Cei."

"Oh no," said Cynon, "you are older, a better story-teller and have seen more marvellous things than I, so you tell your story."

---

* means white phantom
* a large vessel for holding liquor for the table

"No, you begin your story," said Owain "with the best you know."

"I will," answered Cynon.

"I was an only son and I was very ambitious and courageous. I thought nothing in the world was too difficult for me to do and after I had achieved all I could in my own country, I armed myself and set out on a journey through deserts and distant lands. At last I came to the most beautiful valley in the world, where trees grew to the same height. A river ran through the valley with a path alongside. I followed the path until mid-day and continued my journey through the valley until the evening where, at the edge of a plain I saw a large and majestic Castle at the foot of which was a torrent."

"I approached the Castle and saw two young men with yellow curling hair, each with a band of gold around his head. They were both dressed in yellow satin with gold clasps on their shoes. In the hand of each was an ivory bow, strung with the sinews of a stag. Their arrows had shafts of the bone of a whale and were winged with peacock's feathers; the shafts also had golden heads. They had daggers with blades of gold and hilts of whalebone."

"A short distance from them I saw a man in the prime of life with his beard newly shaved, dressed in a robe and cloak of yellow satin decorated with a band of gold lace. He wore shoes of variegated* leather fastened with two studs of gold. I greeted him and courteously he greeted me and we both went towards the Castle."

"There was no one living in the Castle except in the hall where I saw twenty-four ladies embroidering satin at a window. I tell you Cei, the least beautiful of these was more beautiful than any lady you have seen in the Island of Britain and the least lovely of them was more lovely than Gwenhwyfar (Guinevere) the wife of Arthur when she appeared loveliest at the Offering, at the feast of the Nativity or the feast of Easter."

"They got up when I went in and six of them took my horse and took off my armour; six others took my weapons and washed them until they were shining bright. The third six spread cloths on the tables and prepared a meal. The fourth six

---

* many coloured

took off my soiled clothes and put clean ones on me, an under-vest, a doublet* of fine linen, a robe, a surcoat* and a mantle (cloak) of yellow satin with a broad gold band on the cloak. I sat down and they put red cushions around me."

"The six maidens who took my horse, unharnessed him as well as if they had been the best squires (attendants on a knight) in the Island of Britain. They then brought silver bowls of water to wash and linen towels, some green and some white and I washed. In a little while the man sat down at the table. I sat next to him and below sat all the maidens except those who waited on us."

"The table was silver with linen table cloths. The serving vessels were either gold or silver or buffalo horn. Our meal was brought to us and do you know, Cei, I saw every kind of meat and liquor but better than I have ever seen elsewhere?"

"No one spoke to me until the meal was half over, then the man began to speak. I said I was glad to find that someone would speak to me but he said he had not wanted to disturb my meal. 'However,' he said, 'we can talk now.' He asked me who I was and what was the point of my journey. I told him that I was trying to find out whether anyone was better than me or if I could be the master of all men."

"The man looked at me, smiled and said, 'If it would not distress you too much, I will show what you are looking for.' I then became anxious and sad. He could see it and said, 'sleep here tonight, rise early in the morning and take the road through the valley until you come to the wood through which you came. You will see a road branching off to the right which you must take until you come to a sheltered glade* with a mound in the centre'."

"'You will see a big tall black man on top of the mound. He would make the size of two men of this world. He has only one foot and one eye in the middle of his forehead. He holds an iron club – two men would not be able to lift it. He is not a handsome man, in fact he is exceedingly ugly. You will see a

_____

* a close fitting garment worn by men without sleeves
* a loose robe usually worn under armour
* open space between trees

95

thousand wild animals grazing around him. Ask him the way out of the glade. He will tell you briefly the way you must go'."

"That night seemed very long to me. The next morning, I got up, dressed myself, mounted my horse and travelled straight through the valley to the wood. I followed the cross-road which the man had pointed out to me, until, eventually I arrived at the glade. I was three times more amazed at the number of animals that I saw than the man had said. The black man was there on top of the mound. He seemed bigger of build than the man had told me. As for the club he held, I tell you, Cei, it would take four warriors to hold it, not two."

"I asked him what power he had over the animals. 'I'll show you,' he said, as he struck a stag with a great blow which made it bray loudly. At that, all the animals came together so that it was difficult to find room to stand between them. There were serpents, dragons and all sorts of animals. He looked at them, made them go to feed and they obeyed him like a servant would a master."

"The black man then said to me, 'Do you see, little man, what power I have over these animals?' I then asked him the way and his manner became very rough towards me and he asked me where I was going. When I told him who I was and what I was looking for, he directed me. He said, 'Take the path that leads to the top of the glade and go up a steep slope until you come to its summit (top). There you will find an open space like a large valley. In the middle of it a tall tree, whose branches are greener than the greenest pine'."

"'Under this tree is a fountain. By the side of it is a marble slab and on it a silver bowl attached by a chain, so that it may not be carried away. Take the bowl and throw a bowlful of water on the slab and you will hear a great peal of thunder. You will think that heaven and earth are trembling with its fury. Also will come a shower, so heavy, that it will be nearly impossible for you to survive. The shower will be of hailstones. After it the weather will clear but every leaf on the tree will have been carried away by the shower'."

"'Then a flight of birds will land on the tree. In your own country, you will not have heard a song as sweet as that which they shall sing. At that moment of delight at the birds singing, you will hear a murmuring and complaining coming towards you from the valley. You will see a knight upon a coal-black horse, dressed in black velvet and with a pennon* on his lance. He will ride towards you with the greatest speed. If you try to flee, as sure as you are a mounted knight, he will leave you on foot. If you do not find trouble in that adventure, you need not look for it during the rest of your life'."

"So I journeyed on until I reached the summit of the steep slope. There I found everything as the black man had described. I went up to the tree and beneath it I saw a fountain. By its side was a marble slab and the silver bowl fastened by a chain. I took the bowl and threw a bowlful of water on the slab. Then came the thunder and hailstones. I tell you, Cei, no man or beast could survive that shower and live. Each hailstone was big enough to penetrate the flesh to the bone."

"I turned my horse's flank* towards the shower and placed the bottom of my shield over his head and neck and the upper part over my own head. In that way I withstood the shower. When I looked at the tree, there was not a single leaf left on it. Then the sky became clear and the birds lighted on the tree and sang. Cei, I never heard any melody to equal that before or since. When I was being delighted by listening to the birds, a murmuring voice was heard through the valley. It approached me saying, 'Oh, Knight, what has brought you here? What evil have I done to you that you should do this to me and my possessions? Don't you know that the shower today has left neither man nor beast alive in my land?'"

"Just then, a Knight on a black horse appeared, dressed in jet black velvet with a tabard* of black linen over his armour. We charged each other furiously and soon I was thrown down. Then the Knight put the shaft of his lance through the bridle rein of my horse and rode off with the two horses, leaving me where I was. He did not even disarm or imprison me so I returned along the road I had come. When I reached the glade, where the black man was, I tell you, Cei, it's a marvel that I didn't collapse in a pool of liquid at the shame I felt at the black man's mockery of me."

---

* a long narrow flag
* fleshy part of side – between ribs and hip
* a knight's garment over armour

"That night I spent in the same castle where I had spent the previous night and was more agreeably entertained that night than I had been the night before. I was better fed and conversed freely with the people of the castle. None of them mentioned my expedition to the fountain, nor did I mention it to anyone but remained there the night."

"When I got up the next morning, I found a bay palfrey[*], ready for riding, with nostrils as red as scarlet. After putting on my armour, I said goodbye to them all and returned to my own Court. I still have that horse – in the stable over there. I decided that I would not part with him for the best palfrey in the Island of Britain."

"You know, Cei, no one before ever admitted to such an adventure which was so much against himself. Nor have I ever heard of a person, beside myself, having such an adventure, even in King Arthur's Kingdom without anyone else knowing about it."

"Wouldn't it be a good idea to go and try to find that place?" said Owain.

"Oh, Owain," said Cei, "you often say things that you do not intend to carry out."

"Now," said Gwenhwyfar (Guinevere), it would be better if you were hanged than to be so rude towards a man like Owain."

"Good lady," said Cei, "I admire Owain every bit as much as you do, if not more."

With that Arthur woke up and asked if he had been sleeping a little.

"Yes, Lord," answered Owain, "you have slept for a while."

"Is it time to eat?"

"It is, Lord," said Owain.

Then the horn for washing was sounded and the King and all the household sat down to eat. When the meal was over, Owain went back to his lodging and got ready his horse and armour.

The next day, at dawn, he put on his armour, mounted his charger[*] and travelled through distant lands and over desert

---

[*] a reddish brown saddle horse
[*] an officer's horse

mountains. At last he came to the valley which Cynon had described to him. He was certain it was the same. He went along the valley by the side of the river and came to the Castle. As he approached it, he saw the young men with their daggers in the place where Cynon had seen them. The yellow man, to whom the castle belonged, was standing alongside. Owain greeted the man who returned his greeting.

He went towards the Castle where he saw a room where the young ladies were working at satin embroidery. They were sitting on gold chairs. Their beauty and loveliness was far greater than Cynon had described. They served Owain with a meal which gave him more satisfaction than it had Cynon.

In the middle of the meal, the yellow man asked Owain what was the object of his journey. Owain told him, "I am hoping to find the Knight who guards the fountain." The yellow man smiled and said he was reluctant to point out what the adventure had been for Cynon. However, he described what Owain should do and they retired to bed.

The next morning, Owain found his horse made ready for him by the ladies. He set out and came to the glade where the black man was. The build of the black man seemed greater than it had to Cynon. Owain asked him what road to take and he told him.

Owain followed the road, as Cynon had done, till he came to a green tree. He saw the fountain with the slab beside it and the bowl upon it. He took the bowl and threw a bowlful of water over the slab. He then heard the thunder, after which came the shower, much more violent than Cynon had heard. After that the sky became more bright. When Owain looked at the tree, there was not a leaf on it. Immediately the birds came, settled on the tree and sang.

The singing was giving so much pleasure to Owain when he saw a Knight coming towards him through the valley. Owain prepared to meet him but he came violently and they broke both their lances. They drew their swords and fought blade to blade. Then Owain struck the Knight a blow through his helmet, head piece and visor; through skin, flesh and bone and wounded his brain. The Knight realised that he had received a fatal blow and fled. Owain chased him but could not get near enough to strike with his sword again.

Then Owain saw a vast and splendid Castle. They came to the Castle gate. The black Knight was allowed through but the portcullis* was let fall on Owain. It struck his horse behind the saddle and cut it in two. Owain was in a difficult situation. He was trapped on the front of the horse between the two gates and the inner gate was closed. He could see through a gap in the gate, a street facing him, with a row of houses on each side. He saw a young woman with auburn curling hair and a band of gold around her head. She was dressed in yellow satin and her shoes were of different coloured leathers.

She came up to the gate and asked that it should be opened. "Heaven knows," said Owain, "it is not possible for me to open it for you as it is impossible for you to set me free."

"Indeed," said the young woman," it is very sad that you can't be released for every woman should take care of you, for I never saw a more faithful man than you. As a friend you are most sincere and devoted."

"Therefore," she said, "whatever is in my power to do to release you, I will do."

"Take this ring and put it on your finger with the stone inside your hand; close your hand and as long as you hide it, it will hide you. When they have consulted together, they will come to fetch you to kill you. They will be very upset not to find you. I will be on horseback over there. You will be able to see me but not I you. So come and put your hand on my shoulder, so that I know you are near me. By the way I go you will come with me."

She then went away from Owain and he did all that she had told him to do. The people of the Castle came to find him to kill him. When they found nothing but half his horse, they were very displeased.

Owain vanished from there, went to the young woman and put his hand on her shoulder. She then set off, Owain following her, until they came to the door of a large and beautiful room. The girl opened the door and they went in. There was not a single nail in it that wasn't painted with gorgeous colours; not a single panel without images of gold on it.

---

* a heavy metal gate which drops vertically to guard the entrance to a castle

The young woman lit a fire, took water from a bowl, put a linen towel over her shoulder and gave Owain the water to wash. Then she placed before him a silver table, inlaid with gold; upon which was a yellow linen cloth; and she brought him food. Truthfully, Owain had never seen so many sorts of meat so much better cooked than in any other place. He also had not seen such a great display of food and drink that was there. Every drinking vessel was either gold or silver.

He ate and drank until late in the afternoon when they heard a great disturbance in the Castle. Owain asked the girl what it was. "They are administrating extreme unction[*] to the Nobleman who owns the Castle," she said. Owain then went to sleep. The couch which she had prepared for him was good enough for Arthur himself. It was of scarlet, fur, satin, sendal[*] and fine linen.

In the middle of the night they heard a distressing commotion. "What is this noise?" asked Owain. "The Nobleman who owns the Castle is dead," answered the girl. A little before daybreak they heard a loud weeping and wailing. Owain asked her what was the cause of it. "They are bearing the body of the Nobleman who owns the Castle to the church," she answered.

Owain got up, dressed himself, opened the window of the room and looked towards the Castle but he could not see the full number of the people who filled the streets. They were fully armed. A vast number of women were with them, both on foot and horseback and all the priests were singing. It seemed to Owain that the sky resounded with all the sound of the trumpets and the singing of the priests. In the middle of the crowd he saw a bier[*] covered in white linen. Wax tapers[*] were burning beside and around it. No one was lower in rank than a powerful Baron supporting the bier. Owain had never seen such a collection of gorgeous satins, silks and sendal.

Following the procession he saw a lady with blonde hair falling over her shoulders, stained with blood. Her dress of

---

[*] anointing a dying person with oil by a priest
[*] a Medieval silken fabric
[*] a movable stand on which a corpse is taken to the grave.
[*] slender candle

yellow satin was torn. She wore shoes of variegated (multi-coloured) leather. It was amazing that the ends of her fingers were not bruised from the violent way she clapped her hands together. She would have been the most beautiful lady Owain had ever seen, were she in her usual dress. Her cry was louder than the shout of the men or the sound of the trumpets. As soon as he saw her, Owain fell in love with her.

He asked the girl who was the lady. "She is said to be the most beautiful, the most good, the wisest and most noble of women. She is my mistress, who is called the Countess of the Fountain, the wife of him you killed yesterday."

"Well," said Owain, "she is the woman I love the best."

"So," said the young woman, "she will also love you a little."

With that, she got up, lit a fire, filled a pot with water and put it to warm. She brought a white linen towel and put it around Owain's neck. She took a goblet of ivory, a silver bowl and filled them with water with which she washed Owain's head. She then opened a wooden casket, took out a razor with an ivory handle with two gold nails on it. She shaved his beard and dried his head and throat with the towel. Then she brought him food of which Owain had never tasted better or been better served.

When he had finished his meal, the young woman arranged his couch. "Come and sleep here," she said, "and I will go to find your love for you." Owain went to sleep. The young woman shut the door and went towards the Castle. When she arrived there, she found nothing but mourning and sorrow. The Countess in her room would not see anyone because of her grief. Luned[*] (the young woman) asked what was the matter and why she would not see anyone.

"Luned," said the Countess, "what has happened to you, that you did not visit me in my grief? It was wrong of you, my having made you rich, that you did not come to me in my distress."

"Well," said Luned, "I thought you had more sense than that. Is it right for you to mourn that good man or anything you cannot have?"

---

[*] pronounced Linéd

102

"I declare," said the Countess, "that there is no man in the whole world equal to him."

"Not so," said Luned, "for an ugly man would be as good as, or better than he."

"My goodness," said the Countess, "if it were not distasteful for me to put to death one I have brought up, I would have you executed for making such a comparison to me. As it is, I will banish you."

"I am glad," said Luned, "that you have no other cause to do so, since I would have been of great service to you and done something for your benefit."

With that, Luned turned to leave. The Countess rose, followed her to the door and began to cough loudly. When Luned looked back, the Countess beckoned to her and she returned to her. "Well," said the Countess, "even if you are a wicked girl, if you know something that will be to my advantage, tell me."

"I will," said Luned.

"You know that other than by warfare and battle it is impossible for you to protect your lands. Don't delay. Find someone who can help you to defend what you have."

"How can I do that?" asked the Countess. "I will tell you," answered Luned. "Unless you can defend the fountain you cannot hope to hold on to your land and wealth and no one can defend the fountain except a knight of King Arthur's Court. I will go there and I hope nothing bad will happen to me and I can return with a warrior who can guard the fountain as well, if not better, than he who did it before."

"That will be hard to do," said the Countess. "However, go and do what you have promised to do."

Luned set out, pretending to go to Arthur's Court but she went back to the room where she had left Owain. She waited there for such a time as if she were travelling to the Court of King Arthur. At the end of that time, she dressed herself and went to visit the Countess, who was very pleased to see her and asked what news she had from the Court. "I bring you the best of news," said Luned. "I have done what I set out to do. When shall I present the knight to you that I have brought with me here?"

"Bring him here to me tomorrow at midday," said the Countess. "I will gather the people of the town together at that time."

Luned returned home and the next day, at dawn, Owain dressed himself in a coat, a surcoat and mantle (cloak) of yellow satin with a broad band of lace on it. He wore shoes of variegated leather fastened with gold clasps in the form of lions. They then proceeded to the Countess's room.

She was very pleased to see them. She stared at Owain and said to Luned, "This knight doesn't look as if he has travelled."

"Why does that matter lady?" said Luned. "I am certain," said the Countess, "that this man caused the death of my lord."

"So much the better for you, lady," said Luned, "for if he hadn't been the stronger he would not have killed him. There is no cure for what is past, whatever happened."

"Go back home," said the Countess, "and I will take advice."

The next day, the Countess called all her people together and told them that her earldom was left defenceless and that it could not be protected except by military skill. "Therefore," she said, "either one of you take me or give your consent for me to take a husband born elsewhere to defend my lands."

They came to a decision that it were better for her to marry someone from elsewhere. So she sent for the bishops and archbishops to celebrate her marriage to Owain. Then the men of the earldom paid homage to Owain, who, from then on for three years, defended the Fountain with lance and sword. He overthrew any knight who came there and he was greatly loved by his subjects.

Now it happened that one day Gwalchmai (Sir Gawain) was with King Arthur who he saw was very sad and sorrowful. It made him sad to see Arthur in this state and he asked him what was troubling him. "Truthfully, Gwalchmai," said Arthur, "I feel very concerned as to where Owain might be, whom I haven't seen for three years. I shall certainly die if four years pass before I see him, for I am sure it is because of the tale that Cynon told that I have lost Owain."

"There is no need for you to use your whole army to look for him," said Gwalchmai, "for you and the men of your household will be able to avenge Owain if he has been killed;

to set him free if he is in prison and if he is alive, to bring him back to you." It was decided to do as Gwalchmai had suggested. Arthur and his men prepared to go to find Owain. There were three thousand of them together with their attendants. Cynon, the son of Clydno acted as their guide.

Arthur then came to the Castle where Cynon had been before. As he came there, the young men were with their daggers in the same place with the yellow man standing alongside. When he saw Arthur, he greeted him and invited him to the Castle. Arthur accepted his invitation and they entered the Castle together. Even the great number of his men were lost in the vastness of the Castle. The young ladies got up to wait on them and their service was greater than any they had ever had. Even the pages who attended to the horses were no worse than Arthur's servants in his own palace.

The next morning, Arthur set out, with Cynon as his guide, to where the black man was. The build of this man seemed greater to Arthur than had been described to him. They came to the top of the wooded slope, crossed the valley till they reached the green tree, where they saw the fountain, the bowl and the slab. Then Cei came to Arthur and said, "My Lord, I know the meaning of all this and I ask if you will permit me to throw the water on the slab and to experience the first adventure that may happen." Arthur gave his permission.

Cei then threw a bowlful of water over the slab and immediately the thunder came and the shower. They had never known such a thunderstorm before and many attendants were killed by the shower. After that the sky became clear and they looked at the tree which was leafless. The birds then descended upon the tree and sang more sweetly than they had ever heard before.

Then they saw a Knight on a coal-black horse dressed in black satin coming quickly towards them. Cei met him and it was not long before he was thrown from his horse. The Knight departed and Arthur and his men made camp for the night.

When they rose in the morning, they saw a signal for battle on the lance of the Knight. Cei then said to Arthur, "Though I was overthrown yesterday, if it seems right to you, I would gladly meet the Knight again today."

"You may do so," said Arthur.

So Cei went towards the knight and was once again thrown from his horse and was struck on the forehead with the Knight's lance, so that it broke his helmet, his headpiece and pierced his skin and flesh to the bone, so he returned to his companions.

After this, one by one, all of Arthur's men went to fight with the Knight. All were overthrown except Arthur and Gwalchmai (Sir Gawain). Arthur armed himself to fight with the Knight but Gwalchmai asked his permission to fight him first. Arthur gave his permission and Gwalchmai went to meet the Knight, having over himself a satin robe of honour which had been sent to him by the daughter of the Earl of Rhangyw, so that he was disguised and not recognised by any of his men.

They fought all day until the evening, neither being able to unhorse the other. The next day they fought with strong lances but neither was able to master the other. On the third day they fought with even stronger lances furiously until noon. They were both shocked when the girths* of their horses were broken so that they both fell over their horse's cruppers* to the ground. They got up quickly and resumed fighting with their swords.

The people watching had never seen two men so brave and powerful. The Knight gave Gwalchmai such a blow that took his helmet off his face, so that the Knight knew it was Gwalchmai. Then the Knight – who was Owain – said, "My lord Gwalchmai, I did not know you were my cousin, owing to the robe of honour covering you. Take my sword and weapons."

Gwalchmai said, "Owain, you are the winner, take my sword." With that, Arthur saw them speaking to each other and went to them. "My Lord Arthur," said Gwalchmai, "here is Owain who has beaten me but will not take my sword."

"My lord," said Owain, "it is he that has beaten me and will not take my weapons."

"Give me your swords," said Arthur, "then neither of you has beaten the other." Then Owain put his arms around Arthur's neck and all the men pressed forward to see Owain

---

* leather strap to secure the saddle
* the hindquarters of a horse

and hold him. So great was the pressure that the men were nearly killed, then they all returned for the night.

The next day Arthur prepared to leave. "My lord," said Owain, "this is not right. It is three years since I have been away from you. During that time up until today, I have been preparing a banquet for you, knowing that you would come to find me. Stay with me, then, until you and the men have recovered from your journeying."

They all proceeded to the Castle of the Countess of the Fountain and the banquet which had been prepared for three years was eaten and drunk in three months. Never had they had such a delicious banquet. Then Arthur prepared to leave again. He sent a message to the Countess to beg her to allow Owain to go with him for three months, so that they might show him to the nobles and the beautiful women of the Island of Britain.

The Countess gave her consent, although it was very painful to her. So Owain was once again among his family and friends where he remained for three years instead of three months.

As Owain sat eating his meal in the city of Caerleon upon Usk, a young girl came by on a bay* horse with a curly mane. The bridle and saddle were of gold and she was dressed in yellow satin. She came up to Owain, took the ring from off his finger and cried, "You will be treated as a deceiver, a traitor, faithless and disgraced." Then she turned the horse's head and left.

Then Owain remembered his adventure and was sad. Having finished eating, he went to his own home and prepared for the next day. When he got up he didn't go to the Court but wandered to far parts of the earth and to unexplored mountains. He stayed there until his clothes were worn out, his body wasted away and his hair had grown long. He went about with the wild beasts and fed with them until they were friends with him, but eventually he grew so weak that he could not bear their company. He went down from the mountains to the valley, came to a park which was the best in the world and belonged to a widowed Countess.

---

* reddish brown

One day, the Countess and her ladies went for a walk by a lake which was in the middle of the park. They saw the form of a man and were terrified. However, they went near him, touched him and looked at him. They saw that there was life in him but that he was exhausted by the heat of the sun.

When the Countess returned to the Castle, she took a flask of precious ointment and gave it to one of her ladies. "Take this," she said, "that horse over there and that clothing. Place them near the man we just saw. Put the ointment on him near his heart. If there is life in him, the ointment will help to heal him, then watch what he will do."

The girl left and poured all the ointment over Owain and left the horse and clothes nearby. She went a little way off and watched him. Soon she saw him begin to move his arms. He looked at himself and seemed ashamed of his appearance. Then he saw the horse and clothes near him. He crept forward so that he could grasp the clothes from the saddle and began to dress himself. He mounted the horse with difficulty.

The girl then made herself known to him and greeted him. He was very pleased to see her and asked her what land this was. "A widowed Countess owns this land," she said, "on the death of her husband. He left her two Earldoms but now she only has this one Castle that has not been taken from her by a young Earl, her neighbour, who she has refused to marry."

"That is a pity," said Owain as he and the young girl proceeded to the Castle. He alighted from his horse and was shown to a pleasant room. She lit a fire and left him.

The young girl then went to the Countess and gave her the empty flask. "Oh my girl," said the Countess, "where is all the ointment?"

"I have used it all," she said. "Oh my goodness, I can't forgive you for using all this precious ointment on a stranger. However, look after him until he is quite recovered." The girl did so and gave him food and drink. She also provided him with heat, somewhere to stay and medicine until he was well again. In three months he was back to his former self, but even more handsome than ever before.

One day, Owain heard a great commotion and the sound of weapons in the Castle and asked the girl what it was. "The Earl," she said, "who I told you about, has come to subdue the

Countess with a large army." Owain asked her if the Countess had a horse and weapons. "She has the best in the world," said the girl. "Will you go and ask her to lend me the horse and weapons," said Owain, "so that I can go and look at this army?"

"I will," she said.

She went to the Countess and told her what Owain had said. The Countess laughed and said, "Really, I will give him the horse and weapons the like of which he had never seen. I am glad to give them to him in case my enemies take them against my will tomorrow. Yet I don't know what he would do with them.

She gave instructions for a beautiful black horse with a beech saddle to be brought out, together with a suit of armour for man and horse. Owain armed himself and was attended by two pages completely armed with horses and weapons. When they came near to the Earl's army, it was so large, they could not see it all. Owain asked the pages to which troop the Earl belonged. "In that troop," they said, "between four yellow standards (flags), two of them before and two behind."

"Now," said Owain, "you return to the gateway of the Castle and wait for me there." So they did and Owain went forward until he met the Earl. Owain drew him completely out of his saddle and turned the horse's head towards the Castle. With difficulty then he brought the Earl to the gateway, where the pages were waiting for him. They went in and Owain presented the Earl to the Countess as a gift in return for the precious ointment.

The army made camp around the Castle and the Earl restored the two Earldoms to the Countess that he had taken from her, as a ransom for his life. Also, for his freedom, he gave her half of all his lands, all his gold, silver and jewels besides hostages.

Owain took his leave, even though the Countess and all her subjects begged him to stay, but he chose to wander through distant lands and deserts. As he travelled, he heard a loud yelling in a wood. It was repeated a second and third time. Owain went towards the spot and saw a huge craggy mound in the middle of the wood; on the side of which was a grey rock. There was a split in the rock in which there was a serpent. Near the rock stood a black lion. Every time it moved, the serpent darted forward to attack him. Owain unsheathed his sword, approached the rock and as the serpent sprang out, he struck him with his sword and cut him in two. He dried his sword and went on his way but the lion followed him and played around him as though he had been a greyhound he had reared.

They travelled in this way throughout the day, until the evening. When it was time for Owain to rest, he dismounted and turned his horse loose in a flat and wooded meadow. He made a fire and when it was lit, the lion brought him enough fuel to last for three nights. Then the lion disappeared only to return soon carrying a fine large roebuck (male deer.) He threw it down in front of Owain who skinned it and put slices of its flesh upon skewers around the fire. The rest of the buck he gave to the lion to eat.

While he was doing this, he heard a deep sigh near him; and a second and a third. He called out to see if the sigh came from a human being and he had an answer that it did. "Who are you?" asked Owain. "Really," came the voice, "I am Luned, the servant girl of the Countess of the Fountain."

"What are you doing here?" asked Owain. "I am in prison," she answered, "because of the Knight who came from Arthur's Court and married the Countess. He stayed a short time with her but left again for the Court of Arthur and has not returned since. He was the friend I loved the best in the world. Two of the pages of the Countess's court belittled him and called him a deceiver. I told them they were not a match for him so they imprisoned me in the stone vault and said that I should be killed unless he came himself to free me by a certain day and that is the day after tomorrow. I have no one to send to find him. His name is Owain, the son of Urien."

"Are you certain that if he knew this he would come to your rescue?"

"I am most certain of it," she said.

When the meat was cooked, Owain divided it into two between himself and Luned. After they had eaten, they talked together until dawn. The next morning, Owain asked Luned if there was any place where he could get food and entertainment for the night. "There is lord," she said. "Cross over there, go along the side of the river and in a short time you will see a great Castle with many towers. The Earl who owns it is the

110

most hospitable man in the world. You may spend the night there." No sentry kept closer watch over his lord than the lion did over Owain that night.

The next day, Owain mounted his horse and passed by the ford. He came to the Castle, entered it and was welcomed. His horse was also well cared for and fodder (hay) was put in front of him. The lion then went and lay down in the horse's manger, so that none of the people dared to approach him.

Owain was well treated in the Castle, except that everyone was so sad as though death was near. They went into the meal, the Earl sitting on one side of Owain and his only daughter on the other. Owain had not seen anyone as lovely as she. Then the lion came and put himself between Owain's feet and he fed him with the food he was eating himself, but he had never seen such sadness before.

In the middle of the meal, the Earl began to greet Owain. "Then it is time for you to be cheerful," said Owain. "Oh, it is not your coming that makes us sorrowful, but we have good reason to be very sad," said the Earl. "What is that?" asked Owain.

"I have two sons," replied the Earl, "and yesterday they went to the mountains to hunt. Now there is on the mountain a monster who kills men and devours them. He seized my sons and he has threatened to be here tomorrow and will kill my sons unless I give him my daughter. He looks like a man but is built like a giant."

"Oh," said Owain, "that is dreadful. What will you do?"

"Heaven knows," said the Earl, "it would be better that my sons should be killed against my will, then that I should give up my daughter for him to ill-treat and destroy." Then they talked of other things and Owain stayed the night.

The next morning they heard a great disturbance which was the giant coming with the two young men. The Earl was anxious both to protect his Castle and to release his two sons. Then Owain put on his armour, went to meet the Giant and the lion followed him. When the giant saw that Owain was armed, he rushed forward and attacked him. The lion fought the giant more fiercely than Owain did. "Ah," said the giant, "I wouldn't find it so difficult to fight you if it weren't for the animal with you." So Owain took the lion back to the Castle, shut the gate on him and returned to fight the giant.

The lion began to roar loudly because he could hear that Owain wasn't managing to fight the giant very well. He climbed up on the top of the Earl's hall, got on top of the Castle and sprang down from the walls to help Owain. The lion gave the giant a stroke with his paw which tore him from shoulder to hip until his heart was bare. The giant fell down dead and Owain restored the two boys to their father.

The Earl begged Owain to stay with him but he wouldn't and set out towards the meadow where Luned was. When he arrived there he saw a great fire burning and two young men with beautiful curling auburn hair about to put the girl on the fire.

Owain asked what was the charge against her. They told him of the agreement that was between them as Luned had the night before. "So," they said, "Owain has failed to save her, therefore we are taking her to be burnt." Owain said, "But he is a good knight and if he knew Luned was in such danger, it is amazing that he hasn't come to rescue her. If you will accept me instead, I will fight with you."

"We will," they said.

They then attacked Owain and he found it difficult to beat them. With that the lion came to help him and together they got the better of them. "Sir Knight," they said, "it was not agreed to fight you with an animal such as that. It is harder for us to fight you both." So Owain put the lion in the place where Luned had been imprisoned and went back to fight them. However, he didn't have his usual strength and when the lion realised that Owain was in trouble, he roared loudly and burst through the wall until he found a way out. He rushed against the young men and killed them. So Luned was saved from being burned.

Owain returned to the lands of the Countess of the Fountain. When he got there he took the Countess with him to Arthur's Court and she was his wife as long as she lived.

He then took the road that led to the Court of the savage black man. Owain fought with him and the lion did not leave Owain until he had beaten him. When he reached the Court of the black man, he entered the hall and saw twenty-four ladies, the fairest ever seen. The clothes they wore, however, were not worth twenty-four pence and they were as sad as death. Owain asked why they were so sad. They told him, "We are the daughters of Earls and we all came here with our husbands, who are dearly loved. We were welcomed with respect and rejoicing. We were then put in a trance. While we were like that the cruel man who owns this Castle killed all our husbands and took from us our horses, our clothes, our gold and silver. The corpses of our husbands are still in this house and others too. That is why we grieve so and we are so sorry that you come here in case you come to harm."

Owain was sorry too when he heard this. He set off for the Castle and saw a knight approaching him who greeted him in a friendly and cheerful manner, as if he were his brother; but he was the savage black man. "I haven't come in friendship," said Owain. "Then you will find it," he said. With that they charged each other and fought furiously. Owain overcame him and bound his hands behind his back.

The black man then pleaded with Owain to spare his life and said, "My Lord Owain, it was prophesied that you would come here and overcome me and you have done so. I was a robber here and my house was a house of wickedness; but spare me my life and I will become the keeper of an Hospice*. I will keep my house as an Hospice for the weak and the strong as long as I live." Owain accepted this suggestion and stayed that night.

The next day, he took the twenty-four ladies, their horses, clothes, what they had left of their goods and jewels back to Arthur's Court. If Arthur was so pleased to see him after he had lost him the first time, he was even more pleased now. Some ladies stayed in the Court and some who wished to leave, left.

For some time Owain lived at Arthur's court, greatly loved as the head of his household until he went away with his followers which were three hundred ravens which Cenferchyn had left him. Wherever Owain went with them he was victorious.

---

* a house of rest for travellers or a home for down and out and the sick

11. Peredur*, the Son of Efrawc

Earl Efrawc owned the Earldom of the North and he had seven sons. He occupied himself, not so much be tending his own lands, but by attending tournaments, wars and battles. As often happens to those who do this, he was killed, together with six of his sons. The name of the seventh son was Peredur. He was the youngest and not old enough to go to war, otherwise he might have been killed like his father and brothers.

His mother was a scheming and thoughtful woman, who was very anxious about the safety of her only son. So she decided to leave the country where she lived and move to the deserts and wildernesses where no one lived. She only allowed women and boys to accompany her and men who were not accustomed to or capable of fighting. She also did not allow anyone to bring horses or weapons so that her son would not think about them.

The lad went every day to the forest to amuse himself by flinging sticks and staves*. One day he saw his mother's flock of goats with two hinds* standing by them. He was really amazed that these two had no horns, while the others had them. He thought that they must have run wild and lost their horns in that way. Swiftly he drove the goats and hinds together to a barn on the edge of the forest. Then he returned to his mother.

"Oh mother," he said, "I have seen an amazing thing in the forest. Two of your goats have run wild and lost their horns from being missing so long in the wood. I had such trouble putting them in the barn." They all went to see and were astonished when they saw the hinds.

---

* Sir Percival (or Parsifal)
* curved pieces of wood
* female red deer

114

One day, they saw three knights coming along the horse-road on the edge of the forest. The three knights were Gwalchmai son of Gwyar, Geneir Gwystyl and Owain the son of Urien. Owain was tracking and following the knight who had divided the apples in Arthur's Court.

"Mother," said Peredur, "what are those over there?"

"They are angels, my son," she said. "Well," said Peredur, "I will go and become an angel with them," and he went to the road to meet them.

"Tell me, young man," said Owain, "did you see a knight pass this way either today or yesterday?"

"I don't know what a knight is," he answered. "It is someone like me," said Owain. "If you tell me what I ask you, I will tell you what you ask me," said the boy. "Certainly I will," replied Owain.

"What is this?" demanded Peredur, pointing to the saddle. "It is a saddle," said Owain. Then Peredur asked all about the outfits and armour he saw on the men as well as the horses and trappings; what they were for and how they were used. Owain showed him all the things and told him what they were for. "Go the way you are facing," said Peredur, "for I saw someone like that which you asked about and I will follow you."

Then Peredur returned to his mother and her friends and said to her, "Those were not angels but honourable knights." His mother then fainted away. He went to the place where they kept the horses that carried the firewood and that had brought food and drink from the old country to the desert. He took a piebald* horse which seemed to him the strongest of them. He pressed a pack into the form of a saddle and with twisted twigs, he copied the trappings he had seen on the knight's horses.

When he came back to his mother, she had recovered. "My son," she said, "do you want to ride away?"

"Yes I do, with your permission," he said. "Wait a moment while I give you some advice," she said. "I will," he said, "but tell me quickly."

"Go then to the Court of Arthur," she said, "where there are the best, the bravest and the most generous of men. Wherever

---

* two coloured usually black and white

you see a church, go in and say your Paternoster[*]. If you see meat and drink and no one has the kindness or courtesy to offer it to you, take it yourself. If you hear someone cry out, go towards it, especially if it is a woman. If you see a precious jewel, take it and give it to someone else; then you will be praised. If you see a beautiful woman, tell her you admire her, whether she accepts it or no; then you will make yourself a better and more respected man that you were before."

After this talk, Peredur got on his horse and taking a handful of sharp pointed forks in his hand, he rode away.

He travelled for two days and two nights in the woody wilderness and in deserts without food or drink. Then he came to a large wild wood, within which was a glade[*] with a tent in it which to him looked like a church. So he said his Paternoster to it. He went towards it and the door of the tent was open. A golden chair was near the door and sitting on it was a lovely auburn haired girl, with a band of gold on her forehead with sparkling stones in it and with a large gold ring on her hand.

Peredur dismounted and entered the tent. The girl was pleased to see him and welcomed him. At the entrance to the tent he saw food, two flasks full of wine, two loaves of fine wheat flour and slices of the meat of the wild boar.

"My mother told me, wherever I saw meat and drink to take it," said Peredur. "Take it, by all means sir," she said. So he took half of the meat and drink for himself and left the rest to the girl. When he had finished eating, he knelt before the girl and said, "My mother told me that wherever I saw a precious jewel, to take it."

"Do so," she said. So Peredur took the ring, mounted his horse and carried on his journey.

Then the knight who owned the tent came there. He was The Lord of the Glade. He saw the horse's tracks and said to the girl, "Tell me who has been here since I left." She said, "A man of fine bearing" and she described what Peredur's appearance and behaviour had been. "Tell me," he said, "did he do you any harm? "No" said the girl, "he didn't harm me at all."

---

[*] The Lord's Prayer
[*] an open space between forest trees

116

"I don't believe you," cried the knight, "and until I meet him and revenge this insult he has done me and have my vengeance on him, you will not stay two nights in the same house."

Meanwhile, Peredur travelled on to Arthur's Court but before he reached there, another knight had been there who gave a thick gold ring at the door for holding his horse and went into the Hall where Arthur and his household and Gwenhwyfar (Guinevere) and her ladies were gathered. A page was serving Gwenhwyfar with a golden goblet.

The knight then splashed the liquor that was in it in her face and on her stomacher[*] and gave her a violent blow on her face saying, "If any of you have the courage to question what I have just done with the goblet and to revenge the insult to Gwenhwyfar, let him follow me to the meadow and I will wait for him." So he took his horse and rode to the meadow.

All the people there hung down their heads in case any of them would be asked to go and avenge the insult to Gwenhwyfar, for it seemed to them that no one would do such a thing unless he had magic powers, so that no one could take vengeance on him.

Then Peredur entered the Hall upon the bony piebald horse with the rough trappings on it and crossed the whole length of the Hall. In the centre of the Hall stood Cei. "Tell me, tall man," said Peredur, "is that Arthur over there?"

"What would you want with Arthur?" asked Cei.

"My mother told me to go to Arthur and he would make me a knight."

"My goodness," said Cei, "you are very poorly equipped with horse and weapons." Then all the people threw sticks at him when they saw him.

Then a dwarf came forward, who, together with a female dwarf, had been at Arthur's court for a whole year, but had not, in all that time, spoken a word to anyone. "Haha," he said, "welcome to you, good Peredur, son of Efrawc, chief of warriors and flower of knighthood."

---

[*] A part of a woman's dress covering her front & sometimes richly jewelled or embroidered

"Really," said Cei, "you are not well taught enough, to be mute* in Arthur's Court for a whole year and yet now, right in front of Arthur and all his household, to speak out and call this man a chief of warriors and the flower of knighthood." With that, he gave him such a box on the ear that he fell senseless to the ground.

Then the female dwarf exclaimed, "Haha! Good Peredur, son of Efrawc, welcome to you, best of knights and flower of chivalry."

"Truly, lady," said Cei, "you too are ill-bred to be mute for a year at the Court of Arthur, yet to speak as you do of such a man as this" and he kicked her with his foot so that she fell senseless to the ground.

"Tall man," said Peredur, "show me which is Arthur."

"Be quiet," said Cei. "Go after the knight who went out to the meadow and take the goblet from him. Then overthrow him and take possession of his horse and weapons, then you will receive the order of knighthood."

"I will do, tall man," said Peredur and turned his horse towards the meadow.

When he reached there, the knight was riding up and down, proud of his strength, bravery and nobility. "Tell me," he said, "did you see anyone follow me from the Court?"

"The tall man asked me to come and overthrow you, to take the goblet away from you and take your horse and armour for myself," answered Peredur.

"Silence," commanded the knight. "Go back to the Court and tell Arthur from me, either to come himself, or to send someone else to fight with me. Unless he does so quickly, I will not wait for him."

"Well," said Peredur, "whether you choose to willingly or unwillingly, I shall have your horse and weapons and the goblet."

At this, the knight came at him furiously and gave him a violent blow with the staff of his spear between the neck and the shoulders.

"Haha lad!" said Peredur, "my mother's servants were not used to playing with me in this way, so I will play with you."

---

* silent

At that he struck the knight with a sharp pointed fork which hit him in the eye and came out the back of his neck and he fell down lifeless.

"Really," said Owain to Cei, "you were unwise when you sent that madman after the knight. One of two things will happen to him. Either he will be overthrown or killed. If he is overthrown by the knight, he will be seen by him to be an honourable person of the Court and that will forever be a disgrace to Arthur and his warriors. If he is killed, the disgrace will be the same and more than that, the shame will be his. So I will go and see what has happened to him."

Owain, then, went to the meadow and found Peredur dragging the man about. "What are you doing?" asked Owain.

"This iron coat will not come off him, however hard I try," replied Peredur. So Owain unfastened the armour and the knight's clothes.

"Here you are," he said. "Here is a horse and armour better than yours. Take them and come with me to Arthur, to receive the order of knighthood, for you have earned it."

"May I never show my face again if I go," said Peredur, "but you take the goblet to Gwenhwyfar and tell Arthur, that wherever I am, I will be his vassal* and I will do what service to him that I can. Also say that I will not come to Court until I have met up with the tall man that is there, to revenge the hurt he did to the dwarf and dwarfess." So Owain went back to the Court and told all these things to Arthur, Gwenhwyfar and to all the household.

Peredur rode on and met a knight. "Where have you come from?" asked the knight.

"I have come from Arthur's court," said Peredur.

"Are you one of his men?" he asked.

"Yes, I am" he answered.

"It is good to be in Arthur's service," said the knight.

"Why do you say that?" asked Peredur.

"I will tell you," he said. "I have always been Arthur's enemy and all of his men I have met I have killed."

Without any more talk, they fought and it was not long before Peredur brought him to the ground. Then the knight

---

* slave or humble dependant

asked for mercy. "You shall have it," said Peredur, "if you make me a promise that you will go to Arthur's Court and tell them it was I who overthrew you and in service to him. Also say that I will never come to Court until I have avenged the insult to the dwarf and dwarfess." The knight said he would and proceeded to the Court of Arthur. He said what he had promised and also told Cei of Peredur's threat.

Peredur rode on and within that week he met up with sixteen knights and overthrew them all. They all went to Arthur's Court with the same message which the first knight had taken from Peredur and the same threat to Cei who was rebuked* by Arthur which upset Cei very much.

Peredur then rode on further and came to a vast and deserted wood in which was a lake. On the other side was a great castle. On the edge of the lake he saw a grey-haired man sitting on a velvet cushion. He also wore velvet clothes. His attendants were fishing in the lake. When the grey-haired man saw Peredur coming, he got up and went towards the castle. The old man was lame.

Peredur rode to the palace. The door was open and he entered the hall. There was the grey-haired man sitting on a cushion with a large blazing fire in front of him. The people there rose to meet him and helped him off with his cloak. The man asked him to sit on the cushion and they sat and talked.

When it was time for a meal, the tables were laid and they went to eat. When they had finished their meal, the man asked Peredur if he could fight with a sword. "I do not," said Peredur, "but if I were taught, no doubt I would. Whoever can handle a cudgel and shield, will also be able to fight with a sword."

The man had two sons. The one had yellow-hair and the other auburn. "Get up my boys," he said, "and handle the cudgel and the shield." So they did. "Tell me, young sir," said the man, "which of the boys handles them the best?"

Peredur answered, "I think that the yellow-haired boy could draw blood from the other if he chose."

"You take the cudgel and shield from the boy with auburn hair and draw blood from the yellow-haired boy if you can," said the man.

---

* scolded and told off

120

So Peredur got up and went to use the cudgel and shield. He lifted up his arm and struck such a mighty blow that the brow of the yellow-haired boy fell over his eye and he bled. "Ah, young sir," said the man, "come and sit down, for you will become the best fighter with the sword of any of this island. I am your uncle, your mother's brother. You shall stay with me for a while, in order to learn the manners and customs by different countries; and courtesy, gentleness and noble bearing. Forget the ways and talk of your mother. I will be your teacher and will raise you to the rank of knighthood from now on. Also do this. If you see anything strange, do not ask the meaning of it. If no one has the manners to tell you what it is, it will not be your fault but mine because I am your teacher." After this, they were waited on by servants and then went to sleep.

At break of day, Peredur got up, took his horse and with his uncle's permission he rode off. Soon he came to a vast wood, at the end of which was a meadow, on the other side of that was a large castle. He went towards it and found the gate open. He went into the hall and saw a grey-haired man sitting on one side of the hall, with many pages around him who got up to welcome Peredur. They put him by the side of the owner of the palace.

They talked together and he sat by the nobleman at the table when it was time to eat. He asked Peredur whether he could fight with a sword. "I think I could if I were taught," said Peredur. Now, on the floor was a huge staple[*].

"Take that sword," said the man to him, "and strike that iron staple." So Peredur got up and struck the staple, cutting it in two. The sword broke in two parts also. "Place the two parts together and rejoin them," said the man. Peredur then put them together and they became complete as they were before.

He did this a second time and the two parts of the staple and the sword were joined together as before. The third time he did this, the staple nor the sword would join as before. "Young man," said the nobleman, "come and sit down and have my blessing. You fight better with the sword than any man in the kingdom. You have two thirds of your strength. When you gain the other third, no one will be able to compete with you."

---

[*] a U shaped piece of metal

"I am your uncle, your mother's brother. I am also the brother of the man in whose house you were last night." Then they both talked together and they saw two young men come into the hall carrying a huge spear streaming with blood. When all the people saw it they all started to cry out with grief. For all that, the man didn't stop talking to Peredur and as he didn't explain the meaning of what they saw, he did not ask.

When the noise had lessened, two young ladies came in with a large salver* between them on which was a man's head with much blood around it. Then all the people cried out so much that it was trying to be in the same hall with them. Eventually they were silent and when it was time to sleep, Peredur was shown to a pleasant room.

The next day, with his uncle's permission, he set off and came to a wood in which he heard a loud cry. He saw a beautiful woman with auburn hair, a horse with a saddle on it standing near and a corpse by her side. As she tried to put the corpse on the horse, it fell to the ground and she was very upset.

"Tell me, sister," said Peredur, "why are you so upset?"

"Oh! Cursed Peredur, you have never had much pity for my misery."

"Why am I cursed?" asked Peredur.

"Because you are the cause of your mother's death. When you left against her will, it gave her great pain in her heart and she died. That's why you are cursed. The dwarf and dwarfess at Arthur's Court belonged to your father and mother. I am your foster-sister and this was my husband who was killed by the knight who is in the glade* in the wood. Don't you go near him in case you're killed!"

"My sister, you wrongly accuse me, for if I had stayed longer with you, I would never have been able to overcome him, so stop your crying, for it will do no good. I will bury the body, then I will go in search of the knight and hopefully defeat him."

When he had buried the body, they went to the place where the knight was and found him riding proudly along the glade.

---

* a tray usually of silver or gold
* a clear open space between trees

He asked Peredur where he had come from. "I have come from Arthur's Court."

"Are you one of Arthur's men?"

"I am indeed!"

"That is Arthur's gain, I'm sure," said the knight. Without more conversation, they fought each other and Peredur overthrew the knight who asked for mercy.

"You shall have mercy on these terms," said Peredur, "that you take this woman for your wife and honour and respect her greatly, seeing that you, with no reason, killed her husband. You must also go to Arthur's Court, tell him that it was I who overthrew you and that I will never come to the Court again until I have defeated the tall man for his insult to the dwarf and dwarfess.

He accepted the knight's promise that he would do all this. The knight then provided the lady with a horse and suitable clothes and took her with him to Arthur's Court. He told Arthur all that had happened and also told Cei about Peredur's threat. Then Arthur and all the Court told Cei off for having driven such a young man as Peredur from his Court. Owain said, "He will never come back to the Court until Cei has gone from it."

"Well," said Arthur, "I will search all the deserts of the Island of Britain until I find Peredur, then let him and Cei fight it out."

Then Peredur rode off and came to a wood where he saw no tracks of man or animals, just bushes and weeds. At the upper end of the wood, he saw a vast castle with many strong towers. When he came near the gate, he found the weeds taller than elsewhere. He hit the gate with his lance and soon a slim, auburn haired young man came to the battlements. He said, "Do you wish to come in, or shall I announce that you are here?"

"Say that I am here," said Peredur, "and if I may enter, I will go in."

The youth came back, opened the gate for him and he went into the hall and saw eighteen young men, slim and red-headed, of the same height and appearance, of the same dress and age of the one who had opened the gate for him. They were also very well-mannered. They helped him off with his outer cloak and sat down to talk. Then five young girls came from a room into the hall. Peredur had never seen anyone so lovely as the main one. She wore a dress of satin which had once been fine but was now so tattered that her skin could be seen through it. Her skin was whiter than the bloom of crystal. Her hair and eyebrows were blacker than jet and in her cheeks were red spots redder than whatever is reddest.

She welcomed Peredur, put her arms about his neck and made him sit down beside her. Not long after this he saw two nuns enter. One of them carried a flask of wine, the other carried six loaves of bread. "Lady," they said, "there is not as much food and drink as this left in the convent tonight."

They sat down to eat and Peredur saw that the girl wanted to give more of the food and drink to him than any of the others. "Lady," he said, "I will share out the food and liquor."

"Oh no," she said.

"Yes, I will," he said and took the bread and shared it out equally as he did a cup full of the liquor. When it was time for them to sleep, a room was prepared for Peredur and he went to rest.

"Look, sister," said the young men to the loveliest and most noble of the ladies, "we have some advice for you."

"What is it?" she asked. "Go to the man in the upper room and offer to become his wife or his lady if it pleases him."

"That would not be fitting," she said. "Up till now, I have not been any knight's lady. To make him such an offer before he approaches me, I simply cannot do."

"By heaven, unless you agree to do this, we will leave you here to your enemies, to do as they will with you." Being afraid of this threat, she went to Peredur's room.

At the noise of the door opening, Peredur woke up and saw the lady crying and moaning. "Why are you crying my lady?" asked Peredur.

"I'll tell you, lord," she said. "My father owned these lands as their chief. This palace was his and with it he owned the best earldom in the kingdom. The son of another earl then came to claim me for his wife, but I was not willing and my father would not give me against my will, either to him or any other earl in the world. I was my father's only child."

"After my father died, these lands came to me. I was less willing than before to accept him as my husband. So he made war on me and conquered all my possessions, except this one house. Because of the bravery of these men you have seen, who are my foster-brothers and the strength of the house, as long as the food and drink last, it can never be taken."

"Now our provisions are exhausted. As you have seen, we have been fed by the nuns, to whom it is a free country. Soon they will be without supplies and no later than tomorrow, the earl will come and attack this place. If I fall under his power, my fate will be no better than the grooms of his horses. Therefore, lord, I place myself in your hands, so that you can protect me, either by taking me away or by defending me here, whichever you find best."

"Go and sleep now," he said. "I will not leave until I do what you ask or prove whether I can help you or not." She again went to rest. The next morning she came to Peredur and greeted him. "What news do you have?" he asked. "None other than the earl and his army are at the gate. I never saw any place covered with so many tents and knights ready for the fight," she said.

"Have my horse ready," said Peredur. It was and he went to the meadow where there was a knight ready for battle. They met and Peredur threw him off his horse. At the end of the day, another knight challenged him and he overthrew him too. He asked for mercy. "Who are you?" asked Peredur.

"I am the Master of the Household of the Earl," he answered.

"How much of the Countesses possessions do you own?"

"A third," was the answer.

"Then restore to her a third of her possessions in full and all the profit you have made from them. Bring food and drink for a hundred men with their horses and weapons to her court tonight. You will remain her prisoner unless she wishes to have you killed." The knight did this straight away and that night the lady was happy and they feasted well.

The next day Peredur rode to the meadow and defeated much of the army. At the end of the day, a proud and stately knight appeared. Peredur overthrew him and he asked for mercy. "Who are you?" asked Peredur.

"I am the Steward of the Palace," he said.

"How much of the lady's possessions are under your control?"

"One third," came the reply.

"So," said Peredur, "you must fully restore her possessions to the lady, shall give food and drink for two hundred men, their horses and weapons. You will be her prisoner." It was done immediately.

On the third day, Peredur rode to the meadow and defeated more than on either of the preceding days. Again, at the end of the day, an earl came to attack him. Peredur overthrew him and he asked for mercy. "Who are you?" asked Peredur.

"I am the earl," he said, "I will not keep it from you."

"So," said Peredur, "you shall restore the whole of the lady's earldom, give her your own earldom as well as meat and drink for three hundred men and their horses and weapons. You will remain her captive." And so it happened.

Peredur then stayed for three weeks in the country, making sure respect and obedience was paid to the lady and that she should have control of the government. Then he said, "With your permission, I will leave now."

"Do you really wish to?"

"Yes," he said, "if it wasn't that I loved you, I should not have stayed so long."

"Who are you?" she asked.

"I am Peredur, the son of Efrawc from the North. If ever you are in trouble or danger again, let me know and if I can, I will protect you."

Peredur rode on and met a lady on a lean horse which was sweating and she greeted him. "Where have you come from, my lady?" She then told him the reason for her journey. She was the wife of the Lord of the Glade. "So," he said, "I am the knight who is the cause of your trouble, but he will be sorry that he has treated you like this." Then a knight rode up and asked Peredur if he had seen a knight that he was looking for. "Say no more," said Peredur, "I'm the one you are looking for, but you deserve a bad reputation for your treatment of this lady, for she is innocent of anything to do with me."

They fought and it was not long before Peredur overthrew the knight and he begged for mercy. "You shall have mercy," said Peredur, "as long as you go back the way you came and declare this lady is innocent and you will give her the opposite of what you have had from me." The knight promised that he would.

Then Peredur rode on. Above him he saw a castle and went towards it. He struck the gate with his lance. Then a handsome auburn-haired youth opened the gate. He had the build of a warrior but was only a boy. When Peredur came into the hall, there was a tall and stately Countess sitting in a chair with many ladies around her. She was pleased to see him and when it was time, they went to eat.

After their meal was finished, she said, "It would be better if you went elsewhere to sleep, sir."

"Why can't I sleep here?" asked Peredur.

"Nine sorceresses of Gloucester[*] are here with their father and mother. Unless we can escape before daybreak, we shall all be killed. Already they have conquered and laid waste all the country, except this one castle."

"I will stay here tonight," he said, and if you are in trouble, I will help you all I can, but you will not be harmed by me." So they went to rest.

At the break of day, Peredur heard a dreadful disturbance. He got up quickly and, in his vest and doublet[*], with his sword about his neck, he saw a sorceress overtake one of the watch (guards), who cried out violently. Peredur attacked the sorceress and struck her on her head with his sword and flattened her helmet and head-piece so it looked like a plate on her head.

"Have mercy, good Peredur, son of Efrawc, have mercy."

"How do you know that I am Peredur, hag?"

"By destiny and the fore-telling that I should be harmed by you. You will take a horse and armour from me, will learn about chivalry and the use of arms from me."

Peredur said, "You shall have mercy, if you promise that you will no longer injure the Countess's lands." She assured him of this and with the Countess's permission, he left with the sorceress to the palace of the sorceresses. There he stayed for

---

[*] Caer Loyw
[*] a close fitting garment with or without sleeves

three weeks. He then chose a horse and weapons and went on his way.

In the evening, he came to a valley at the head of which was a hermit's cottage. The hermit welcomed him and there he spent the night. In the morning he got up and when he went outside, a shower of snow had fallen in the night and a hawk had killed a wild fowl in front of the cottage. The noise of the horse had scared the hawk away and a raven had landed on the bird.

Peredur stood and compared the blackness of the raven, the whiteness of the snow and the redness of the blood to the hair of the lady which he loved most which was blacker than jet, to the skin which was whiter than the snow, and to the two red spots on her cheeks which were redder than the blood on the snow appeared to be.

Now Arthur and his men were searching for Peredur. Arthur said, "Do you know who is the knight with the long spear who stands by the brook over there?"

"Lord," said one of them, "I will go to find out who he is." He reached the place where Peredur was, asked what he was doing and who he was. Because he was thinking so intently about the lady he loved most, he didn't answer. Then the young man came at Peredur with his lance. Peredur turned on him and struck him off his horse to the ground. After this twenty-four young men came at him and he defeated them all bringing them to the ground with a single blow.

Then Cei came and spoke to Peredur rudely and angrily. Peredur hit him under the jaw with his lance. He attacked him so that he broke his arm and his shoulder blade. He rode over him twenty times. Cei lay on the ground stunned with the violence of the pain he suffered and his horse returned wildly. When the men saw the horse come back without his rider, they rode to the place where the attack had been. They first thought that Cei had been killed but then realised that with a good doctor, he might live.

Peredur didn't move from his deep thoughts, on seeing the crowd that had gathered around Cei, who was brought to Arthur's tent. He had skilled doctors to see to him. Arthur was very upset that Cei had suffered so, for he was very fond of him.

Gwalchmai then said, "It is not right that anyone should disturb an honourable knight who is deep in thought; for either he is pondering some injury he had had, or he is thinking about the lady he loves the most. Such rudeness was perhaps shown by someone he has met last. With your permission, lord, I will go to him and see if he has changed his thinking. If he has, I will ask him to come to meet you."

Then Cei was furious and spoke angrily with spiteful words. "Gwalchmai," he said, "I know you will bring him because he is worn out. It is no great feat to defeat a weary knight who is tired of fighting. A coat of fine linen would be enough armour for you. You need not break either your sword or lance in fighting the knight, the state he is in."

Gwalchmai then said to Cei, "You might use more pleasant words, were you so inclined. It doesn't look well on you to be so angry and displeased with me. I think I will bring the knight here with me without breaking either my arm or my shoulder." Then Arthur said to Gwalchmai, "You speak like a wise and prudent man. Go and arm yourself and choose a horse." Gwalchmai armed himself and rode quickly to where Peredur was.

He was resting on the shaft of his spear, still deep in thought. Gwalchmai approached in a friendly manner and said to him, "If I thought it would be agreeable to you, as it would to me, I would like to talk with you. I also have a message from Arthur for you asking if you would come to visit him. Two men have done this before."

"That is true," said Peredur, "but very unfriendly they were. They attacked me which made me annoyed, for I didn't want to come out of the deep thought I was in. I was thinking of the lady who I love best. I was reminded of her because I was looking at the snow, the raven and the drops of blood of the bird that the hawk had killed on the snow. I thought that her whiteness was like that of the snow; the blackness of her hair and eyebrows like that of the raven and the two red spots on her cheeks were like the drops of blood."

"That was a gentle thought and I am not surprised that you would not want to be disturbed from it," said Gwalchmai.

"Tell me," said Peredur, "is Cei in Arthur's Court?"

"He is," he answered, "for he is the knight who last fought with you and has had a broken arm and shoulder from falling from your spear."

"Truly," said Peredur, "I am not sorry that I have begun to avenge the insult to the dwarf and dwarfess."

Gwalchmai was amazed to hear him speak of the dwarf and dwarfess. He threw his arms around him and asked his name. "Peredur, the son of Efrawc am I," he said "and who are you?"

"My name is Gwalchmai," he replied.

"I am really glad to meet you," said Peredur, "for in every country I have been, I have heard of your famous bravery and honesty. I am proud to ask for your friendship."

"You shall have it and grant me yours."

"I will, with great pleasure," answered Peredur.

So they rode joyfully together to where Arthur was and when Cei saw them coming, he said, "I knew that Gwalchmai didn't need to fight the knight. No wonder he is famous; he can do more by fair words than I can by the strength of my arm."

Peredur than went with Gwalchmai into his tent where they both took off their armour. Peredur got dressed in clothes the same as Gwalchmai wore. They went to Arthur and greeted him. "Look, my lord," said Gwalchmai, "here is he for whom you have looked, for so long."

"Welcome to you," said Arthur to Peredur. "You shall stay with me, for had I known how brave you were, you should never have left me as you did. Nevertheless, it was predicted by the dwarf and dwarfess whom Cei ill-treated and whom you have avenged." Then the Queen and her ladies came in. Peredur greeted them, for they were happy to see him and greeted him. Arthur showed him great honour and respect as they returned towards Caerleon.

The first night Peredur was at Arthur's Court in Caerleon, as he walked in the city after his meal, he met Angharad Law Eurawc (Angharad Golden-hand). "My goodness sister," he said, "you are a most beautiful and lovely lady. If it would please you, I would love you more than any woman."

"I promise," she said, "that I do not love you or will ever love you."

"I also promise," said Peredur, "that I will never speak a word to any Christian again, until you will love me more than any other man."

The next day, Peredur went on up the high road, along a mountain ridge until he saw a round valley which was craggy and wooded. There were ploughed lands between the meadows and the woods. In the middle of the woods, he saw large black houses, roughly built. He dismounted and led his horse towards the woods in which he saw a rocky ledge where a lion was lying and sleeping. It was held by a chain. Beneath the lion he saw a deep, immense pit, full of the bones of men and animals.

Peredur drew his sword and struck the lion so that it fell into the mouth of the pit and hung there by the chain. With a second blow he struck the chain, broke it and the lion fell into the pit. He then led his horse over the rocky ledge and into the valley, in the centre of which he saw a fair castle and he went towards it.

By the castle sat a huge grey haired man who was larger than any man he had seen before. Two young pages were shooting the hilts of their daggers made of the bone of the sea-horse. One of the pages had yellow hair, the other auburn. They went before him to where the grey man was and Peredur said Good-day to him. The grey man said, "Shame on my porter!" Peredur realised that he meant the lion which was the porter. He followed the grey man and the pages into the castle. It was a fine place and the hall they entered was laid with plenty of food and drink.

He saw an old woman and a young one come from another room. They were the most stately women he had ever seen. Then they all washed and went to eat. They grey man sat at the head of the table with the old woman next to him. Peredur and the young woman were sitting together and the two pages served them.

The young woman gazed sadly at Peredur so he asked her why she was so sad. "For you, my friend; for when I first saw you, I loved you more than all men. It saddens me to know that so gentle a young man should have such a fate that awaits you tomorrow. Did you see the many black houses in the middle of the wood? All those belong to the vassals* of the grey man over there, who is my father. Tomorrow they will attack and kill you."

"Listen, fair lady," he said, "will you make sure my horse and armour be in the same place where I will lodge tonight?"

"Certainly, I will if I can," she said.

When it was time to sleep rather than make merry, they went to bed. The lady put Peredur's horse and armour near where he lodged for the night. The next morning he heard a great noise of men and horses around the castle. He got up, armed himself and his horse and went to the meadow. The old woman and the young one came to the grey man and said, "Lord, take the word of the young man that he will never reveal what he has seen here and we will guarantee that he keeps it."

"I will not do so," said the grey man. So Peredur fought with the army and killed one third of it without being hurt himself.

The old woman then said, "Look, much of your army has been killed by the young man. Will you now be merciful to him?"

"I will not," he said. When the two women were on the battlements looking out, they saw Peredur meet the yellow-haired youth and kill him. "Now will you grant him mercy?" asked the young woman.

"I will not do it," the grey man replied. Then Peredur attacked the auburn haired youth and killed him as well.

"It would have been better if you had granted him mercy before he killed your two sons, for you will not escape from him now," said the old woman.

"Go girl and ask him to grant mercy to us, for we put ourselves in his hands," said the grey haired man.

So the girl went up to Peredur and asked for mercy for her father and for his vassals who had escaped alive. "You shall have it on condition that your father and all who follow him, go to pay homage to Arthur and tell him it was I who did him this service."

"We will, certainly," said the grey haired man. "You will also be baptised and I will send a message to Arthur asking him

---

* holders of land under the medieval feudal system

to give you the valley for you and your heirs for ever," said Peredur.

Then they went in and the grey man said to Peredur, "Since I have owned this valley, I haven't seen any Christian leave here with his life, except you. We will go to pay homage to Arthur and become Christian and be baptised."

Peredur then said, "I thank Heaven that I have not broken my promise to the lady I love best, which was that I would not speak one word to any Christian."

They stayed there the night and the next morning, the grey man, with his company, set out for Arthur's Court. They paid homage to him and he had them baptised. The grey man then told Arthur that it was Peredur who had conquered them and Arthur gave the valley to the grey man and his family for ever as Peredur had requested. With Arthur's permission, the grey man returned to the Round Valley.

Peredur rode on the next day and crossed a vast empty desert with no houses to be seen. At long last, he came to a small poor-looking house where he heard that there was a serpent lying on a gold ring making it impossible for anyone to live nearby for seven miles around. He came to the place where the serpent was and angrily, furiously and desperately he fought with the serpent when at last he killed it and took away the ring for himself.

From then on he spoke to no Christian and therefore lost his colour and his appearance for he longed for Arthur's Court and the lady whom he loved the best.

Then he made for Arthur's Court and on the road he met with some of Arthur's men with Cei at the front. He knew them but they didn't recognise him. "Where are you coming to?" asked Cei. He said it two or three times but received no answer. So Cei pushed his lance through Peredur's thigh, who, in case he would break his vow, didn't cry out or respond but rode on.

Gwalchmai said to Cei, "Indeed, it was very wrong of you to hurt that young man who cannot speak." Then he returned with Peredur to Arthur's Court. He said to Gwenhwyfar (Guinevere), "Lady, look at the damage Cei has done to the young man. Please give him medical care before I come back and I will pay you for doing so."

Before the men returned from their mission, a knight came to the meadow beside Arthur's Palace, to dare someone for a fight. His challenge was accepted by Peredur who fought and defeated him. For a week he defeated a knight every day.

One day, Arthur and his followers were going to church when he saw a knight who had raised a signal for battle. "Men," said Arthur, "I will not go any further until I have my horse and weapons to defeat this 'peasant'." Then his attendants went to fetch his horse and weapons, but Peredur met them on their way back and took the horse and weapons from them. He proceeded to the meadow, and all those who saw him go to fight the knight went upon the tops of houses, mounds and high places to see the battle. Then Peredur beckoned to the knight with his hand to start the fight. The knight charged at him but he didn't move from the spot. Peredur then spurred his horse and charged fiercely and furiously, severely wounding him under his jaw, raising him out of his saddle. He threw him to the ground away from him. Peredur then went back and left the horse and weapons with the attendants as before and went to the Palace on foot. He was then known as the Dumb Knight.

Angharad Golden-hand met him and said, "I declare to Heaven, it is such a pity that you cannot speak, for if you could, I would love you better than any man. Even though you can't speak, I believe I will still love you more than any man."

"May Heaven reward you, lady," he said, "I will love you too." Then it was clear that he was Peredur, for he had spoken to a Christian. He then renewed his friendship with Gwalchmai, Owain and all the others and remained in Arthur's Court.

Arthur was in Caerleon upon Usk when he went hunting with Peredur who let his dog loose upon a hart*. The dog killed the hart in a desert place. A little way off he saw a Palace with a hall, at the door of which were three bald swarthy* youths playing gwyddbwyll (a kind of chess). When he entered, he saw three ladies sitting on a bench all dressed alike as suitable to those of noble birth.

---

* male deer
* dark complexioned

As he sat down by them on the bench, he noticed that one of the ladies was crying and he asked her why. "I am so sorry to see such a handsome young man as you killed," she said.

"Who will kill me?" he asked.

"If you dare to stay here tonight, I will tell you," she said.

"However great the danger is, tell me now," said Peredur.

"This Palace is owned by my father," she said, "who kills everyone who comes here without his permission."

"What kind of man does that?" asked Peredur.

"A man who is violent to his neighbours and shows mercy to no one," said the lady.

He then saw the young men get up and clear the chessmen from the board. He heard a great commotion after which a huge black one-eyed man came in. The ladies went to meet him and helped him off with his coat. He sat down and after a while he looked at Peredur and asked who the knight was. "Lord," said one of the ladies, "he is the fairest and most noble young man you ever could see. For Heaven's sake, deal gently with him?"

"For your sake, I will deal gently with him and spare his life tonight," he said.

Then Peredur came to them near the fire, had food and drink and talked with the ladies. Being affected by the drink he had taken, Peredur had the courage to ask the black man, "If you are so mighty a man, who could have put out your eye?"

"It is one of my habits," said the black man, "that anyone who asks me that, shall not escape with his life, either freely or at any price."

"Lord," said the lady, "whatever he said to you as a joke or as a result of the liquor he has drunk, remember your promise."

"I will, certainly," he said. "For your sake, I will grant him his life for tonight." So they left it at that, for that night.

The next day, the black man got up, put on his armour and said to Peredur, "Get up, man, to be put to death." Peredur said to him, "Do one of two things, if you are going to fight with me, either take off your armour or give me some so that I can fight with you fairly."

"Why, man, could you fight, if you had armour? Choose some then." The lady then brought some armour to Peredur so he fought with the black man until he asked for mercy.

"You shall have mercy, black man, provided that you tell me who you are and who put out your eye?"

"Lord, I will tell you, I lost it fighting with the Black Serpent of the Carn*. There is a mound, called the Mound of Mourning on which there is a barrow*. Inside that is a serpent, on the tail of which is a stone. Whoever holds the stone in one hand shall have in his other hand as much gold as he wishes. I am called the Black Oppressor. The reason for this is that there is no one around who I have not oppressed and I show justice to no one."

"How far is it to the mound?" asked Peredur. "The same day as you set out you will come to the Court of the Sons of the King of Suffering."

"Why are they called that?"

"The Addanc* of the Lake kills them once every day. When you go on, you will come to the Court of the Countess of the Achievements."

"What achievements are there?" asked Peredur. "Three hundred men are in her Court and sit down next to the lady to tell of the achievements of the men of her Court. When you leave there you will reach the Mound of Mourning, where there are three hundred tents, the owners of which are guarding the serpent."

"Since you have been an oppressor for so long," said Peredur, "I will see that you are no longer one." So he killed him.

The lady then said to him, "If you were poor when you came here, from now on you will be rich because of the treasure belonging to the black man you killed. Of all the lovely ladies there are in this Court, you shall have the one you like best for your wife."

"Lady, I didn't come here to find a wife, you should take for your husbands the young men that are here. Neither do I wish for your wealth for I don't need it."

Peredur rode on and came to the Palace of the Sons of the King of Suffering. When he entered, he saw only women, who

---

* a barrow – an archaeological grave
* as above
* a lake monster. Also 'afanc' pronounced 'avanc'

were very pleased to see him. As they began to talk with him, a horse arrived with a saddle on it with a corpse in the saddle. One of the women got up, took the corpse from the saddle and bathed it in a tub of warm water which was below the door. She also smoothed precious ointment on it. The man got up alive and came to Peredur and welcomed him. Two other men came in on their saddles and were treated the same. Peredur asked why this was so. They told him there was an Addanc in a cave which killed them once every day. So they left it at that, that night.

The young men set off next morning and Peredur asked to go with them. They refused him saying, "It you should be killed there would be no one to bring you back to life again." They rode on and Peredur followed them. After they had disappeared out of sight, he came to a mound on which sat the fairest lady he had ever seen. "I know what you intend to do," she said. "You are going to find the Addanc who will kill you, not by courage, but by cunning. He has a cave, at the entrance of which is a stone pillar. He sees everyone who enters but they can't see him and from behind the pillar he kills everyone with a poisonous dart. If you would promise to love me above all the other women, I will give you a stone so that you will see him when you go in but he won't see you."

"I will certainly promise," said Peredur, "for when I first saw you I loved you. Where shall I find you?"

"When you look for me, look in the direction of India." She vanished after placing a stone in Peredur's hand.

He came towards a valley, through which ran a river. The edges of the valley were wooded and on each side of the river were level meadows. On one side of the river, he saw a flock of white sheep and on the other a flock of black sheep. Whenever one of the white sheep bleated, one of the black sheep would cross over and become white and whenever one of the black sheep bleated, one of the white sheep would cross over and become black.

He then saw a tall tree by the side of the river, one half of which was in flames from the root to the top. The other half was green and in full leaf. Nearby he saw a young man sitting on a mound with two greyhounds white breasted and spotted, on leashes, lying by his side. He was certain he had never seen one of such noble bearing as he. In the wood opposite he heard hounds chasing a herd of deer.

Peredur greeted the young man who greeted him in return. There were three roads leading from the mound; two of them were wide roads, the third more narrow. Peredur enquired where the roads went. "One of them goes to my palace," said the young man, "I would advise you to do one of two things; either go to my palace, where you will find my wife, or else stay here to see the hounds chasing the deer from the wood to the plain. You will see the best greyhounds you ever saw killing the stags by the water. When it is time to go to eat, my page will bring me my horse and you can stay in my palace tonight."

"Thank you very much," said Peredur, "but I can't stay, I must be on my way."

"The other road leads to the town which is near, where you could buy food and drink. The narrow road leads to the cave of the Addanc," said the young man. "With your permission, I will go that way," said Peredur.

He went towards the cave with the stone in his left hand and his lance in his right. As he went in, he saw the Addanc, pierced him through with his lance and cut off his head. As he came out of the cave, his three friends were at the entrance. They greeted him and said it was a prophecy that he should kill the monster. Peredur gave the head to the young men and they offered him any of the three sisters he would choose for his wife and half their kingdom with her. "I didn't come here for a wife," said Peredur, "but if I did I would prefer your sister to all others."

He rode on and heard a noise behind him. Looking back, he saw a man in red armour riding a red horse. He rode up and saluted him and Peredur greeted him kindly. "Lord, I come to ask something of you," he said.

"What is that?"

"That you would take me for your attendant."

"Who would I be taking for an attendant?" asked Peredur.

"I will not hide my identity from you. Etlyn Gleddyf Coch (Edlym Red-sword) is my name, an earl from the Eastern Country."

"I am amazed that you would be an attendant to someone who has no more land than you, for I too have an Earldom; but since you wish to be my attendant, I will gladly take you on," said Peredur.

They then went on to the Court of the Countess. They were all pleased to see them. They were placed at table below the members of the Court, but that was the custom of the Court and no disrespect to them. Whoever would overthrow the three hundred men of her household would then sit next to the Countess and she would love him above all men. Peredur then overthrew three hundred men, sat down at her side and she said, "Thank goodness I have such a brave and handsome man as you, for I have not had the man I love best."

"Who is he?" asked Peredur.

"It is Edlym Red-sword who I love best and I have never seen him," she said. "Why, Edlym is my attendant and for his sake I came to joust with your men. He could have done it better than I if he had wished. I will give him to you."

"Heaven reward you," said the Countess. "I will take the man I love best." That night the Countess became Edlym's bride.

The next day, Peredur set out for the Mound of Mourning. "I will go with you," said Edlym. So they went on till they came to the mound and the tents.

"Go to the men over there," said Peredur, "and ask them to come and do homage to me."

So Edlym went to them and said, "Come and do homage to my lord."

"Who is your lord?" they asked.

"Peredur Longspear is my lord," answered Edlym.

"If it were allowed to kill a messenger, you wouldn't be going back alive for arrogantly demanding Kings, Earls and Barons to do him homage." With that Edlym returned to Peredur who asked him to go back to them saying, either they do him homage or fight with him. They chose to fight.

That day he overthrew the owners of a hundred tents; the next day the owners of a hundred more. The third day the remaining hundred decided after discussion to do homage to Peredur. He asked them, then, why they were there. They told him they were guarding the serpent until it died. "Then we will fight amongst ourselves over the stone. Whoever should win would have the stone."

"Wait here," said Peredur, "I will go to find the serpent."

"No, Lord," they said, "we will all go together."

"I will not have that," he said, "for I will not have more fame than you if the serpent is killed." Then he went to the place where the serpent was and killed it. He came back and said, "Add up what you have spent here and I will repay you," which he did. He asked them that they should be his men and said to Edlym, "Go back to her you love best and I will reward you," and he gave him the stone. "May Heaven repay and protect you," said Edlym.

Peredur rode off and came to the loveliest valley he had ever seen, through which ran a river and where he saw many tents of various colours. He was amazed at the number of water mills and wind-mills that he saw. There rode up to him a tall auburn haired man, in workman's clothes and Peredur asked him who he was. "I am the chief miller of all the mills about," he said.

"Will you give me a place to stay?" asked Peredur.

"I will, certainly," he answered.

They came to the miller's home which was very pleasant. Peredur asked the miller for money as a loan so that he might buy meat and drink for himself and the people of the house. He promised to repay him before he left. He also asked the miller why so many people were gathered there. The miller said to Peredur, "Either you are from far away or you are a fool. The Empress of Cristinobyl (Constantinople) the Great is here and she will only have a man who is very brave for she doesn't need riches. It was impossible to bring enough food for the thousands that are here. That's why all the mills were constructed." They then went to bed.

The next day Peredur rose and armed himself and his horse for the tournament. Among the tents he saw in one, a beautiful girl leaning her head out of the tent. He had never seen a more lovely girl than she. She wore a dress of gold satin. He stared at her and fell in love with her. He stayed there gazing at her from morning to midday and from midday to evening. Then the tournament ended so he went to his lodging and took off his armour.

140

He then asked the miller for money as a loan. The miller's wife was angry with Peredur; nevertheless the miller loaned him the money. The next day he did the same thing again and at night came to his lodging and borrowed money from the miller as before. The third day, as he was in the same place, gazing at the girl, he felt a hard blow between his neck and shoulder. Looking behind him, he saw it was the miller, who said, "Do one of two things: either turn your head away or go to the tournament."

Peredur smiled at the miller and went to the tournament. All that he fought that day he threw to the ground and sent them to the Empress as a gift. Their horses and armour he sent as a gift to the miller's wife in payment of what he owed. Back at the tournament, Peredur overthrew all the men he fought there. He sent them to the Empress's prison and their horses and armour to the miller's wife in payment of the borrowed money.

The Empress sent to him – now known as The Knight of the Mill – to ask him to visit her. Peredur didn't go at the first message or the second but the third time she sent a hundred knights to bring him against his will. He fought with them and had them bound like stags and thrown in the mill-dyke. The Empress took advice from a wise man, who said, "With your permission, I'll go to him myself," which he did and asked Peredur to come to the Empress for the sake of his lady-love. So, together with the miller, Peredur came and sat by the Empress and talked for a short while, then left for his lodging.

The next day when he visited her, all the rooms were well-decorated for they didn't know where he would sit. He did sit beside the Empress and spoke with her politely. While they talked together, they saw a black man enter with a full goblet of wine in his hand. He dropped to his knee before the Empress and implored her to give it to someone who would fight him for it. She looked at Peredur, who said, "Lady, give me the goblet." He drank the wine and gave the goblet to the miller's wife.

"While they were there, another black man of bigger built than the other, came in with a wild beast's claw in his hand in the shape of a goblet and filled with wine. He presented it to the Empress and pleaded with her to give it to no one who would not fight for it. "Lady," said Peredur, "give it to me." She gave it to him. He drank the wine and gave the goblet to the miller's wife.

Then a rough looking red curly headed man came in with a bowl of wine in his hand. He went down on his knee and begged the Empress to give it to no one but that would fight him for it. She gave it to Peredur who in turn sent it to the miller's wife. He returned to his lodging that night and the next day armed himself and his horse, went out to the meadow and killed the three men. He then went to the tent and the Empress said to him, "Good Peredur, remember the promise you made when I gave you the stone and you killed the Addanc."

"Lady, I do remember," he said, and he ruled with the Empress for fourteen years, as the story goes.

Arthur was in his main palace at Caerleon upon Usk. On the floor in the middle of the hall sat four men on a carpet of velvet: Owain the son of Urien, Gwalchmai the son of Gwyar, Hywel the son of Emyr Llydaw and Peredur Longspear. There soon entered a black curly headed girl on a yellow mule who was rather ugly. She had high cheeks, a long face and a short nose. One eye was a most piercing mottled grey, the other was black as jet sunk into her head. Her teeth were long and yellow, more yellow than the flower of the broom. Her stomach rose from her breast-bone higher than her chin and her back was crooked. Her legs were long and bony and she had had huge feet.

She greeted Arthur and all his men except Peredur to whom she spoke angrily. "Peredur," she said, "I don't greet you because you don't deserve it. Fate was blind when it gave you fame and favour. When you were in the Court of the Lame King and saw a young man carrying a streaming spear with blood dripping from it on to the young man's hand and you saw many other amazing things, you did not ask about them. If you had, the King would now have health and peace in his kingdom, whereas he now has war and battles; knights killed, women left widowed and young women left without hope and all because of you."

Then she said to Arthur, "With your permission, lord, my home is far away near the stately Proud Castle. I don't know if you've ever heard of it. There live five hundred and sixty-six knights of the order of Chivalry and each has a woman he loves best. Whoever wishes to gain fame and honour, I know where he may find it. There is a castle on a high mountain, inside which is a lady who is a prisoner there. Whoever would set her free would become famous throughout the world." At that she rode away.

Gwalchmai then said, "I will not rest until I know whether I can set the lady free." Many of Arthur's men agreed, but Peredur said, "In the same way, I will not rest until I know the story and the meaning of the spear the black girl spoke of." Then as everyone was getting ready, a knight appeared at the gate looking the size and strength of a great warrior with his horse and armour. He greeted Arthur and all his men except Gwalchmai. On the knight's shoulder was a gold shield with an azure blue bar on it and all his armour was of the same colour.

He said to Gwalchmai, "You killed my lord with your deceit and treachery and that I will prove to you."

Up got Gwalchmai and said, "Here is my gage* to you, here or where you'd like, that I am not a deceiver or traitor."

"Before the King, who I obey, I will fight you to prove you're wrong," said the knight.

"Certainly," said Gwalchmai, "go on and I will follow you." So the knight went on and Gwalchmai got ready. Many a suit of armour was offered to him but he refused it all preferring his own. When he and Peredur were ready, they set out to follow the knight, not together, but each on his own.

Next day at dawn, Gwalchmai came to a valley where there was a fortress, inside which was a vast palace with high towers around it. He saw a knight on a gleaming, black, prancing, but sure of foot palfrey coming out of the gate. He was the owner of the court. Gwalchmai greeted him and was asked by the knight from where he had come. "I come from Arthur's Court," said Gwalchmai.

"Are you Arthur's man?"

"I am, sir," he replied.

"I can see that you are tired and weary. Go to my palace where you can rest for the night. Take this ring as a token to the porter. You will find my sister there."

---

* challenge to fight

Gwalchmai went to the gate, showed the ring to the porter and made for the tower. There he saw a great blazing smokeless fire and a beautiful, stately girl sitting on a chair near the fire. She was pleased to see him and they sat down to a meal and had pleasant conversation. Then a handsome grey haired man entered the room. "You bad girl," he said, "if you only knew how wrong it is that you should sit and talk with this man, you wouldn't do it." With that he turned his head and disappeared.

"Sir," said the girl, "if you would take my advice, I should lock the door in case he has a trap for you." Gwalchmai got up and went to the door where the man, with sixty others, fully armed, were entering the tower. He defended the door with a gwyddbwyll (chess) board, in case anyone should come up before the man returned from hunting.

The Earl then came and asked what was happening. "It is a sad thing," said the grey haired man, "that the girl over there has sat and talked with the man who killed your father. He is Gwalchmai son of Gwyar."

"Hold on then," said the Earl, "I will go in." He made Gwalchmai welcome. "Sir" he said, "it was wrong of you to come to this court if you knew you had killed our father. Even though we will not avenge, God will."

"Friend," said Gwalchmai, "this is how it is. I didn't come here to admit or deny killing your father. I am on a mission for Arthur. I ask you for a year until I have completed it. Then will I admit or deny it." The Earl granted him that and he stayed the night. He set out the following day but no more is known of Gwalchmai's adventure in this story.

Peredur went on his way and wandered over the whole island searching for news of the black girl but heard of none. He came to an unknown land in the middle of a valley by a river. As he was crossing the valley, he saw a rider dressed as a priest coming towards him. He asked for his blessing.

"Wretched man," he said, "you have no right to receive a blessing dressed in armour on this day."

"What day is this?" asked Peredur. "Today is Good Friday."

"Don't blame me for not knowing," said Peredur, "for it is a year since I left my own country." He then dismounted and led his horse by hand.

It was not long, as he went along the high road, that he came to a crossroad through a wood. On the far side of the wood he could see a towerless castle which appeared to be inhabited. At the castle gate, he met the priest he had met before and asked for his blessing which he gave saying, "It is more fitting to travel dressed like this. You can stay the night with me," which he did.

The next day, Peredur intended to leave, but the priest said, "This is no day for anyone to travel. Stay with me today, tomorrow and the day after and I will give you directions to find the place for which you are looking." On the fourth day, Peredur decided to leave, but asked the priest to guide him to the Castle of Wonders. "As much as I know, I will tell you," he said. "Go over the mountain where there is a river valley in which there is a king's court. The king was there at Easter. If you were to get news of the whereabouts of the Castle of Wonders, it would be there."

Peredur went on his way and came to the river valley where he met a number of men going to hunt. Among them was a man of high rank, who, after Peredur greeted him, said, "Either come with me to the hunt or go to my court. I will send one of my pages to accompany you and commend you to my daughter who will give you foot and drink until I return from hunting. Whatever you wish to know, I will gladly tell you then." The king sent a yellow-haired page along with him. When they came to the court, the lady had risen and was washing before having a meal, which they had together. Everything Peredur said to her, she laughed loudly at and the page said to her, "If he is not your husband already, he soon will be, for I see your heart and mind are set on him."

The short yellow haired page went back to the king and said that he thought it likely that the man he had met would soon be his daughter's husband, if he were not already. "What is your advice?" asked the king.

"My advice would be to set strong men on him and hold him until you know that for certain." So he set men on Peredur and imprisoned him.

The lady went to her father to ask why Peredur had been sent to prison. "Surely," he said, "he will not be free tonight, nor tomorrow, nor the next day after."

She said nothing more to the king but went to Peredur and said to him, "Is it unpleasant for you to be here?"

"I would not mind if it were," he replied.

She said, "Your bed shall not be less comfortable than the king's, you shall have the best entertainment the court can provide and I shall have my bed in here so that we can cheerfully talk together."

"This I can't refuse," he said. He stayed in prison that night and the lady provided all she had promised him.

The next day, Peredur heard an uproar in the town and asked the lady what it was. "The King and his men are coming to this town today," she said.

"What do they want here?" he asked. "There is an earl near here who owns two Earldoms and is as powerful as the King. They intend to fight today."

"I ask you to get me a horse and armour so that I can see the encounter. I promise I will return to my prison." So she provided him with a horse and armour together with a bright scarlet surcoat[*] with a yellow shield on his shoulder.

Peredur went to the battle, defeated all the earl's men that he met that day and returned to his prison. The lady asked him what had happened but he didn't answer her. She therefore asked her father, who of his men had been the best in battle. He said he didn't know but a knight with a red robe of honour and a yellow shield was the most successful. She smiled and went to where Peredur was and paid great attention to him that night.

For three days Peredur killed the earl's men but before anyone could tell who he was, he returned to the prison. On the fourth day, he killed the Earl himself. The lady went to her father to ask what news there was. "Good news," he said. "The earl is dead now and the two earldoms are now mine."

"Do you know who killed him?" she asked. "The knight in the red robe and yellow shield," he answered.

"Lord, I know who that is," she said.

"Who is he?" he exclaimed.

---

[*] a robe of honour

"Lord, it is the knight you have in prison," she said.

The king went to Peredur, greeted him and told him he would reward the service he paid him. When they sat down to eat, Peredur was placed beside the King with the lady on the other side. After the meal, the King said to Peredur, "I will give you my daughter in marriage, half my kingdom and the two earldoms as a gift."

"Thank you, Lord," said Peredur, "but I didn't come here to take a wife."

"What are you looking for then?" asked the king.

"I am looking for news of the Castle of Wonders," said Peredur.

"That is a great undertaking you wish to pursue," said the lady, "but you shall have news of the Castle and men to guide you through my father's lands together with ample provision for your journey. You are the man I love best. Go over the mountain over there where you will see a lake. The castle is within the lake and is called the Castle of Wonders, but we do not know what the wonders are."

Peredur came to the castle, the gate of which was open. When he went into the hall, the door was also open and he entered. There were chessmen playing chess against each other. The side he supported, lost the game whereupon the other side shouted out as if they were living men. Peredur became angry, took the chessmen in his lap and then threw the chessboard into the lake.

As he was doing so, the black girl coming in said to him, "You are not welcome here for you have done more harm than good."

"What are you complaining about girl?" asked Peredur.

"You have thrown the Empress's chessboard into the lake which she values as much as her empire," she answered.

"Is there a way in which it can be recovered?" There is. Go to the Castle of Ysbidinongyl, where there is a black man who destroys much of the Empress's lands; kill him and you will recover the chessboard, but if you do this, you will not return alive."

"Will you show me the way?" he said.

"Yes, I will," she said.

He reached the castle of Ysbidinongyl and fought with the black man who pleaded for mercy.

"I will grant you mercy," said Peredur, "if you see that the chessboard is replaced in the hall where I first saw it." Then the girl came to him and said, "A curse on you for leaving him alive; the board is not in its place. Go back and kill him."

He went back and killed the black man. When he returned to the court the girl was there[*]. "Where is the Empress?" asked Peredur.

"You will not see her until you kill the monster which is in the forest there."

"What kind of monster is it?"

"It is a stag that is as swift as the swiftest bird, with a horn on its forehead as sharp as a spear. It destroys the branches of the tops of trees, kills every animal it finds and the others die of hunger. It also comes every night and drains the fish pond so that all the fish die for want of water."

"Will you show me this animal?" asked Peredur.

"No, I will not," she answered. "No human being has dared enter the forest for a year; but there is the lapdog belonging to the Empress that will disturb the stag and bring it to you so that the stag will attack you."

The lapdog went as a guide to Peredur, disturbed the stag that rushed at Peredur who let it pass by him and struck off its head with his sword. While he was looking at the stag's head, he could see a lady on horseback approaching. She took the lapdog up in the sleeve of her cape. The stag and its head were on the ground beneath her with a red gold collar round its neck.

"Sir Knight," she said, "you have acted discourteously, killing the fairest jewel in my kingdom."

"I was asked to do so," he said. "Is there any way I can gain your friendship?"

"There is," she said. "Go to the mountain over there and you will see a small wood in which there is a cromlech[*]. There you must challenge a man three times to fight. You will then have my friendship."

---

[*] and the board one assumes!!

[*] a boulder or stone slab

Peredur went on his way, came to the side of the wood and challenged any man to fight. A black man emerged from beneath the boulder with a bony horse beneath him. Both he and his horse were covered in huge rusty armour. They fought and as often as Peredur would throw him to the ground, he would get up again on to his horse. Peredur dismounted and drew his sword. The black man disappeared with his horse and Peredur's horse so that he could not see him a second time.

Peredur walked along the mountain and on the far side he could see a castle in a river valley. He went to the castle and entered the hall, for the door was open. There he saw a lame grey-headed man sitting on one side of the hall with Gwalchmai beside him. They made Peredur welcome and were glad to see him. He saw his horse in the same stall as Gwalchmai's.

A young man with yellow hair knelt before Peredur and said, "Lord, it was I who came in the form of a black girl to Arthur's Court and when you threw away the board, killed the black man from Ysbidinongyl; when you killed the stag and when you fought against the black man of the cromlech (boulder). I also came with the head all bloody on the salver[*] and with the lance that streamed with blood. The head was your cousin's and he was killed by the sorceress of Caer Loyw (Gloucester). It was they that made your uncle lame. I am your cousin and it is foretold that you will avenge all this."

So Peredur and Gwalchmai decided to send to Arthur and his men to ask him to come against the witches. They fought against them and one of the witches killed one of Arthur's men before Peredur's eyes. He asked her to stop. A second time, the sorceress killed a man before Peredur's eyes. Again he asked her to stop. A third time the witch killed a man before him. This time he drew his sword and struck the sorceress on the top of her helmet and split it in two. She screamed and called the others to flee saying that this was Peredur, the man who had learned chivalry from them and by whom they were destined to be killed.

---

[*] silver dish

Then Arthur and his men fell upon the witches and killed them. So all the sorceresses of Caer Loyw (Gloucester) were killed and that is the story of the Castle of Wonders.

12. Geraint, the Son of Erbin

It was the custom of Arthur to hold his Court at Caerleon upon Usk. He held it there for seven Easters and five Christmases. Once upon a time he held Court there at Whitsuntide, for Caerleon was the most accessible place in his Kingdom by sea and land. He gathered about him nine crowned kings, who were his vassals* and with them earls and barons. Those would be his invited guests at all high festivals unless they were prevented somehow.

While he was at Caerleon, holding Court, thirteen churches would be set apart for his Masses; one for Arthur, his kings and guests; the second for Gwenhwyfar (Guinevere) and her ladies; the third for the Steward of the Household; the fourth for the King of the Franks and all other officers; nine other churches were for the Masters of the Household but chiefly for Gwalchmai (Sir Gawain) above all because of his fame and noble birth.

Glewlwyd Gafaelfawr (Mighty-grasp) was the chief porter but he only served Arthur at high festivals. Seven men under him served at other times. On Whit Tuesday, as the Emperor was sitting at his banquet, a tall auburn-haired young man came in, in a coat and tunic of ribbed brocaded silk, a gold hilted sword about his neck and low leather shoes on his feet. He came to Arthur, was welcomed and asked if he had any news. "I have, lord," he said, "but am surprised that you do not know me. I am one of your foresters in the Forest of Dean. Madawg is my name, son of Twrgadarn."

"Tell me your news," said Arthur.

"I have seen a stag in the forest, the like of which I have never seen before."

---

* holders of land by feudal tenure

"What is there about it that you have never seen before?" asked Arthur.

"He is pure white, lord, and does not herd with the other animals, so proud and royal bearing has he. I have come for your advice as what to do about him."

"I shall do what seems best to me," said Arthur. "I will go and hunt it tomorrow in the early morning. Give notice to all in the Court and to Rhyferys (his chief huntsman) and Elifri (his chief groom)." So it was arranged, with the forester leaving before him.

Then Gwenhwyfar said to Arthur, "Lord, will you permit me to go tomorrow to see and hear the hunt for the stag which the young man spoke of?"

"I will, gladly," said Arthur. "Then I shall go," said Gwenhwyfar. She also asked Arthur, "Would you also permit the one who kills the stag to cut off its head and give it to either his own lady-love or to his friend's lady?"

"Certainly, I will," answered Arthur, "but I will blame the Steward if everyone is not ready for the hunt in the morning." They then spent the night singing, playing games and telling stories, until it was time to sleep.

The next day, they got up and Arthur called his attendants to help him dress. He wondered that Gwenhwyfar did not wake up but said, "Let her sleep, don't disturb her, for she would rather sleep than go hunting." Then, as Arthur went on his way, he could hear two horns sounding, one near the lodging of the chief huntsman and one from the lodging of the head groom. Then all his men gathered and they set out for the forest.

After Arthur had left the Court, Gwenhwyfar woke up and called her ladies to dress her. She said, "Ladies, I had permission last night to go see the hunting. One of you go to the stables and get a horse suitable for a woman to ride." One of them went but found only two horses, so Gwenhwyfar and one of her ladies mounted them and went through the Usk, following the trail of the men and horses.

As they rode, they heard a loud rushing sound and looked back to see a knight on a huge horse which was stately, swift and proud. He as a fair-headed youth, bare legged and of princely stature. He had a gold-hilted sword on his thigh and wore a tunic and surcoat of brocaded silk with low leather boots on his feet. Around his neck was a scarf of blue-purple with an apple in each of the corners.

He overtook Gwenhwyfar and greeted her. She said, "Welcome to you Geraint. I knew you as soon as I saw you. Why haven't you gone hunting with my lord?"

"Because I didn't know he was going," answered Geraint. "I am also surprised that he went without letting me know," said Gwenhwyfar. "I was asleep, lady, so I didn't know that he had gone."

"You will be the most agreeable companion for me," said Gwenhwyfar, "for we shall hear the horns when they sound and the dogs when they are let loose and bark."

They came to the edge of the forest and stopped. Soon they heard a loud noise. They looked back and saw a dwarf riding a horse which was stately, strong, foaming and spirited. He held in his hand a whip. Near him was a lady on a beautiful white horse of steady and proud even pace. She wore a royal robe of gold brocaded silk. Near to her was a knight on a large war-horse with heavy and bright armour upon him as well as the knight. They had never seen a man and armour of great remarkable size for each of them was near to the other.

"Geraint," said Gwenhwyfar, "do you know that knight?"

"No," he said, "for that strange armour prevents me seeing his face or features."

"Go, girl," said Gwenhwyfar, "and ask the dwarf who that knight is." The girl went up to the dwarf who waited for her when he saw her coming towards him. She asked him, "Who is that knight?"

"I will not tell you," he answered.

"Since your manners are so bad, I will ask him myself," she said. "You will not do that," he cried.

"Why?" she asked.

"Because you are not noble enough to speak to my lord," he answered. She then turned her horse's head toward the knight. With that the dwarf struck her across her face and eyes drawing blood. She returned to the Queen complaining of the pain of the blow.

"You were treated most cruelly by the dwarf," said Geraint. "I will go myself to find out who is the knight."

"Yes you go," said Gwenhwyfar.

Geraint went up to the dwarf and asked, "Who is the knight?"

"I will not tell you," said the dwarf.

"I will ask him in person then," said Geraint.

"No, you will not," said the dwarf. "You are not honourable enough to speak to my lord."

"I have spoken to men of equal rank," said Geraint and turned his horse's head towards the knight. The dwarf overtook him, struck him as he had done the girl and the blood stained the cloak which Geraint was wearing. He put his hand on the hilt of his sword, but thought better of killing the dwarf when the armoured knight might attack him, so he returned to Gwenhwyfar.

"You acted wisely and discreetly," she said.

"Lady, I will go after him again with your permission. When he comes to an uninhabited place I will provide myself armour either on loan or on hire, so that I can pit myself against him."

"Go, then, but do not attack him until you have good armour. I will be anxious for news of you."

"You will hear from me by tomorrow afternoon," he said and set off.

The way they went was below the palace of Caerleon, across the ford on the Usk, travelling on high ground until they came to a walled town with a Fortress and a Castle[*]. As the knight passed through, the people of every house called out and made him welcome. When Geraint came to the town, he looked at every house to see whether he knew anyone who would lend or hire him armour, but he recognised no one. Every house he saw was full of men, armour and horses being shod. Shields were being polished, swords furbished and armour burnished.

The knight, the lady and the dwarf rode up to the castle and were welcomed there. Everyone risked their necks from the battlements to see them. Geraint wondered whether the knight would stay at the castle. He looked around for lodgings for himself and saw, a short distance from the town, an old palace which had fallen into decay. Because he knew no one in the town, he went towards the court where he saw a ruined hall

---

[*] Caerdydd (Cardiff)

154

with a stairway leading up to a room. On the stairway sat a grey-haired old man wearing old tattered clothes. Geraint stared at him for a long while when the man said to him, "Young man, what are you thinking?"

"I am wondering where I can stay the night," he said.

"Come on in," said the man, "and you will have the best I can offer you."

Geraint followed the grey-haired man into the hall where he dismounted and left his horse there. They went up into the room where he saw a very old woman sitting on a cushion in old tattered clothes of brocaded silk. He saw that in her young days she would have been very beautiful. A girl was sitting near her who wore a shift and veil which were old and going threadbare. He was certain he had never seen a more beautiful or graceful girl than she.

The grey-haired man said to the girl, "There is no attendant for this young man and his horse but you."

She said, "I will give the best service that I can both to him and his horse." She then helped Geraint off with his outer clothes and boots and gave his horse straw and corn. She went to the hall as before and came back into the room. The grey-haired man then said to her, "Go into the town and bring back the best food and drink you can find."

"I will surely, lord," she said and went into the town.

They talked together while she was in the town. On her return, she came, with a manservant, a bottle of mead* and a quarter of a young ox. In her hands she carried a helping of white bread and a manchet loaf* in her cloak. As she came into the room she said, "I failed to get anything better than this, for I wouldn't have been given credit for more."

"This will do well enough," said Geraint. They boiled the meat and when the food was ready, they sat down to eat with Geraint between the grey-haired man and his wife. The girl waited on them and they ate and drank.

When they had finished eating, Geraint began a conversation with the grey-haired man. He asked him to whom

---

* an alcoholic drink of fermented honey and water
* a medieval loaf of very good quality – shaped like a batch

the palace that he was in belonged. "I built it and the castle and the city you have seen," he said.

"How is it that you have lost them now?" asked Geraint.

"I lost an Earldom as well," he replied, "and this is how I lost them. I had a nephew, my brother's son, whose lands I took over with my own. When he came of age, he demanded to have his property back which I refused to do, so he declared war on me and took from me all that I possessed."

"Good sir," said Geraint, "will you tell me why the knight, the lady and the dwarf came to the city and why I saw preparations for war?"

"I will," said the grey man. "The preparations are for the game to be held tomorrow by the young Earl which will be like this. In the middle of the meadow here there will be two forks set up, on them a silver rod upon which will be a Sparrow Hawk. There will be a tournament for the Sparrow Hawk and all the people you see gathered in the city will attend. Each knight will go with the lady he loves best. No man can joust without the lady he loves best. The knight you saw has won the Sparrow Hawk these last two years. If he wins it the third year, it will be given to him and he will then be known as the Knight of the Sparrow Hawk from then on."

"Sir," said Geraint, "what do you advise concerning the injury I received from the dwarf and also that to the lady-in-waiting to Gwenhwyfar?"

"It is not easy for me to advise you," said the grey man, "for you have no lady to joust for but if you would like, you can take my horse, which is better than yours as well as my armour."

"Thank you, kind sir," said Geraint, "but my own horse and arms will be sufficient for me. However, if you will permit it, I will take your daughter to the tournament. If I come back from there unhurt I will be loyal to and love your daughter as long as I live. If I do not escape, she will be as free as before."

"I will gladly permit it," said the grey-haired man, "and since you are determined on this, your horse and armour shall be ready early in the morning, for the Knight of the Sparrow Hawk will announce that his lady take the Sparrow Hawk. 'For,' he will say, 'you are the loveliest of women and have possessed it last year and year before. If anyone denies it you today, I will by force defend it for you.' Therefore," said the grey-haired man, "you need to be ready before day-break and we three will be with you." So it was settled and they went to rest for the night.

Before dawn they rose, dressed and by the time it was daylight they were all four in the meadow. There was the Knight of the Sparrow Hawk making the proclamation and asking his lady-love to fetch the Sparrow Hawk. "Do not fetch it," said Geraint, "for here is a lady more fair, noble and beautiful who has a better claim to it than you."

"If you think the Sparrow Hawk is hers, come and do battle with me," said the knight. So Geraint went forward to the end of the meadow, and, covered with rusty and worthless armour – as was his horse – they met to fight one another.

They broke several sets of spears; all that were brought to them. When the Earl and his company saw the Knight of the Sparrow Hawk gaining the upper hand, they were shouting with joy and happiness but the grey-haired man and his wife and daughter were very sad. He gave Geraint many lances as often as he broke them and the dwarf served the Knight of the Sparrow Hawk in the same way. Then the grey-haired man said to Geraint, "Oh my young lord, here is the lance which I held in my hand when I gained the honour of knighthood and from that time on I have never broken it. It has an excellent point to it." Geraint took it and thanked him.

Then the dwarf also took a lance to his lord saying, "Here is a lance no less good than his and no knight has ever withstood this one."

Geraint said, "I swear that unless I am suddenly killed he shall be more the better for your help." Then he spurred his horse and attacked the knight, after a warning, and gave him such a savage blow that he split his shield in two, broke his armour and burst his girths*, so that he and his saddle were thrown to the ground over the horse's cruppers*.

Geraint dismounted quickly and, in a rage, drew his sword and attacked the knight who also got up and drew his sword against Geraint. They fought on foot with sparks flying like fire

---

* a leather or cloth bank to secure the saddle of the horse
* hind-quarters of a horse

from their armour and sweat and blood keeping the light from their eyes. When Geraint was winning, the grey-haired man, his wife and daughter were glad but when the knight prevailed the Earl and his party rejoiced.

When the grey-haired man saw Geraint receive a severe blow, he went to him and said, "Remember the treatment you had from the dwarf and the insult to Gwenhwyfar – Arthur's wife." This gave Geraint added strength and remembering all that, he lifted his sword and struck the knight on the crown of his head, breaking all his head-armour, cutting through all skin and flesh to the bone.

The knight fell to his knees, threw his sword away and begged for mercy. "I am sorry to Heaven for my sins and wish to speak to a priest even if you grant me mercy," he said.

"I will do so on one condition," said Geraint, "that you go to Gwenhwyfar the wife of Arthur, to make amends for the injury done to her lady-in-waiting by your dwarf. As for me, I am content with what I have done to you."

"I will do that gladly, but who are you?" asked the knight.

"I am Geraint the son of Erbin. Tell me who you are."

"I am Edeyrn the son of Nudd," he said as he mounted his horse and went towards Arthur's Court. The lady he loved best went with him as did the dwarf in great sorrow. That is this story so far.

Then the young Earl and his men came up to Geraint and invited him to his castle. "No, thank you," said Geraint, "I will stay where I stayed last night."

"Since you'll not come, I shall send all that I have for your comfort as well as ointment for your wounds so that you may recover from your tiredness and fatigue," said the young Earl.

"Thank you very much," said Geraint. "I shall go to my lodging." So he went with the Earl Ynwyl (the grey-haired man), his wife and his daughter. When he reached the room, the servants and attendants of the Earl arrived at the court. They arranged the living quarters with straw and a fire. Soon the bath and ointment were ready and they washed Geraint's head.

The young Earl, with forty knights who were at the tournament, came as Geraint finished his bath. He was asked to go to the hall to eat. "Where is the Earl Ynwyl, his wife and daughter?" asked Geraint. "They are in the upper room over there," said the earl's chamberlain[*], dressing themselves in clothes the Earl has brought for them."

"See that the girl does not dress in those clothes until she comes to Arthur's Court, when Gwenhwyfar shall choose clothes for her." So the girl did not dress in the clothes provided by the Earl.

They all entered the hall, washed and sat down to eat. On one side of Geraint sat the young Earl with Earl Ynwyl beside him. On the other side of Geraint were the girl and her mother. Other people sat according to their rank and they ate, being served very well with many sorts of dishes. The young Earl wanted Geraint to visit him the next day, but Geraint said, "No I won't, for tomorrow I must go to Arthur's Court with the young lady. Also, as long as Earl Ynwyl is poor and in trouble, I mean to restore to him his lands and all the possessions he has lost."

"Sir Knight," said the young Earl, "it is not my fault that Earl Ynwyl is without his lands."

"To be sure," said Geraint, "he shall not be without them any longer, unless I die suddenly."

The young Earl said, "With regard to the disagreement between me and Ynwyl, I will take your advice and put things right between us."

"All I ask," said Geraint, "is that you restore to him what is rightfully his and all he has lost in between."

"I will gladly do that, for your sake," said the Earl.

"Then," said Geraint, "all who owe homage to Ynywl, let him come forward and do it here now." All the men did so and it was all agreed. His castle, his town and all his possessions were restored to Ynywl. He received all he had lost, down to the smallest jewel.

Earl Ynwl then said to Geraint, "Here is the young lady you fought for in the tournament. I give her to you."

"She shall go with me," said Geraint, "to the Court of Arthur and Gwenhwyfar so that they will do with her what they wish. The next day they set out for Arthur's Court and this is the story so far concerning Geraint.

---

[*] the officer at the head of a noble's court

159

Now this is how Arthur hunted the stag. The man and the dogs were divided into hunting parties and the dogs were let loose upon the stag. The last dog let loose was Arthur's favourite hunting dog named Cafall who left all the other dogs behind him and turned the stag. Arthur cut off his head before anyone else could. They sounded the death horn and all gathered round. Then Cadyrieith said to Arthur, "Lord, here comes Gwenhwyfar with just one lady-in-waiting."

"Tell Gildas the son of Caw and all the scholars of the Court to accompany Gwenhwyfar to the Palace." So they did.

They then all set out for the Palace, talking together about the stag's head and to whom it should be given. One wished it to be given to the lady he loved best, another to the lady he loved best. They were all arguing sharply over the head of the stag. They came to the palace and when Arthur and Gwenhwyfar heard them bickering over the head, Gwenhwyfar said to Arthur, "My lord, I think I know what should be done with the stag's head. Let it not be given away until Geraint the son of Erbin returns from his mission." She told Arthur what it was and he agreed. So it was decided.

The next day, Gwenhwyfar posted watchmen to look out for Geraint. After midday they saw an unshapely little man on a horse, after him a woman or girl also on horseback and after her a large knight, bowed down, hanging his head low and sadly with armour which looked broken and worthless.

Before they came to the gate, one of the watchers went to Gwenhwyfar, told her what they had seen and what a sorry sight they were. "I don't know who they are," he said. "I know," said Gwenhwyfar, "that is the knight that Geraint was after and I think he doesn't come of his own free will. If Geraint has caught up with him, he has avenged in full the injury done to my lady-in-waiting."

A porter came to her now and said, "My Lady, there is a knight at the gate. I never saw so pitiful a sight. He is as miserable and broken as the armour he wears which is covered with dry and discoloured blood."

"Do you know his name?" she asked.

"I do," he said. "He tells me he is Edeyrn the son of Nudd."

"Then," she said, "I don't know him either."

She went to the gate to meet the knight and as he entered she was sorry that he was in such a poor condition, even though he was accompanied by the churlish dwarf. Edeyrn greeted the Queen and she welcomed him. "Lady," he said, "Geraint the son of Erbin sends greetings to you."

"Did he meet you?" she asked.

"Yes, but it was not to my advantage, not his fault but mine, Lady. He compels me to do as you bid for the injury done by the dwarf to your lady-in-waiting. He forgives the insult to himself, since he has beaten me and put me in danger of my life. He insists I do justice to you for the injury you have suffered, Lady."

"Where did he overtake you?" asked Gwenhwyfar.

"In a place where we were jousting and contending the Sparrow Hawk in a town which is now called Caerdydd (Cardiff). There were three people with him in tattered clothes; a grey-haired old man, an old woman and a fair young lady. It was for her that Geraint jousted in the tournament for the Sparrow Hawk for he said she was more entitled to the Sparrow Hawk than this lady who is with me. We fought and he left me as you see me."

"Sir," said the Queen, "when do you think Geraint will be here?"

"I think he will be here tomorrow, Lady, with the young woman."

Then Arthur came to him and he greeted Arthur who gazed at him a long time, amazed to see him in that state. Thinking he knew him, he said, "Aren't you Edeyrn the son of Nudd?"

"I am, Lord," he answered "and I have met with such trouble and terrible wounds." Then he told Arthur all of his misadventure.

"Well," said Arthur "it is right that Gwenhwyfar be merciful to you, from what I hear."

"Whatever you recommend for him I shall agree to," said Gwenhwyfar, "for it was as much an insult to you as to me."

"That will be the best thing to do," said Arthur, "let him have medical care until it is decided whether he may live. If he should be allowed to live, let him make amends as shall be judged by the nobles of the Court who will take sureties* to that effect."

"I am pleased with that," said Gwenhwyfar, so Arthur became surety for Edeyrn as did Caradawc the son of Llyr (Lear), Owain the son of Nudd, Gwalchmai and many others.

Arthur then had Morgan Tud brought to him, who was his chief physician. "Take Edeyrn the son of Nudd, have a room prepared for him and treat him as you would myself, if I were wounded. Let no one disturb him save yourself and your helpers."

"I will gladly do that, Lord," said Morgan Tud. Then the steward of the household asked Arthur where the young woman should go.

"Take her to Gwenhwyfar and her ladies," he said. The steward did so. That is the story so far.

The next day Geraint approached the Court and Gwenhwyfar had set watchmen on the ramparts in case he came unnoticed. One of the watchers came to where Gwenhwyfar was and said, "Lady, I think I see Geraint and a young woman with him. He is on horseback but in walking gear. The woman, however, appears to be in a white linen garment."

"Come, my women, come to meet Geraint, to welcome him and wish him well," said the Queen. She and her ladies went to meet Geraint. He greeted her and she welcomed him profusely for what he had done so well in making amends for her.

"Lady," he said, "I wanted to make amends for you according to your wishes and here is the young lady who helped to have your revenge."

"I truly welcome her," said Gwenhwyfar. "It is right that we should receive her joyfully." They then went in and dismounted. Geraint came to where Arthur was and greeted him.

"You are very welcome," said Arthur. "Since Edeyrn the son of Nudd has received what he deserved at your hands, you were successful in your mission."

---

* Guarantees or pledges. It was important that knights stood surety for each other.

"It is not me who is to blame for that," said Geraint, "but the arrogance of Edeyrn son of Nudd who would not tell me his name. I wouldn't leave him alive until he told me who he was or until one would vanquish the other."

"Now," said Arthur, "where is the lady for whom you challenged at the tournament?"

"She is gone with Gwenhwyfar to her chamber." Then Arthur went to see the lady and he and all his Court were glad to see her for they had never seen any lady as beautiful as she. She was then dressed in the clothes that Gwenhwyfar had chosen for her and she made wonderful sight. Arthur then gave her to Geraint and they all celebrated with music, food and drink for the whole day and evening. When it was time for bed, Geraint and Enid (for that was the lady's name) slept together as man and wife. In the morning, many gifts were given to them and she made her home in the palace with many companions who respected her more highly than any lady, other than the Queen, in the Island of Britain.

Then Gwenhwyfar said, "I judged rightly regarding the stag's head, that it should not be given to anyone until Geraint's return; so this is the proper occasion to give it to Enid, the daughter of Ynywl who has fame throughout the land. No one will begrudge her, for there is nothing here but fellowship and love for her." This was approved by Arthur also and the head of the stag was given to Enid so that her fame increased and she had more friends than ever. Geraint from that time on, loved the stag and took part in tournaments and combat from which he would be victorious. After a year, a second year and a third year he did this, until he was famous all over the Kingdom.

Once upon a time, when Arthur was holding court in Caerleon-upon-Usk at Whitsuntide, there came to him learnéd and knowledgeable messengers who greeted him. "Welcome to you," said Arthur, "from where do you come?"

"We come, Lord, from Cornwall," they said, "from Erbin the son of Custennin, your uncle, who sends an important message to you as an uncle should greet his nephew and as a vassal greets his Lord. He says to you that he is getting old, frail and weary and his neighbouring chiefs, knowing this, encroach on his boundaries and covet his lands. He earnestly begs you to allow Geraint, his son, to return to him and protect his possessions. He says it would be better for Geraint to do this, to protect his inheritance, than to take part in tournaments which bring no profit although he wins glory from them."

"Yes," said Arthur, "go and change your clothes, have a meal, refresh yourselves after your journey and then you will have my answer." So they went to eat.

Arthur thought how difficult it would be for him to let Geraint go from him and his Court, but neither did he think it fair that he should be prevented from going to protect his lands, seeing that his father was unable to do so. It would also be sad for Gwenhwyfar and her ladies to let Enid go away from them. All that day and night was spent in feasting and Arthur told Geraint of the message from his father.

"Whether it is to my advantage or disadvantage, I will do what you decide," said Geraint.

"Even though it will be painful for me to lose you, it is right that you go to defend your boundaries," said Arthur. "Take as many men with you as you wish from my faithful ones."

"Thank you, Lord, I will," said Geraint.

"What do I hear you discussing?" asked Gwenhwyfar, "Is it about the messengers come to take Geraint from us?"

"It is," said Arthur.

"Then I must choose suitable companions for Enid who will go with her," said Gwenhwyfar.

"You will do well to do that," said Arthur.

That night they went to sleep and the next day the messengers were allowed to leave. They were told that Geraint would follow them. On the third day Geraint set out with many of Arthur's knights including Gwalchmai the son of Gwyar, Bedwyr the son of Bedrawd, Cei the son of Cynyr, Peredur the son of Efrawg and Edeyrn the son of Nudd of whom Geraint said, "I think he is well enough to ride," but Arthur said that would not be fitting for Geraint to take Edeyrn with him until peace is made between him and Gwenhwyfar.

"Gwenhwyfar can allow him to go with me if he gives sureties," (see above) said Geraint.

164

"If she pleases, she can let him go without sureties," said Arthur, "for he has suffered enough for the insult which the lady-in-waiting received from the dwarf."

"If you and Geraint both agree, I will do this gladly, Lord" said Gwenhwyfar. Then she allowed Edeyrn to go with Geraint freely.

They set out towards the Severn where, on the other side, were the nobles of Erbin the son of Custennin and his foster father in the lead to welcome Geraint warmly. Also there were many women of the Court with his mother to receive Enid the daughter of Ynywl, his wife. There was great rejoicing in the Court and throughout the whole country at the coming of Geraint whom they greatly loved and knew of the fame he had gained since he had left them and because he intended to protect his lands.

They arrived at the Court where there was great feasting and entertainment of music and games. To do honour to Geraint, all the nobles of the land were invited to visit him. The day and night passed with great enjoyment. At dawn, the next day, Erbin rose and called Geraint to him, together with the nobles who had accompanied him on his journey from Wales saying, "I am a feeble old man and while I was able I maintained my lands for you and for myself, but you are young, at the best of your youth and strength, so from now on you shall look after your lands."

Geraint said, "You shall not give power over your lands into my hands nor take me from Arthur's Court."

"I shall give the lands to you," said Erbin, "and from today you will receive the homage of your subjects."

Then Gwalchmai said, "It would be better if you grant favours to those who come to you today and tomorrow receive the homage of your subjects." Cadyrieith then came to them and asked for what they wished. Arthur's men began to give gifts, so did the men of Cornwall. They were not long in giving, so eager were they to give gifts to Geraint. No one went away unsatisfied and had what they desired. That day and night were spent in the greatest enjoyment.

The next day, at dawn, Erbin asked Geraint to send messengers to the men, to ask whether they were agreeable that Geraint should come to receive their homage. This Geraint did, to the men of Cornwall who said it would be a great and joyful honour to pay him homage. So he received their homage and they stayed with him until the third night.

The day after, Arthur's followers intended to leave but Geraint said, "It is too soon for you to go away. Stay with me until I have received the homage of my chief men." So they remained with him until he had done so. Then they set out for the Court of Arthur. Geraint and Enid accompanied them as far as Diganhwy (Dyngannon) where they parted.

Ondyaw, the son of the Duke of Burgundy said to Geraint, "Go to visit the far parts of your territories and if you have any trouble, send for us."

"Thank you, I will do that," said Geraint. He travelled to the boundaries of his lands with experienced guides and the chief men of his own country went with him. He took possession of the furthest lands he saw.

Then, as he used to do when he was at Arthur's Court, he started taking part in tournaments again. He became famous as he had before and enriched his Court and his friends with the best horses, armour and most valuable jewels. He didn't stop until his fame had spread all over the region when he began to love easy living and pleasure. He loved his wife and stayed with her until his nobles felt rejected. He lost their friendship and there was gossiping in the Court that he was spending too much time with his wife Enid and ignoring his friends.

His father, Erbin got to hear of this and asked Enid whether it was she who had encouraged Geraint to act this way.

"No, indeed," said Enid, "nothing is more hateful to me than this." She didn't know what to do, for although it was difficult for her to speak of this to Geraint, it was not easy either for her to hear of this without telling Geraint of it, so she was very sad.

One morning, in the summer time, they were on their bed, Geraint sleeping on the edge of it. Enid was wide awake in this room with glass windows letting the sun in on to the bed. Geraint was asleep without the bedclothes on his body. Enid gazed at the beauty of him and said to herself, "Oh dear, am I the cause of the loss of his fame and glory which he so enjoyed?" As she said this, tears dropped from her eyes and fell upon his chest. Her words and tears woke him and he had the idea that she was thinking and speaking of another man who she loved more than him and wished to be with.

Geraint was therefore troubled in his mind and called to his squire[*] who came to him. "Prepare my horse and armour quickly," he said to him and to Enid he said, "Go and dress yourself and have your horse made ready. Dress in the worst riding-dress you have and shame on me if you return here until you know whether I have lost my strength so completely as you say, then it would be easy for you to meet with him whom you wish for." So she got up and dressed in a simple dress. "I do not understand what you mean, Lord," she said.

"Nor will you know as yet," he said.

Geraint then went to see his father, Erbin, "Sir," he said, "I am going on a quest and I don't know when I will be back so please look after your possessions until I return."

"I will," he said, "but I am amazed that you go so suddenly. Who is going with you, for you are not strong enough yet to travel to the land of Lloegyr (England) alone?"

"Only one person will go with me," said Geraint.

"I hope many will go with you in Lloegyr," said his father.

Geraint went to where his horse was, which was covered with heavy armour. He ordered Enid to mount her horse and ride a long way in front of him. "Whatever you see or hear about me," he said, "do not turn back and unless I speak to you, do not say a word either."

They set out but he didn't choose the most pleasant or frequented road to travel but one on which were likely to be thieves, robbers and poisonous animals. They came to a high road, which they followed until they came to a vast forest. They went towards it when they saw four armed horsemen coming from the forest.

When the horsemen saw them, one said to the others, "Look, this is a good place for us to take two horses and armour and a lady too. We should have no difficulty in doing so looking at the lone knight who hands his head so heavily and thoughtfully." Enid heard this but she didn't know what to do for fear of Geraint, who had told her to be silent.

---

[*] an attendant on a knight

"May Heaven punish me," she said to herself, "but I should prefer to be killed by him than any other and though he might kill me, I shall tell him in case _he_ is killed unawares." She waited until Geraint was nearer to her, then said, "Lord, did you hear what those men were saying about you?"

He looked up angrily at her, "You have only to hold your peace as I told you, not bother about that," he said. "Though you wish me killed by those men, I am not afraid."

Then the first horseman came at Geraint with his lance, but he let the lance go by him then thrust the lance through the man's shield, which split in two and pierced his body which fell to earth from his horse. The second knight attacked him furiously, but with one thrust, Geraint overthrew him also and killed him as he had done the first one. Then the third one came at him who be killed in the same way. He also killed the fourth one.

Enid was sad to see this but Geraint dismounted from his horse, took the armour of the men he had killed and placed them on their saddles. He tied together their reins and mounted his horse again. "This is what you must do," he said. "Take the four horses, drive them before you and go in front as I told you before. Speak not one word until I speak to you and I promise you that if you do, you will be punished."

"I will do as you say, Lord," said Enid.

They went through the forest and came to a vast plain in the centre of which was a thickly tangled copse[*]. Out of it came three horsemen towards them, fully armoured – both they and their horses. Enid looked at them closely, then heard them say, one to another, "Look there, this is a good find for us. Without any effort we find four horses with four suits of armour on them. We can easily take them from that droopy knight and the girl will be in our power too."

Enid thought, "This is only too true, for my Lord is exhausted from his previous fighting. I will be very sorry if I do not warn him of this danger." She waited a while until Geraint came near, then said, "Lord, did you hear that conversation between those men about you?"

"What was it?" he asked.

---

[*] small wood

"They are saying that they will easily be able to take away all these goods."

"I vow to Heaven," he answered, "that I am less worried about what they say than you will not be silent and obey my orders."

"My Lord," she said, "I am afraid that they could take you unawares."

"Hold your tongue then," he said, "haven't I asked for silence?"

Just then one of the horsemen attacked Geraint with his lance – he thought with some success, but Geraint struck it aside. Then he rushed at him, aimed at his middle so that his spear pierced the shield, through his body which fell from the horse to the ground. Both the other horsemen came at him in turn but neither was more successful than his companions.

Enid stood by, looking at all this fearing on one hand that Geraint would be wounded and on the other hand glad to see him victorious. He then dismounted, bound the three suits of armour upon the three saddles, fastening the reins of the horses together, so that he had seven horses with him. He mounted his horse and told Enid to drive the others forward. "It is no good telling you not to speak for you will not take my advice," he said to her.

She said, "I will do so if I can Lord, but I can't keep quiet if I hear threats against your person from strange people which haunt this wilderness."

"I say again," he said, "I want nothing but peace, so be silent."

"I will, Lord, if I can," she said.

She went on with the horses ahead of her. They travelled across open country, high, level and beautiful, until they came to a wood, which was so large, they could not see the end of it. Out of the wood came five horsemen, eager, bold, mighty and strong, mounted on powerful chargers* which were snorting proudly. When they drew near, Enid heard them say, "Look, here is a good find for us, which we can take easily, without much trouble; the woman too, from that single knight who looks so dreary and sad."

---

* knight's or officer's horses

169

Enid was extremely disturbed on hearing these words, but didn't know what in the world she should do. At last, however, she decided to warn Geraint; so she turned her horse's head towards him. "Lord," she said, "if you had heard what I did you would be more worried than you are."

Angrily and bitterly he grinned at her saying, "I hear you going against everything I have said to you, for which you may be sorry."

Immediately the men came at him but he overcame them all, placed the five suits of armour on the five saddles, tied together the reins of the now twelve horses and gave them over to Enid. "I don't know whether it is any good to order you," he said, "but this time I especially command you to obey me." So she went forward towards the wood, keeping her distance from Geraint, as he had told her. He was sorry for her, as far as his anger would allow, to see a lady so highly born struggling with the horses.

As they reached the wood, night fell. As the wood was so deep and vast, he said, "Lady, it is not wise to go on."

She said, "Well, Lord, whatever you wish me to do."

"It is best to turn out of the wood to rest and wait for daylight to pursue our journey," he said.

"So we will," said Enid.

He dismounted, lifted her to the ground and said, "I must sleep, I am so tired, so you look after the horses but do not sleep."

"I will, Lord," she replied.

He then went to sleep in his armour and the night passed quickly because of the season. When she saw the dawn come up she looked to see if he was awake which he was. She said, "I have wanted to speak to you for a while, Lord," but he said nothing to her for he had not given her permission to speak. Then he got up and said, "Go, take the horses and ride on as you did yesterday." She left the wood and came to open country with meadows on either side where men were mowing the meadows with scythes. They then came to a river where the horses bent down to drink.

They went up to a steep hill where they met a slender lad with a satchel around his neck. There was something in the satchel but they didn't know what it was. He had a small blue pitcher* in his hand and a bowl on the mouth of the pitcher. The lad greeted Geraint who returned his greeting and asked from where he had come. "I come from the town you see before you. Would it displease you if I asked where you come from?"

"By no means," said Geraint. "I came through that wood over there."

"You came through the wood today?"

"No, we were in the wood last night."

"I should think the conditions there were not pleasant for you and you have had no food or drink."

"No," said Geraint.

"Then will you please take my advice," said the lad "and have this meal from me."

"What sort of meal?" asked Geraint. "One that is meant for the mowers," said the young lad, "nothing less than bread, meat and wine. You may have it if you like."

"We are most grateful for it," said Geraint.

He dismounted, the lad took Enid from her horse, then they washed and ate their meal. The lad sliced the bread, gave them drink and waited on them. When they had finished, he got up and said to Geraint, "My Lord, with your permission, I will go now to fetch food for the mowers."

"Go first to the town and take the best lodging you can find for me and the horses. You may take any horse and armour in payment for your services."

"Thank you, Lord," said the lad, "this would be more than enough for what I have done for you."

He went to the town and found the most comfortable lodging he could. Then he went to the court to see the Earl and tell him of his adventure. "I'll go now to meet the knight and lead him to his lodging," he said to the Earl, who said,

"Yes, go gladly and tell the knight he is welcome to the court if he so wishes." The young lad went to meet Geraint and told him he would be well-received by the Earl if he wished, but Geraint preferred to go to his lodging. It was a comfortable room with plenty of straw and coverings and there was a roomy place for the horses. The lad had prepared food for them.

---

* an earthenware jar used for holding liquids

After they had taken off their outer clothes, Geraint said to Enid, "Go to the other side of the room and you may call the woman of the house if you wish."

"I will do as you say, Lord," she said.

Soon the man of the house came to Geraint and asked, "Sir, have you eaten?"

"I have," he said. Then the lad asked him if he would drink something before he met the Earl. "Yes, I will," said Geraint, so the lad went into the town to bring them drink. They drank but then Geraint said, "I must sleep."

"Yes," said the lad, "while you are sleeping, I will go to the Earl."

"Go", said Geraint, "but come back here when I need you." So Geraint and Enid went to sleep.

The young lad then went to the place where the Earl was, who asked him where was the knight's lodging. He told him and said, "I must go soon to wait upon him."

"Go," said the Earl. "Take my greetings to him and tell him I will see him in the evening."

"I will," said the lad and he came to where they were when it was time for them to wake up. They got up and had a meal which the lad served them. Geraint then asked the man of the house if there were any of his friends he wished to invite to him and he said there were.

"Bring them here," said Geraint, "and entertain them at my expense with the best you can buy in the town," which he did.

Soon the Earl came to visit Geraint with his twelve honourable knights. Geraint rose and welcomed him. "Heaven protect you," said the Earl. Then they all sat down and the Earl talked with Geraint. He asked him what was the object of his journey.

"I have none," said Geraint, "except to find adventures and to follow my inclination." The Earl then stared at Enid closely and thought he had never seen a lady more fair or beautiful than she and he set his heart on her. He then asked Geraint, "Have I your permission to go to speak with that lady over there, for I see that she is apart from you?"

"You have it willingly," said Geraint.

"Oh Lady," he said, "it cannot be pleasant for you to travel in this way with that man over there!"

"It is not unpleasant," she said, "to travel the same road which he travels."

"You have neither men nor women to serve you," he said.

"Yes," she said, "but it is better for me to follow that man than to be served by men and women."

"Take my advice," said the Earl, "I will give you all my Earldom if you stay with me."

"I will not," she said. "That man over there was the first I was promised to and I will not be unfaithful to him."

"You are wrong," said the Earl. "If I kill him, I can keep you with me as long as I choose and when you no longer please me, I can turn you away. If you come, however, on your own free will, there will be faithfulness between us as long as I live." She thought about his words and decided it was best to encourage him in what he asked. "Well sir," she said, "this would be best unless I am accused of being very unfaithful, come here tomorrow to take me away as if I knew nothing about it."

"I will do that," he said, taking his leave with his attendants. Enid didn't tell Geraint anything of the conversation she had had with the Earl, in case it made him angry and cause him distress.

At the usual time, they went to sleep, but Enid slept little and at midnight she got up, placed all Geraint's armour together so that it would be ready to put on. She was quite fearful when she went to Geraint's side of the bed and woke him saying; "My Lord, get up and dress." She then told him of all the Earl had said to her. Although he was angry, he took her warning and dressed himself. She lit a candle so that he would have light to do so.

"Leave the candle there," he said. "Call the man of the house to come here." She did so and the man of the house came. "Do you know how much I owe you?" asked Geraint.

"You owe very little," he said.

"Take the eleven horses and eleven suits of armour."

"My Lord," he said, "I didn't spend the value of one suit of armour on you."

"For that reason," replied Geraint, "you will be that much richer. Now will you come to guide me out of the town?"

"I will gladly. Which way did you want to go?" he asked.

173

"I wish to leave the town by a different way from that which I entered," said Geraint.

The man of the lodging accompanied him as far as he wanted. Geraint then told Enid to go on in front of him as before and the man returned to his home. As he reached his house, there was a great commotion. When he looked out he saw fourscore[*] knights headed by the Dwnn Earl. "Where is the knight that was here?" he asked.

"Oh Sir, he went away some time ago."

"Why villain, did you let him go without informing me?"

"My Lord, you did not command me to do so or else I wouldn't have allowed him to go."

"What way did he go?"

"I don't know except that he took the high road."

They turned their horse's heads that way and seeing the tracks of the horses on the high road, they followed. When Enid saw the dawn come up, she looked back and saw vast clouds of dust coming nearer and nearer to her. This troubled her. She thought it was the Earl and his men coming after them. She then saw a knight appearing out of the mist. "Oh dear" she said, "It would be better for me to be killed by my lord than to see him killed without warning him."

"My Lord," she said to him, "do you see that man over there hurrying after you with many others behind him?"

"I do," he said "and in spite of my orders, you still cannot keep silent."

Then he turned on the knight and with the first thrust he threw him down under his horse's feet. He did the same with all the rest of the eighty knights – thrusting his spear, as they all, from the weakest to the strongest, were overthrown. Last of all, the Earl came at him, broke one spear, then another when Geraint attacked him. He asked for mercy as he was trampled by the horses so Geraint granted him mercy. Through the hardness of the ground and the violence of the strokes they had received from Geraint, not one knight survived without being fatally wounded.

Geraint, then, went on his way along the high road he was on and Enid went first and kept her distance. Nearby they saw

---

[*] a score is 20 so fourscore is eighty (80)

the most beautiful valley they had ever seen which had a large river running through it. There was a bridge over the river where they saw a walled town – the best anyone had ever seen. As they approached the bridge, Geraint saw coming towards him, from a small thick copse, a man on a large and lofty horse, very spirited but manageable.

"Ah, Knight," said Geraint, "from where have you come?"

"I come," he said, "from the valley below us."

"Can you tell me who is the owner of this fair valley and the walled town over there?"

"I will, gladly," said the knight. "The English and French call him Gwiffred Petit, but the Welsh call him Y Brenhin Bychan," (The Little King)."

"Can I go by the bridge and by the lower road beneath the walled town?" asked Geraint.

The knight answered, "You may not go that way unless you intend to fight him, for it is usual for him to fight everyone who comes upon his lands."

"I will, however, go that way on my journey," said Geraint.

"If you do, you will probably meet with shame and humiliation," said the knight.

Then Geraint proceeded along the road that led to the town, which brought him to ground that was hard and rough. As he travelled he became aware of a knight following him on a war-horse that was strong, large and powerful. On it he had never seen so small a man. They were both completely armed. When the knight had overtaken Geraint he said, "Tell me sir, whether it is through ignorance or presumption that you insult my dignity and break my rules?"

"No," said Geraint, "I did not know this road was forbidden to anyone."

"You did know it" said the other, "so come with me to my Court to give me satisfaction*."

"That I will not," said Geraint. "I would not ever go to your Lord's Court unless Arthur himself was your Lord."

"By the hand of Arthur himself," said the knight, "I will have satisfaction of you or be defeated by you."

---

* opportunity to fighting a duel

Immediately, they charged at each other. A squire of his brought him lances as he broke them. They gave each other such violent strokes that their shields lost all their colour, but it was very difficult for Geraint to fight such a small man. They, however, fought, until their horses were brought to their knees. They went on fighting on foot, giving each other such fierce blows, so frequently and so severely powerful, that their helmets were pierced, their skull caps broken, their armour shattered and the light of their eyes was darkened by sweat and blood.

At last, Geraint became so angry that he gathered all his strength and furiously determined, he lifted his sword and struck the knight on the crown of his head a blow so powerful that it pierced through his head armour, his skin and flesh until it wounded the very bone. The sword flew out of the Little King's hand and landed far away from him.

He asked Geraint for mercy. "Though you have neither been courteous or just," said Geraint, "you shall have mercy, upon condition that you will become my ally, never fight me again and will come to my assistance whenever you hear I am in trouble."

"I will do this gladly, Lord," promised the Little King. "Now come to my Court to recover from your tiredness and fatigue."

"I will not," said Geraint.

Then the Little King looked at Enid where she stood and was sorry to see a lady of her nobility so greatly distressed. He said to Geraint, "My Lord, you are wrong not to take a rest and refresh yourself for a while, for if you meet any trouble in your present state, it will not be easy for you to overcome it." However, Geraint wished only to go on his journey, bloodstained and in pain. Enid went first but kept her distance.

They travelled towards the wood which they saw in front of them. The heat of the sun was very great and because of the blood and sweat, Geraint's armour stuck to him and he was more aware of his pain than when he received it, so he stood under a tree to shelter from the sun. Enid stood under another tree.

Soon they heard the sound of horns and a great noise. Arthur and his company had come down to the road. While

Geraint was considering which way he would go to avoid them, he was noticed by a page, who was an attendant to the Steward of the Household. He went to him and told him what kind of man he had seen in the wood. The Steward had his horse saddled, took his lance and shield and went to the place where Geraint was.

"Sir Knight," he said, "what are you doing here?"

"I am standing under a shady tree to avoid the heat of the sun."

"What journey are you on and who are you?"

"I look for adventure and go where I please," said Geraint.

"Indeed," said Cei*, (for it was he) "then come with me to see Arthur who is nearby."

"I will not," said Geraint.

"You must come," said Cei, then Geraint knew who he was but Cei didn't know Geraint. Cei attacked him as best he could but Geraint became angry and struck him with the shaft of his lance so that he rolled headlong to the ground. He didn't want to do more to him than that.

Scared and in a wild manner, Cei got up, mounted his horse and went back to his lodging. Then he went to Gwalchmai's† tent and said, "I have been told by one of the servants that he has seen a wounded knight in the wood in battered armour. Will you go and see if this is true?"

"I don't mind going," said Gwalchmai.

"Take then your horse and some armour," said Cei, "for I hear he is none too courteous to anyone who approaches him." So Gwalchmai took his spear and shield, mounted his horse and arrived at the spot where Geraint was.

"Sir Knight," he said, "what kind of journey are you on?

"I journey for my own pleasure and to look for adventures."

"Will you tell me who you are or will you come to see Arthur who is close by?"

"I will not tell you who I am, neither will I go to see Arthur," answered Geraint who knew it was Gwalchmai but Gwalchmai didn't know him.

---

* Sir Kay
† Sir Gawain

"I don't intend to leave you until I know who you are," said Gwalchmai, charging him with his lance and striking him on his shield so that the shaft shivered into splinters and their horses were head to head.

Then Gwalchmai looked at him closely and realised who he was. "Oh Geraint," he said, "is it you?"

"I am not Geraint," he replied.

"I am sure you are Geraint," he said, "and this is an ill-advised expedition you are on." He then looked round and saw Enid and welcomed her warmly.

"Geraint," said Gwalchmai, "come to visit Arthur; he is your lord and cousin."

"I will not," said Geraint, "for I am not in a fit state to see anyone." Then one of the pages came to speak to Gwalchmai who whispered to him to tell Arthur that Geraint was here wounded and would not go to see him although he was in a pitiful state.

"Ask Arthur to move his tent nearer to the road, for Geraint will not meet him willingly and he cannot be forced – the mood he is in." So the page went to Arthur and told him this.

Arthur had his tent moved to the side of the road and Enid was happy in her heart. Gwalchmai led Geraint along the road to where Arthur was camped. "Lord," said Geraint "all hail."

"God bless you," said Arthur, "but who are you?"

"This is Geraint," said Gwalchmai. "He has come against his own free will to meet you."

"He has lost his reason," said Arthur. Then Enid came and greeted Arthur who asked one of the pages to help her down from her horse and blessed her.

"So Enid," said Arthur, "what journey is this?"

"I don't know, Lord," said Enid, "just that I must go where he goes."

"My Lord," said Geraint, "with your permission we will leave and be on our way."

"Why must you go?" asked Arthur. "You cannot go now unless it is to your death."

"He will not allow me to make him stay," said Gwalchmai.

"He will obey me," said Arthur "and more than that, he must not go from here until he is healed."

"I would rather you let me go, Lord," said Geraint.

"I will not, by Heaven," said Arthur, who then had a girl conduct Enid to Gwenhwyfar's room in her tent.

Gwenhwyfar and all her ladies were so pleased to see her. They took off her riding habit and dressed her in other clothes. Arthur also called Cadyrieith, ordered him to pitch a tent for Geraint and have everything ready that was needed for the doctor to attend Geraint. Cadyrieith did this and Morgan Tud (the doctor) was called with his helpers to heal Geraint.

Arthur and his men stayed there for nearly a month while Geraint was being healed. When he was fully recovered he came to Arthur and asked his permission to leave. "I do not know whether you are well enough," said Arthur.

"I am, Lord," said Geraint.

"I don't believe you, only the doctors that tended you will I believe," said Arthur. He summoned the doctors to come to him and asked if it were true.

"It is, Lord," said Morgan Tud, so the next day Arthur allowed Geraint to leave and continue his journey.

On the same day, Arthur left too and Geraint asked Enid to go before him as usual as she went along the high road. As they travelled they heard a loud shrieking. "Stay here," said Geraint, "I will go to see what is the meaning of this noise."

"I will," she said. He went to an open clearing where he saw two horses, one with a man's saddle and the other a woman's saddle on it. He saw a knight lying dead in his armour and a young woman in a riding dress standing over him, crying loudly.

"Oh, Lady," said Geraint, "what has happened to you?"

"I was travelling here with my dear husband when three giants came up to us and without any reason in the world, they killed him."

"Which way did they go?" asked Geraint.

"Up there on the high road," she replied.

He returned to Enid and said, "Go to the lady over there and wait with her until I come back." She was sad when he ordered her to do this but did it nevertheless. She went to the lady, who was pitiful to hear, but she felt that Geraint would never return.

Meanwhile, Geraint followed the giants and overtook them. Each of them was bigger than three men and each carried a huge club over his shoulder. Geraint rushed at one of them and pierced him through the middle with his spear. Drawing it out again, he pierced the second giant in the same way. The third giant turned on him, struck him with his club, split his shield and crushed his shoulder which reopened his wounds which made him bleed again. However, Geraint drew his sword and attacked the giant, giving him a blow on his head so severe, violent and fierce that his head and neck were split down to his shoulders and he fell dead.

Geraint left them there and returned to Enid. When he saw her, he fell lifeless from his horse. She let out a piercing cry and came to stand over him. At the sound of her cries, the Earl of Limours (Limwris) and his men came along. He said, "What has happened to you?"

"Oh, good Sir," she said, "the man I love and shall always love has been killed." Then he said to the other woman, "what is the reason for your distress?"

"They have killed my beloved husband also."

"Who was it that killed them?"

"Some giants killed the man I loved best and the other knight went after them and came back in the state you see. It could be that he killed some, if not all of the giants."

The Earl had the knight that was dead buried, but he thought that there was still some life in Geraint yet. To see if he would live, he had him carried in the hollow of his shield upon a bier[*]. The two ladies went to the Court were Geraint was laid on a couch near the table in the hall. They all took off their travelling clothes except Enid. She would not change because she was so sad. The Earl tried to persuade her to change her clothes and to eat something, but she refused. He tried many times to get her to eat but she would not. He offered her his Earldom with himself whether Geraint lived or died so that she be happy and joyful. She said, "I will not be joyful as long as I live."

"Come and eat then," he said.

"I will not until that man on the bier will eat also."

"That cannot be," said the Earl "for that man is dead already."

---

[*] a movable stand for a coffin or corpse

"I will prove that I can," said Enid. Then he offered her a goblet of wine to change her mind. "I will not drink unless he does too," she said.

"Well," said the Earl, "there is no point in my being gentle with you or not," and with that he gave her a box on the ear and she shrieked loudly. The sound of that made Geraint come to himself and sit up. Finding his sword in the hollow of his shield he picked it up and struck the Earl a fiercely-wounding, mighty great blow on his head, so that it cut him in two and the sword was stopped by the table. All then left the table and ran away – not so much in fear of living but of seeing a dead man come to life to kill them.

Then Geraint looked at Enid and he was sad for two reasons, one was to see that she had gone pale and wan and the other to see that she was right. "Lady," he said, "do you know where our horses are?"

"I know where your horse is, Lord, but not the other," she said. So he went to the horse, mounted him and took Enid up on the horse behind him.

Away they went along a road between two hedges. Night was falling then they saw behind them shining shafts of spears. They also heard the trampling of horses' hooves and the noise of men approaching. "I hear something following us," he said. "I will put you on the other side of the hedge," which he did. A knight came towards brandishing his spear. When Enid saw this she cried out, "Oh Sir, what glory will you win killing a dead man?"

"Oh my goodness," he replied, "is it Geraint?"

"Yes, it is," she said, "and who are you?"

"I am the Little King," he answered, "coming to your rescue after hearing you were in trouble. If you had followed my advice, none of this would have happened."

"Nothing can happen without the will of Heaven," said Geraint, "although some good may be gained with advice."

"Yes," said the Little King, "and I have good advice for you now. Come with me to the court of a son-in-law of my sister, which is nearby and you shall have the best medical attention in the kingdom."

"I will do so willingly," said Geraint. Enid was put on one of the squires' horses and they went forward to the Baron's palace where they were welcomed and treated with good hospitality.

The next morning they went to look for doctors who soon came and who treated Geraint until he was well. While Geraint was under medical care, the Little King had his armour repaired until was as good as new. They stayed there for a fortnight and a month.

Then the Little King said to Geraint, "Now we will go on to my own Court to rest and amuse ourselves."

"No," said Geraint, "if it pleases you, we will travel one more day and then return."

"Certainly," said the Little King, "you go then." So early the next day they set out and Enid was happier than she had ever been. They came to a main road which divided into two and they saw a man coming on foot along one of these roads.

Gwiffert (the Little King) asked him from where he had come. "I come from doing errands in the country," the man said.

"Tell me," said Geraint, "which of these roads is the best for me to follow?"

"It is best to travel on that road," he answered, "for if you take this road you will never return. Down below there is a hedge of mist and with it enchanted games. No one who has ever gone there has returned. The Court of Earl Owain is there and he permits no one to lodge in the town, rather that they go to his Court."

"We will go along the lower road," said Geraint.

They went along it until they came to the town where they took the most pleasant lodging. As they were doing so, a young man came up to them, greeted them asking what they were doing there. "We are taking up our lodging to spend the night."

"It is not the custom of the man who owns the town to allow those of gentle birth to stay but to come to the Court. Therefore please come to the Court."

"We will be pleased to come," said Geraint.

As they approached the Court, they were made welcome by the Earl who ordered tables to be prepared. They washed and sat down in this order: Geraint was on one side of the Earl with Enid on the other. Next to her was the Little King, then the Countess next to Geraint and the next according to their rank.

Then Geraint remembered the games and thought that he would not be allowed to take part, so he stopped eating. The Earl saw this and thought it was because of the games and he was sorry that he had ever established those games, not wishing to lose such a young man as Geraint. If Geraint asked him to abolish the games, he would do so.

The Earl then asked Geraint, "What are you thinking about, since you are not eating? If you do not wish to go to the games, you need not."

"Thank you," said Geraint, "but I wish nothing better than to go to the games and to be shown the way there."

"If this is what you want, you shall have it," said the Earl.

"I do indeed," said Geraint. Then they ate well, with much food and drink served to them.

When the meal was over, they got up and Geraint called for his horse and his armour and dressed himself and the horse. All the men moved to the side of the hedge, which was so high that it reached as high as they could see in the air. Upon every stake in the hedge, except two, there was a head of a man and there were a great number of stakes. "May no one go with this knight?" asked the Little King. "No one may," answered Earl Owain.

"Which way is the entrance?" enquired Geraint.

"I don't know," said Owain, "but enter the easiest way you can see."

Then, fearlessly, without delay, Geraint dashed forward into the mist. On leaving the mist, he came to a large orchard where he saw a big space in which there was a tent of red satin, the door of which was open. An apple tree stood in front of the door and on a branch hung a huge hunting horn. He dismounted and went into the tent. There was no one in there except one lady sitting on a golden chair with an empty chair opposite her.

Geraint went to the empty chair and sat down. "Oh Sir," said the lady, "I would not advise you to sit on that chair."

"Why not," asked Geraint. "The man who owns that chair has not allowed anyone else to sit on it."

"I don't care if it displeases him that I sit on this chair," said Geraint. Immediately there was a great commotion outside the tent. Geraint looked to see what it was and saw a knight mounted on a large high-spirited war-horse. There was a cloak in two parts upon him and the horse.

"Tell me, Sir Knight," he said, "who asked you to sit there?"

"I did," said Geraint.

"It was wrong of you to pay me disrespect and disgrace. Come, do me satisfaction for your insolence."

Geraint then got up and they started to fight straight away. They broke a set of lances, a second set and a third giving each other frequent strokes. At last Geraint became angry, urged on his horse, rushed upon him and thrust his sword through his shield splitting it in two and he fell headlong to the ground.

"Oh, my lord," he said, "have mercy and you can have all you want."

"I only wish that these games shall no longer exist, nor the hedge of mist, nor magic, nor enchantment."

"You shall have it, willingly," he said.

"Then see to it," said Geraint.

"Sound that horn over there and when you sound it all mist will vanish but it will not go unless it is blown by the knight who has beaten me," he said.

Enid was sad and anxious where she was for the safety of Geraint, who sounded the horn. At the first blast, the mist vanished and all the people came together and made peace with each other. The Earl invited Geraint and the Little King to stay with him that night.

The next morning they separated and Geraint went towards his own lands where he reigned prosperously and his fame and splendour lasted and brought honour and renown to him and Enid from that time on.

Taliesin

Taliesin literally the 'radiant brow' was a Welsh Bard of the sixth century. He was invited by Emperor Arthur to his court at Caerleon upon Usk, where he became highly celebrated for his poetic genius and his knowledge of the sciences.

The various poems recited in the Tale of Taliesin appear to have been composed at different periods.

Synopsis of A Tale of Taliesin

After many adventures of being chased by Caridwen and taking
the forms of various animals, he eventually became a grain of
wheat which she ate after having made herself into a black hen.
She was pregnant with him for nine months and he was so
beautiful that she couldn't kill him. Instead, she put him into a
leather bag and threw him into the sea. He was found by Elffin
and being a very intelligent child, he grew very quickly and
became a bard.

Elffin is imprisoned by his uncle, the King, for saying that
his wife was more beautiful and virtuous than the King's, and
that his bard (Taliesin) was the best. The King tries to prove
that Elffin's wife is not virtuous by sending his son Rhun to his
house, but Taliesin hears of this and warns her. He tells her to
change places with her maid and dress as her, putting jewellery
on the fingers of the maid as if she were her mistress.

Rhun gets the maid drunk, thinking she is the mistress, and
cuts off her little finger with a ring on it that Elffin had given
his wife. He takes it back to the King to prove that Elffin's wife
was in a drunken stupor when he cut it off.

Elffin is released from prison and gives three reasons why
it is not his wife's finger, and that his wife is virtuous and
Taliesin is the greatest bard.

A Tale of Taliesin

Long ago there lived in Penllyn, a man of wellborn descent, named Tegid *Foel. His house was in the middle of the Lake Tegid, and his wife was called Caridwen. They had a son named Morfran ab* Tegid, also a daughter named Creirwy, the most beautiful girl in the world. There was another brother, an ugly fellow named Afagddu. Now, his mother Caridwen thought that, because of his ugliness, he would not be accepted among men of noble birth, unless he had some great talent or knowledge, for it was the beginning of Arthur's time and of the Round Table.

So, according to the magic spells in the books of the Feryllt, she decided to boil a cauldron* of inspiration and science for her son, so that he might be honourably received because of his knowledge of the mysteries of the future state of the world.

She then began to boil the cauldron, which was not to stop boiling for a year and a day, until three blessed drops were obtained of the grace of inspiration. She put Gwion Bach, the son of Gwreang of Llanfair in Caereinion, in Powys, to stir the cauldron and a blind man named Morda to tend the fire beneath it. She told them that it must not stop boiling for a year and a day. She also, according to the books of the astronomers and in the hours of the planets, gathered all charm-bearing herbs every day.

---

* Pronounced 'V'
* son of ...
* a large pot for boiling

One day, towards the end of the year as Caridwen was pulling plants and making incantations*, it happened that three drops of the magic liquid flew out of the cauldron and fell on the finger of Gwion Bach. Because they were so hot, he put his finger into his mouth and immediately as he did so, he foresaw everything that was to come. He also saw that his main concern was to guard himself against the cunning of Caridwen, for her skill was so great.

Very much afraid, he fled towards his own land and the cauldron burst into two because all the liquid in it, except the three charm-bearing drops, was poisonous. The horses belonging to a man called Gwyddno Garanhir were poisoned by the water of the stream into which the liquid from the cauldron had run. From then on, the stream was called The Poison of the Horses of Gwyddno.

Caridwen came in and saw all the work of a whole year lost. She picked up a piece of wood and struck the blind Morda on the head until one of his eyes fell out upon his cheek. He said, "You have wrongfully disfigured me, for I am innocent. Your loss was not because of me."

"You are right," said Caridwen, "it was Gwion Bach who robbed me."

She ran after him and when he saw her, he changed himself into a hare and ran off. She then changed herself into a greyhound and chased him. He ran towards the river and became a fish. She then took the form of a female otter and swam after him under the water, until it was necessary for him to turn himself into a bird. She, as a hawk, followed him and gave him no rest in the sky.

Just as she was about to swoop upon him and he was afraid of death, he spotted a heap of grains of wheat and turned himself into one of them. Then she transformed herself into a high-crested black hen, went to the wheat, which she scratched with her feet, found him and swallowed him.

As the story says, she was pregnant with him for nine months and when he was delivered, she could not find it in her heart to kill him because he was so beautiful. So she wrapped

---

* magic spells

him in a leather bag and threw him into the sea on the twenty-ninth day of April, hoping for the mercy of Nature.

At that time, the weir of Gwyddno was on the strand* between Dyfi and Aberystwyth near to his own castle and a hundred pounds worth (in money) of fish was taken from that weir every May eve (last day of April). In those days, Gwyddno had an only son named Elffin, a most useless young man lacking in intelligence.

It made his father very sad, for he thought he must have been born at an evil hour. On the advice of his council, his father had allowed him to fish in the weir that year, to see if he would have some good luck and to give him something with which he could face the world.

The next day when Elffin went to look, there was nothing there, but as he turned back, he saw a leather bag on a pole in the weir. One of the men who guarded it then said to him, "You were never unlucky until tonight, but now you have destroyed the goodness of the weir which always gave the value of a hundred pounds every May eve. Tonight, there is nothing but the leather skin bag in it."

"Well now," said Elffin, "there may be something of value of a hundred pounds in the bag." They lifted up the bag and the one who opened it saw the forehead of a boy and said to Elffin, "Look, a radiant brow!"

"He shall be called Taliesin," said Elffin as he lifted the boy in his arms and regretting his bad luck, he put him sadly up behind him. He made his horse amble gently, for before he had been trotting and carried him as gently as if he had been sitting on the easiest chair in the world. Soon, the boy sang a song of consolation and praise to Elffin and predicted great honour for him. *The Consolation* was as follows—

'Fair Elffin, do not be sad!
Let no one be displeased with his lot,
To despair will bring you no gain.
No man sees what supports him;
The prayer of Cynllo will not be in vain;
God will not break his promise.

---

* a piece of sea, lake or river

Never in Gwyddno's weir—
Was there such good luck as this night.
Fair Elffin dry your cheeks!
Being too sad will not avail.
Although you think you've no gain,
Too much grief will bring you no good;
Do not doubt the miracles of God:
Although I am small I am clever.
From seas and from mountains,
And from the depth of rivers,
God brings wealth to the fortunate man.

Elffin of lively qualities,
Your attitude is really unmanly;
You must not be over sorrowful:
Better to trust in God than to anticipate evil.
Weak and small as I am,
On the foaming beach of the ocean,
In the day of trouble I shall be
Of more service to you than three hundred salmon.

Elffin of notable qualities,
Don't be displeased at your misfortune;
Although I lie weak in my bag,
There is goodness in my voice.
While I continue your protector
You have not much to fear;
Rememb'ring the names of the Trinity,
None shall be able to harm you.'

****

This was the first poem that Taliesin ever sang, attempting
to comfort Elffin in his disappointment that the fish in the weir
were lost and, what was worse, that everyone would think that
it was his fault and his bad luck. Then, Elffin asked Taliesin
what he was, whether man or spirit, so he sang this song—

"Firstly I was made a handsome looking fellow.
Then, given speech, I was liberated

By a smiling black old hag who, when irritated
Dreadful her demand, when she pursued me:
I have fled with speed, fled as a frog,
Fled as a crow, never finding rest;
I've fled as a deer into a tangled thicket;
Fled as a wolf, fled as a fox,
I've fled as a squirrel that hides in vain,
I've fled as a grain of pure white wheat,
Then I was thrown into a dark leather bag,
On an endless sea I was set adrift;
Which seemed to me that I was tenderly nursed,
And the Lord God then set me free."

****

Then Elffin came to his father Gwyddno's house or court
together with Taliesin. Gwyddno asked him if he had had a
good haul at the weir. Elffin told him that he had something
which was better than fish. "What is that?" asked Gwyddno. "A
bard," answered Elffin. Then Gwyddno said, "What good will
that do you?" Taliesin himself replied, "He will do him more
good than the weir ever gave you!" Gwyddno then asked, "Are
you able to speak, being so little?" Taliesin answered him, "I
am better able to speak than you are to question me."

"Let me hear what you can say," said Gwyddno. Then
Taliesin sang:

"In water there's a quality which is blest;
To meditate aright on God is most just;
To pray to Him in thoughtfulness is proper too.
For he will not refuse to you a reward.
Three times I have been born, I know by meditation;
A person would be unhappy not to know
All the sciences of the world that are in my heart,
For I know what has been and what will be.
I will ask my Lord to keep me safe,
The Son of Mary whom I trust is my delight.
For in Him continually is the world upheld.
God has instructed me and raised my hopes,
The true Creator of Heav'n protects me;

It is right that all saints should daily pray,
For God, who makes all things new, will bring them to Him."
****

So Elffin gave his 'catch' to his wife, who nursed him tenderly and lovingly. From then on, Elffin became richer day after day, in love and favour with the king, and Taliesin stayed there until he was thirteen years old. Elffin was then invited to spend Christmas with his uncle Maelgwn Gwynedd who, soon after, held open court at Christmastime in the castle of Dyganwy, for all his lords, both spiritual (bishops and archbishops) and temporal* (secular* lords). There were also a great number of knights and squires, who began to talk and discuss among themselves. This is what was said:

"Is there in the whole world a king so great as Maelgwn, or one on whom Heaven has bestowed as many gifts as upon him? First, form and beauty, meekness and strength, as well as all the powers of the soul?" Together with these, they said that Heaven had given one gift that bettered all others, which was the beauty, grace, wisdom and modesty of his queen, whose attributes were greater than those of all the ladies and noble young women throughout the whole kingdom.

Then, they questioned one another as to who had the braver men, the fairer or fastest horses or greyhounds; who had the cleverer or wiser bards than Maelgwn?

Now, at that time, the bards were great favourites of those in power in the kingdom. Then, none of them were heralds, unless they were learnéd men, not only expert in the service of kings and princes, but studious and well-versed in the ancestry, arms and exploits of princes and kings; in discussions about the foreign kingdoms, the ancient things of this kingdom and chiefly in the histories of the first nobles; who were also prepared always with their answers in various languages, Latin, French, Welsh and English. Together with this, they were great chroniclers* and recorders; they were skilful in making up verses and composing englyns (songs or rhymes) in every one

_____

* non-religious
* non-religious
* relaters of past events

192

of those languages. At that feast in Maelgwn's palace, there were as many as twenty-four of these bards, the chief one of all was one named Heinin Fardd.

When they had all finished praising the king and his gifts, Elffin spoke and said, "Truthfully, I would say that no one but a king may compare with a king; but if he were not a king, I would say that my wife was as virtuous as any lady in the kingdom, also that I have a bard more clever than all the king's bards." Soon, some of his 'friends' told the king of all his boasting, and the king ordered him to be thrown into a strong prison, until he knew the truth as to the virtues of his wife and the wisdom of his bard.

Now when Elffin had been put in a tower of the castle with a thick chain around his feet (it is said that is was a silver chain because he was of royal blood), the king, as the story is told, sent his son Rhun to find out about the appearance of Elffin's wife. It seems that Rhun was the most boorish man in the world. He didn't have a good word to say about any woman or girl to whom he had spoken.

When Rhun hurried to Elffin's home, determined to bring disgrace upon his wife, Taliesin told his mistress how the king had put her husband in prison and that Rhun was coming shortly to try and bring disgrace upon her. So he advised his mistress to dress one of the kitchen maids in her clothes, which the noble lady gladly did. She also loaded her hands with the best rings that she and her husband possessed.

Then, Taliesin asked his mistress to put the maid to sit at her supper table in her room while she herself acted as the maid. When they were sitting like that, Rhun suddenly arrived at Elffin's home and was joyfully welcomed by the servants who knew him well. They took him to their mistress's room, where the maid, disguised as the mistress, also welcomed him.

She then sat down to supper with Rhun who began joking with the maid (disguised as the mistress). The story tells that she became so drunk that she fell asleep, probably from a powder which Rhun had put into her drink. She slept so soundly that she never felt it when he cut off her little finger from her hand, which had on it a signet ring that Elffin had given to his wife as a token only a short time before.

Rhun returned to the king with the finger and the ring as proof to show he had cut it from her hand without waking her from her drunken sleep. The king was extremely pleased at this news and sent for his councillors to whom he told the whole story from the beginning. He ordered that Elffin should be brought from his prison and told him off because of his boast. He said to Elffin, "You must know now, beyond doubt, how foolish it is for a man to trust in the virtues of his wife further than he can see her. You can be certain of your wife's foulness, when you look at her finger with your signet ring on it, which was cut from her hand last night when she was in a drunken stupor."

Then Elffin spoke up and said, "With your permission, mighty king, I cannot deny that it is my ring, for it is well-known; but I insist that the finger it is around was never attached to my wife's hand, for there are three important things about it which can prove that it never belonged to any of my wife's fingers."

"Firstly, it is certain, that wherever my wife is at present, sitting, standing or lying down, this ring would never stay on her thumb, whereas you can plainly see that it was difficult to pull it over the joint of the little finger of the hand from which it was cut. The second thing is, that my wife always filed her nails on a Saturday as long as I have known her and the nail of this little finger hasn't been filed for a month. Thirdly, the hand this came from was kneading rye dough within three days of this finger being cut off and I can assure you that my wife has never kneaded rye dough since she has been my wife."

The king was very angry with Elffin for standing up to him so strongly concerning the goodness of his wife, so he ordered him to prison for the second time, saying that he should not be freed until he had proved the truth of his boast, as well as the wisdom of his bard and the virtue of his wife.

In the meantime, his wife and Taliesin remained happily at his house where Taliesin told his mistress how Elffin was in prison because of them, but he also told her to be glad for he would go to Maelgwn's court to free his master. She asked how he would do this and he answered her—

"A journey I will make

And to the gate I'll come,
I'll go into the hall
And sing my little song:
To silence royal bards
Before their mighty chief,
Upon them will I break
And Elffin I will free.
Should argument arise
Before the mighty prince,
I'll summon all the bards
For sweet and flowing song.
Taliesin, chief of bards
With Druid's wise old words
Will set kind Elffin free
From haughty tyrant's bonds.

Let neither grace nor health
Be to the mighty king,
There soon shall be an end
To all this force and wrong.
And may there be much harm
To Rhun and all his race,
Short be his length of life
And all his lands laid waste.
Long exile be assigned
To Maelgwn Gwynedd."

****

After this, he left his mistress and eventually arrived at the Court of Maelgwn, who was going to dine in royal state in his hall, as was the custom in those days for kings and princes to do at every chief feast.

As soon as Taliesin entered the hall, he put himself in a quiet corner, near to the place where the bards and minstrels would be coming to do service and duty to the king as was customary at high festivals when the gift of the king is announced. So, then the bards and minstrels came to proclaim the generosity of the king as well as his power and strength.

At the moment when they passed by the corner where he was crouching, Taliesin pouted out his lips after them and played "Blerwm, blerwm," with his finger upon his lips. They didn't take much notice of him but came before the king to whom they bowed down without speaking a single word but pouting their lips and making mouths at the king, playing "Blerwm, blerwm," upon their lips, as they had seen the boy do.

This made the king assume that they were all drunk, so he commanded one of his lords, who served at the table, to go and tell them to collect their wits, remember where they were and how they were expected to behave. The lord did this willingly but they didn't stop what they were doing. They were asked a second and a third time, then told to leave the hall.

At last, the king told one of his squires to strike a blow on the chief of them named Heinen Fardd, so the squire took a broom and struck him on the head so that he fell back in his seat. He then got up and knelt before the king to plead that it was not their fault but from the influence of some spirit that was in the hall.

Heinen said, "Oh Honourable King, I must tell your grace that it is not from strength of drink or of too much liquor that we are without power of speech like drunken men, but through the influence of a spirit that sits in the corner over there in the form of a child." The king then commanded the squire to fetch him. He went to the nook where Taliesin sat and brought him before the king, who asked him what he was and where he came from. He answered the king in verse[*]:

"Primary chief bard am I to Elffin,
And my original country is the region of the summer stars;
Idno and Heinen called me Merddin,
Soon every king will call me Taliesin.
I was with my Lord in the highest sphere,
On the fall of Lucifer into the depth of hell.
I have borne a banner before Alexander;
I know the names of the stars from north to south;
I was in Canaan when Absalom was killed;

---

[*] spoken by Taliesin

I was in the court of Don before the birth of Gwdion

I was talkative before being given the gift of speech,
I was at the place of the crucifixion to the merciful Son of God;
I have been three times in the prison of Arianod;
I have been the chief director of the work of the tower of
Nimrod;

I am a wonder whose origin is not known.
I have been in Asia with Noah in the Ark,
I have seen the destruction of Sodom and Gomorra;
I have been in India when Rome was built.

I have been with my Lord in the manger of the ass;
I strengthened Moses through the water of Jordan;
I have been in the heavens with Mary Magdalene;
I have obtained the muse from the Cauldron of Caridwen;
I have been bard of the harp to Lleon of Lochlin

For a day and a year in stocks and fetters
I have suffered hunger for the Son of the Virgin.
I have been teacher to all intelligences,
I am able to instruct the whole universe.
I shall be until the day of doom in the face of the earth;
And it is not known whether my body is flesh or fish."

"Then I was for nine months
In the womb of Caridwen
I was first little Gwion
And at last am Taliesin."

****

When the king and his nobles had heard the song, they
were amazed, for they had never heard the like from a boy so
young as he. However, when the king knew that he was Elffin's
bard, he asked Heinin, he first and wisest bard, to answer
Taliesin and to compete with him; but when he tried, he
couldn't do anything but play 'blerwn' on his lips. When he
sent for the other twenty-four bards, they all did the same and

197

couldn't do anything else. Maelgwm then asked the boy
Taliesin why he was there, and he answered him in song—

"O you puny* bards,
I am trying
To secure the prize
If I can.
By a gentle song
I am really trying
Trying to retrieve
My great loss.
May I have success
For Elffin is in trouble
In Teganwy jail
All in chains.
Strengthened by my muse
I am so powerful;
Three hundred spells and more
Are in the songs I sing.

I am Taliesin,
Chief of all the bards,
I'll make fair Elffin free,
Free from chains.

If you're primary bards
To the master of sciences,
Declare the mysteries
Of mankind.
You are blundering bards
Being much too troubled;
Cannot celebrate
The Kingdom of the Britons.
I am Taliesin
Chief of all the bards,
I'll make fair Elffin free,
Free from chains."

****

* weak, feeble

"*Be silent, then you unlucky rhyming bards,
For you cannot judge between truth and falsehood.
If you are primary bards formed by heaven,
Tell your king what his fate will be.
It is I who am a prophet and a leading bard,
And know every passage in the country of your king;
I shall liberate Elffin from the depths of the stony tower;
And will tell your king what will befall him.
A most strange creature will come from the sea marsh of Rhianedd
As a punishment of wickedness on Maelgwn Gwynedd;
His hair, his teeth and his eyes being as gold,
And this will bring destruction upon Maelgwm Gwynedd."

******

"Discover you will
What is the strong creature?
Which came before,
Before the flood
No flesh, no bone,
No vein, no blood.

Without head,
Without feet,
It will be neither
Older nor younger
Than as it was
At the beginning.

Great are its gusts
When it comes from the south;
It's in the field,
It's in the wood,
No hand, no foot,

* spoken by Taliesin

No signs of old age.

It was not born,
Nor was it seen,
It will cause fear
Wherever God wills;
On sea, on land,
It's beyond compare.

It is strong,
It is bold,
It's good, it's bad,
It's extremely harmful;
It's here, it's there,
It's everywhere.

One Being has prepared it,
Out of all creatures,
By a tremendous blast,
To wreak vengeance
On Maelgwm Gwynedd."

****

While he was singing his verse near the door, a mighty storm of
wind came up, so that the king and all his nobles thought that
the castle would fall on their heads. The king then ordered them
to quickly fetch Elffin from his dungeon and to place him
before Taliesin. It is said, that, as soon as he sang a verse, the
chains opened from around his feet.
"I adore the Supreme, Lord of all animation,
He that supports the heavens and Ruler of all.
He that made water good, gave each gift and blest it;
May abundance of mead be given to Maelgwm,
Who supplies us all from his foaming mead horns?
With the choicest liquor he can supply;
Since bees do collect, but do not enjoy,
We have sparkling 'stilled mead, universally praised.

I entreat the Supreme, the sov'reign of peace,
To liberate Elffin from banishment.
This man gave me wine and ale as well as mead,
With large princely steeds so beautiful to see;
May God of his grace to grant me, in honour,
A great many years of peace and goodwill,
O Elffin, great knight, may you have long life."

****

      Afterwards, he sang the ode which is called *The Excellence
of the Bards*.
"What was the first man?
Made by the God of heaven
What the fairest flattering speech
Prepared by the youngest;
What meat, what drink,
What roof was his shelter?
What the first impression
Of his first thought;
What became his clothing?
Which was a disguise,
Because of the wild country
In the beginning?
Why should a stone be hard?
A thorn sharp-pointed?
Who is hard like flint?
Who is salt like brine?
Who is sweet like honey?
Who rides on the gale?
Why is the nose ridged?
Why is a wheel round?
Why the tongue should be gifted with speech
Rather than any other part?
If your bards, O Heinin, are so clever,
Let them reply to me, Taliesin."

****

After that he sang the address which is called 'The Reproof of the Bards'.

"If you are a bard completely inspired
With genius not to be controlled,
Do not be uncontrollable
Within the court of your king;
Until your rigmarole shall be known;
You must be silent, Heinin,
As to the name of your verse,
And to the name of your boasting;
And as to the name of your grandfather
Before he was baptised.
And the name of the sphere,
And the name of the element,
And the name of your language,
And the name of your region.
Be gone, you bards above,
Be gone, you bards below!

It is certain that you do not know
How to understand the song I sing,
Nor clearly how to tell
Between the truth and what is false;
A bard that will not silence me,
A silence may he not obtain,
Until he goes to be covered
Beneath some gravel and some stones;
And they who will listen here to me,
May God listen to him."

Then he sang the piece called 'The Spite of the Bards.'

"Minstrels persevere in their own way,
Immoral songs are their delight;
Vain and tasteless praise they recite,
Falsehood at all times do they say.
Innocent persons they deride,
Married women they destroy,
Virgins of Mary they corrupt,
Vainly pass their lives away.

Nightly drunk, they sleep all day,
In idleness they feed themselves.

The Church they hate, the tavern frequent,
With thieves and criminals they make friends;
At courts they request some feasting,
Ev'ry senseless word they do say;
Ev'ry deadly sin they praise,
Ev'ry vile way of life they lead;
Through ev'ry village and town they stroll,
They do not think of the grip of death,
Neither lodging nor charity do they give;
Always eating to excess.

Psalms or prayers they do not say,
Tithes or offerings to God do not pay.
Do not worship on Sundays or holidays,
Vigils or festivals they do not heed.
The birds do fly, the fish do swim,
Bees collect honey, worms do crawl,
Ev'rthing works to find its food,
Except minstrels and useless thieves.

I deride neither song nor minstrelsy,
For they're given by God to lighten thought;
But him who abuses them
For blaspheming Jesus and His grace."

****

Taliesin, having set his master free from prison, having
protected the innocence of his wife and silenced the bards, so
that not one of them dared say a word, now brought Elffin's
wife before them and showed that she had not one finger
missing. Elffin and Taliesin were very pleased.

Then he told Elffin to bet with the king that he had a horse
both better and faster than any of the king's horses. This Elffin
did and the day, time and place were fixed. The place is now
called Morfa Rhianedd; the king went there with all his people

and twenty-four of the fastest horses he had. After a long process, the course was marked and the horses were placed for running.

Taliesin then came with twenty-four twigs of holly, which he burnt black. He told the young man who was to ride his master's horse to place them in his belt. He ordered him to let all the king's horses go before him and as he overtook each one, to take one of the twigs and strike each horse over the crupper[*], then let that twig fall. After that to take another twig and do the same to every one of the king's horses as he overtook them making sure that the horseman noticed when his own horse stumbled and to throw his cap on the spot.

All these things the young man did, giving a blow to every one of the king's horses and throwing down his cap where his horse stumbled. Taliesin brought Elffin to the spot after his horse had won the race. He asked him to make workmen to dig a hole there. When they had dug deep enough, they found a large cauldron full of gold.

Taliesin then said, "Elffin, this is the payment and reward to you, for having taken me out of the weir and having brought me up from that time until now." On this spot stands a pool of water which is call Pwllbair right up to this day.

After all this, the king ordered that Taliesin be brought before him. He asked him to recite something about the creation of man from the beginning. Taliesin then said the poem which is now called:

'One of the Four Pillars of Song[*]'

A.

"The Almighty made,
Down the Hebron vale,
With his moulding hands,
Adam's fair form.

And five hundred years,
Void of any help,

---

[*] hind quarter of a horse
[*] spoken by Taliesin

204

There he remained and lay
Without a Soul

He again did form,
In calm paradise,
From a left-side rib,
Bliss-throbbing Eve.

Seven hours they were
The orchard keeping,
Till Satan brought strife,
With wiliest* from hell.

From there they were driven,
Cold and shivering,
To gain their living,
Into this world.

And once, not hidden
She brought forth Abel
And Cain the forlorn,
The homicide.

To him and his mate
Was given a spade
To break up the soil,
So to get bread.

The wheat pure and white,
Summer soil to sow,
Everyman to feed,
Till great Christmas feast.

An angelic hand
From the high Father,
Brought seed for growing
That Eve might sow."

---

* tricks and cunning ways

B.

"But then she did hide
Of the gift a tenth,
And all did not sow
Of what was dug.

Black rye then was found,
And not pure wheat grain,
To show the mischief
So of thieving.

For this thievish act,
It is required,
That all men should pay
A tenth to God.

Of the rosy wine,
Planted on sunny days,
And on new-moon nights;
And the white wine.

The wheat rich in grain
And red flowing wine
Christ's pure body make,
Son of God.

The wafer is flesh,
The wine is spilt blood,
The Trinity's words
Sanctify them.

Solomon did obtain
In Babel's tower,
All the sciences
In Asia land.

So did I obtain
In my bardic books,
All the sciences
Of Europe and Africa.

Their course, their bearing,
Their permitted way,
And their fate I know,
Unto the end."

C.

"Oh! What misery,
Though extreme of woe,
Prophecy will show
Oh Britain's race!

A coiling serpent
Proud and merciless,
On her golden wings,
From Germany.

She will overrun
England and Scotland
From Lychlyn* sea-shore
To the Severn.

Then will the Britons
Be as prisoners,
By strangers swayed,
From Saxony."

D.

"Their Lord they will praise,
Their speech they will keep,
Their land they will lose,
Except wild Wales.

Till some change shall come,
After long penance,
When equally rife
The two crimes come.

---

* Welsh word for Norway

Britons then shall have
Their land and their crown,
And the stranger swarm
Shall disappear.

All the angel's words,
As to peace and war,
Will be fulfilled
To Britain's race."

****

He told the king further various prophesies of things that
would be in the world, in songs, as follows:

****

[*The manuscript from which Lady Guest made her
translation breaks off at this point.*]

End Song by Margery Hargest Jones
'So Much We Know...'

So much we know of the tale of Taliesin,
Primary bard in all of Wales,
With his wit and with his wisdom,
He freed Elffin from his chains;
He was wise, so bright and clever,
Skilled in verse and skilled in song;
His name will live in Wales forever.
Be revered all ages long.

'A Voice from Long Ago'
Toriad y Dydd   (Taliesin's Prophesy)

A voice from long ago
Still echoes in our hills;
The Prophet Bard Taliesin's words
The countryside yet fills.
For so the poet saw it,

And put it into rhyme,
These very true tho' ancient words
From very ancient time.
"Their God they'll ever worship,
Their language will retain,
They'll lose their land for evermore,
Yet wild Wales shall remain."
He tells us that for always
We'll keep our lovely land,
In which the beauty and the music
Live by Freedom's hand.

In our green isle of splendour,
He saw an ancient race,
Being driven from their father's home,
Make hills their dwelling-place.
He saw from this great kingdom
The sceptre disappear,
And many bards, and chiefs and princes
Ever gone from here.
"Their God they'll ever worship,
Their language will retain,
He tells us that for always
We'll keep our lovely land,
In which the beauty and the music
Live by Freedom's hand."